Em

Christmas
at the Little
Cottage
on the
Hill

Bookouture

Published by Bookouture in 2018

An imprint of StoryFire Ltd.

Carmelite House
50 Victoria Embankment
London EC4Y 0DZ

www.bookouture.com

ISBN: 978-1-78681-572-9
eBook ISBN: 978-1-78681-571-2

For Ade

Chapter 29 – I bet you're so relieved everything turned out okay…

Chapter 1

Maddie had been staring out of the window for at least the last fifteen minutes. It was ridiculous to be as excited as she was, but she couldn't help it; she'd always been that way about Christmas, and she was about to enjoy her first at Joy's Acre.

The kitchen was blissfully warm and suffused with the smell of sliced oranges and cinnamon coming from a pan on the stove. At the sound of wheels on gravel, she flashed Trixie a huge grin and shot through into the hallway and out the front door, practically running across the courtyard to where Seth had just manoeuvred the pickup truck into its usual spot. She let it come to a complete stop before opening the gate and hurrying through.

She opened the cab door and waited impatiently while Tom climbed from the passenger seat.

'I thought you'd never get here,' she said. 'Talk about keeping a girl in suspense.'

Seth emerged from the other side of the truck. 'It took rather longer than expected,' he said, grinning at Tom. 'I swear this tree is even bigger than the one we had last year. Are you sure it's going to fit?'

Tom pulled on a pair of thick leather gloves. 'I think we're about to find out.' He moved to the rear of the truck and let down the tailgate, turning his head to one side as the branches of a huge twelve-foot-tall tree brushed across his face. 'Although, we probably shouldn't worry. Angus will just pick it up and thrust it into the ground with his bare hands anyway,' he joked.

'There is that,' replied Seth, nodding as a battered Land Rover turned across the parking area and pulled up beside them. 'Speak of the devil…'

Maddie turned and watched while the other vehicle drew up alongside them. She'd only met Angus the woodcutter once so far and had been so in awe that she'd hardly said a word; he was quite possibly the biggest man she had *ever* seen. By contrast, he was also the most softly spoken, with a quiet and utterly beguiling manner that seemed totally at odds with his size.

A couple of moments later all four of them were standing at the rear of the truck contemplating the task at hand.

'Good morning, Maddie,' said Angus. 'Isn't she beautiful?'

Maddie returned the greeting, nodding at the huge tree.

'I can't wait to see it in place. It will be like our very own Trafalgar Square.'

Angus nodded. 'Well, Summersmeade Hall has provided the tree for Joy's Acre for quite a number of years now. It will look beautiful, that I can guarantee. Did you ever see the tree in London when you were there, Maddie?'

She beamed at him in excitement. 'Every year,' she said, 'without fail. It wouldn't have been Christmas without it.' She glanced at Seth. 'In fact, this year will be the first in a very long time that I won't get to see it, but you know what, I don't mind one little bit. There's nowhere else I'd rather be.'

'Then we must make sure she looks her very best. Just for you.'

Angus laid a huge hand on the tree trunk. 'Gentlemen, are we ready?'

He tugged on the trunk and the tree slithered gracefully from the back of the truck onto the ground. 'I'll take the thick end,' he said. 'And if I might suggest, Seth, as the shortest among us, that you go in the middle, leaving Tom to take the top end. If we can get her up on our shoulders it will save the branches from snagging on the ground. If not, gently does it please.'

Seth grimaced at Tom as Maddie smothered a smile. Not only was Angus about six inches taller than even Tom, he was also very broad and muscular from years of working outdoors. He completely dwarfed them all.

'And one last thing,' said Angus, directing a look at Tom. 'No swearing please, there is a lady present.' But his words were delivered with a wink and Tom just laughed.

The three men grunted and groaned as the tree was hefted into the air, branches completely engulfing them, and Maddie ran on ahead to grab Trixie, taking a deep appreciative breath as she re-entered the kitchen; the aroma was just as intoxicating as before.

'I always think the smell of mulled wine is like Christmas bottled, don't you?' she said as Trixie turned away from the huge saucepan she was stirring to greet her.

'And with perfect timing, this is just about ready. I'll let it steep for a bit and then once the tree is up, we can all have a glass and offer up a toast.' Her dark eyes were shining. 'Christmas at Joy's Acre, Maddie. Who'd have thought it?'

Maddie crossed the room to give her a hug. 'I know,' she said, pulling away. 'The year has gone so fast since we came in the spring, and now it's the first of December. I still can't believe everything that's happened. Tom is working on thatching the last of the holiday cottages, the other three are all occupied, the barn is almost ready... Some days I really do think I'm dreaming. Honestly, could it get any better than this?'

She gave Trixie a warm smile as the room darkened for a moment, the light through the window blocked momentarily as the huge tree passed by.

'Come on, I can't wait to see it up.'

Maddie pulled at Trixie's arm and the two of them practically ran down the hallway to the other end of the house and out of the back door, where the full extent of Joy's Acre opened out in front of them.

Across the gardens, in a rough semi-circle, stood the farm's four holiday cottages, three of which were now finished, leaving the fourth, to their left, still to be renovated. Its half-finished thatch stuck up like tufts of badly cut hair, but it wouldn't be long before it too was complete. Come the new year, with the barn done as well, a whole raft of new plans would be ready to put into place. Even on a bitterly cold day like today, the sight of it all warmed Maddie's heart.

As resident cook, the kitchen was very definitely Trixie's domain, but out here was where Clara lavished her care and attention, and there wasn't an inch of the garden that hadn't flourished as a result. Clara had been at Joy's Acre for several years and had transformed the badly neglected area, returning it to its original Victorian splendour. In the very centre of the garden was a lawn, but on every side, bisected by numerous paths, were large beds planted with so many different flowers and shrubs that Maddie still didn't know the names of half of them. Between these were numerous vegetable patches, and it was deep in one of these that Maddie spied Clara now, her long blonde hair tied into two thick plaits that hung underneath a bright red knitted hat. Maddie didn't know how Clara could stand being outside in all weathers, but Clara seemed to thrive on it. It was a full-time job ensuring that the garden produced a constant stream of vegetables for the kitchen.

Intent on her digging, Clara didn't notice Maddie and Trixie until they were both nearly standing in front of her and she pulled a pair of headphones from her ears, laughing.

'Michael Bublé,' she explained. 'I'm not allowed him on until December as I have a tendency to overdose, so today…' she smiled, 'he is on repeat.'

Trixie rolled her eyes. 'You'll be sorry,' she said.

'I know, I'll probably be sick of him by next week, but you've got to, haven't you; it's Christmas!'

Maddie nodded, her eyes catching on something over Clara's shoulder. 'It most certainly is, and here it comes now.'

Clara thrust the fork she was digging with into the soil, turned, and stood with her hands on her hips.

'There's nothing quite like the sight of three gorgeous men carrying a Christmas tree to warm the cockles, is there?'

'Clara! Wash your mouth out,' said Trixie. 'You're spoken for. As are Seth and Tom for that matter.'

Clara blushed. 'Oh, I didn't mean it like that. Just that it's such a quintessential Christmas scene, isn't it? Declan would love it.'

Maddie exchanged a look with Trixie and smiled. Declan was a TV producer who had arrived at Joy's Acre a couple of months ago with a view to making a television series. Although it had caused no end of problems, it had also sparked a relationship between Clara and Declan, which was still going strong.

'And how is the lovely Declan?' asked Maddie, her eyes twinkling.

Clara blushed again. 'Well, he's… lovely!' she exclaimed. 'And he moves in two weeks! I still can't quite get my head around the fact that he's going to be living next door.'

Trixie nodded several times. 'Like I said, it won't be long before you're Lady of the Manor…'

'Nuh-uh,' she replied. 'It ought to be Maddie's turn first.'

Maddie just grinned and turned her attention back towards the three men and the Christmas tree. 'I'm not sure I dare watch, in case it all goes horribly wrong.'

'It doesn't usually,' replied Clara. 'We've pretty much got it down to a fine art over the years, and besides, I've never met a tree yet who would dare argue with Angus.'

'That's practically what Seth said,' Maddie replied. 'I know he's a giant, but he seems really nice, and it will be a big help to us having him around. I can't help but wonder if there's a story there though; Seth mentioned that he lives alone and has done for quite some time. I'm not sure how old he is exactly, but doesn't that strike you as odd?'

Clara looked anguished. 'Don't even go there, Maddie,' she warned. 'Seriously. He is a lovely man, the gentlest you could ever wish to meet, but he's a very private person, so don't go prying.'

Trixie picked up on her tone of voice. 'That sounds to me like you know an awful lot more than you're letting on.'

'How perceptive,' Clara replied, then seamlessly changed the subject. 'Oh, I love it when the tree goes up. Somehow it quite transforms the garden, especially at night with its lights on. The last hour before I go home, when the dusk is just settling, is the best. Quiet and still, but hopeful somehow, like a beacon in the night. Seth usually strings fairylights right along the side of the main house, but this year, imagine how beautiful it will look with all the cottages lit up as well.'

Maddie followed her line of sight, feeling a sudden rush of happiness. These next few weeks could well prove to be some of their busiest yet, but no one at Joy's Acre was afraid of hard work, and she couldn't think of anywhere she'd rather be, or any group of people she'd rather be with. She'd often had cause to think about why things worked the way they did at Joy's Acre, but in the end she had come to the conclusion that sometimes the right people just came together at the right time. Put them in the right place also and what you had was… well, it was the closest thing to magic Maddie could think of.

A shout went up from across the garden and, as one, the three women made their way across the grass to where the tree was now erected – its branches still trussed, but the trunk firmly anchored in its base. It towered above their heads.

'Can you give me a hand with the ladder, Seth?' asked Tom, grinning at them all as he moved past. As a thatcher, Tom had no shortage of ladders, and one of them was nearby, leaning against the roof of the Woodcutter's Cottage.

Maddie stared up at the top of the tree and inwardly shuddered. She had been up Tom's ladders a few times in the past, but the experience always left her with legs feeling like jelly. Rather him than me, she thought. Tom scaled ladders like he was running up stairs and came down them the same way too. With absolutely no fear of heights, he was the perfect person to not only cut the ties from the tree, but also to adorn it with its first decoration: a handmade willow star for the very top, which Maddie had helped Clara to make the previous weekend. She'd watched in awe as Clara had deftly woven together whips of willow, bending them into two triangles which she then laid against one another to form a six-pointed star. Where the triangles met, she had tied each joint with bright red ribbon. Once the basic shape was formed the star was decorated with foliage and berries, much like a wreath.

It had seemed to take Clara only a matter of minutes, and when she was done she started all over again on four smaller versions; one for the door of the main house and the other three for each of the cottages ahead of the arrival of a new party of guests. By then of course, each of the cottages would also have its own, smaller Christmas tree set up in the living room.

Trixie gave Maddie's arm a sudden nudge. 'Back in a minute,' she said. 'Don't let Tom put the star up until I'm back, will you? I want to see it go up.'

Maddie nodded, suspecting that Trixie would be returning with a glass of mulled wine for each of them.

'I'll come with you,' said Clara, and Maddie smiled. Clara and Trixie had had their friendship tested to the limits by the arrival of the film crew a few months back, but their generosity of spirit had won out and made them realise what a perfect double act they were. Joy's Acre would simply not function without either of them.

Ten minutes later, and it was all done. As soon as Trixie and Clara had returned, Tom had shinned up the ladder and firmly tied the star to the top before carefully cutting through the ropes that bound the tree's branches. A collective 'aahhh' went up as soon as the last were released, revealing the spectacular tree in all its glory.

Tom returned to stand with them, accepting his glass of mulled wine from Angus and raising it to him. 'You've done us proud,' he said, 'and no mistake.'

'Well, I can't take all the credit; Mother Nature did most of the work. But she is a fine tree, I can't argue with that.' Angus raised his own glass, and was about to say something further when Seth cut in.

'I know you always toast the tree, Angus, but this year I wondered if I might say something?'

'Of course… Christmas will be a little… different than usual,' he replied, smiling in Maddie's direction.

She frowned slightly, confused by his words, and was about to ask what he meant when Seth cut in again.

'It's definitely been a year that's seen a lot of firsts—'

'Yeah, you've stopped being such a grumpy bugger for one,' quipped Tom, winking at Maddie.

Seth pretended to look hurt. 'Me?' he queried. 'When we all know that you're a changed man since a certain lady violinist began to tug at your heart strings…'

Tom blushed. 'Well, I walked straight into that one, didn't I?' he muttered. 'Carry on. As you were, Seth.'

'Christmas has always been a happy time at Joy's Acre and now, with Maddie and Trixie here too, this year looks set to go off the scale.' He gave Maddie a look that made her insides somersault.

'And now things are changing up at the Hall as well. With Agatha moving out and gifting us part of the estate, it could have caused huge problems for Angus so I'm mightily relieved that he's agreed to come and work for me, lending us another pair of – extraordinarily large – hands. So, I'd like to officially welcome Angus to Joy's Acre, and indeed thank Mother Nature for providing us with a little of her Christmas spirit.' He paused to raise his glass in the air.

'It's going to be a very busy few weeks, but… Happy Christmas everyone.'

'Happy Christmas!'

Chapter 2

'Oh, this is heaven, isn't it?'

Maddie lay back on the sofa, snuggling closer to Seth and stretching her feet out towards the fire. Even with her thick stripy socks on, her toes were only just beginning to thaw out.

After the tree had gone up, she and Clara had spent the remainder of the afternoon collecting holly and ivy from the woodland behind Joy's Acre. Most of it would be used to provide decoration for the cottages, wreaths for the front doors, or garlands for the mantelpieces in each living room. Even though they had carried it all back to one of the greenhouses to begin their work, the panes of glass there afforded little protection from the bitter chill of the day outside and the stone floor was as cold as ice. Maddie had hardly been able to feel her toes all through dinner.

Now though, she leaned her head against Seth's shoulder, and felt the delicious waves of warmth wash over her. One hand lay in her lap, the other entwined with Seth's beside her. There were a million and one things to think about, but her mind was blissfully empty as she savoured a rare evening off.

Her breathing became heavier and heavier. She was about to close her eyes when she realised that Seth had not answered her. She lifted her head slightly, wondering if he had already nodded off, and was surprised to find him staring at the fire, an oddly intense expression on his face.

'Penny for them?' she said, nudging him gently.

It wasn't unusual for Seth to be lost in thought – there was so much still to attend to with the renovations, and always one problem or another to tackle – and he often had to be reminded to share his concerns instead of keeping them to himself. Maddie knew that he was anxious to get the barn finished as soon as possible, not only because he had promised Clara and Trixie that they could move in there after the new year, but also with Christmas looming…

'Is it the party?' she prompted when he still didn't reply. 'Because if it is, I know it's utter madness, but it *will* happen, Seth. You know what we can do if we put our minds to it, and I'm pretty sure that we can count on the villagers to help as well. Everyone I've spoken to is madly excited.'

'Please tell me you love me?'

The question came so out of the blue that Maddie's stomach flipped in shock. She sat up and stared at Seth, feeling her heart beat faster. What on earth had happened to cause him to doubt her? He had seemed so happy earlier…

She took one look at his face and broke into a broad smile, a wave of love rushing over her. She pushed against him, her lips finding his.

'Of course I love you, you muppet,' she said. 'Why wouldn't I?' She kissed him again. 'Besides, didn't anyone tell you that it's Christmas soon, which is probably *the* most romantic time of year. And I get to spend it with you…'

'Except that we're going to be so busy, by the time Christmas actually arrives we'll be too knackered to enjoy it.'

He looked a little happier, even if his words were still filled with doubt. Perhaps he was just tired himself; they *had* had rather a busy day.

'I know,' she agreed. 'We never seem to do things by halves, do we? But think about it… would we really want it any other way? I know throwing a party for the whole of Summersmeade isn't just going to happen all by itself, but with Declan moving in to the Hall, it's the perfect time to resurrect the village tradition. After all, we'd already decided to go ahead with the annual summer fete next year, and this is what makes life here so wonderful. It's hard work but it doesn't have to feel like it. In fact, with all of us pulling together, it rarely does. Not many people get to do something they love day in, day out.' She took hold of his hand. 'And with someone they love…'

To her surprise, Seth didn't look totally convinced as he stared back towards the fire. She felt a flicker of unease in the pit of her stomach. He cleared his throat, and she suddenly realised that he looked nervous more than stressed.

'The trouble is though, it's not just the party…' He paused, then turned back to her, his face soft in the dim light, his eyes dark with longing. 'I think I've landed everyone with a whole lot more work, and you'll probably never forgive me, but it seemed such a brilliant idea at the time… I hope it still is…'

She frowned gently, catching the wistful note in his voice. 'What did, Seth?' she asked.

He suddenly let go of her hand, shuffling forward until he was perched right on the edge of the sofa, almost on his knees.

'I can't imagine doing any of this without you, Maddie. And I really don't want to have to. When I first moved to Joy's Acre with Jen we had such hopes for the future, yet when she died so soon after I thought my life was over, that I was being punished in some way for daring to dream.'

'Oh, Seth…'

He put a finger on her lips. 'Shhh,' he said, softly. 'I know that sounds melodramatic, but I'd sunk so low I didn't think there would ever be a way to get out of the pit I'd fallen into, and frankly I didn't much care.'

He paused briefly to compose himself. 'It took you to make me realise that I had everything I needed to start climbing out. It was right here under my nose all the time, I just couldn't see it. But once I understood what I needed to make me happy, I realised that there was just one thing missing. Or rather, that there wasn't anything missing, because you were right there in front of me… no, at my side. I hope you'll never leave.'

His words caught in Maddie's throat as she breathed them in, forming a lump that grew with every passing second. There were tears shining in his eyes, just as there were in hers. She opened her mouth to speak, but Seth gave a slight shake of his head.

'I love you so much,' he said, this time sinking to his knees in front of her. 'I know it's Christmas and there are already a million and one things to do… It's possibly the worst timing ever, but… Would you marry me, Maddie Porter?' He wrinkled up his face. 'And please say yes, because, dear God, it's all arranged.'

Her hand flew to her mouth as a rush of emotion threatened to spill out, and then she just let it anyway, because she didn't care what she looked like. She nodded, grabbing hold of his hands, and then nodding again, laughing, crying, sniffing all at the same time.

'Yes!' she finally managed. 'Yes! Oh God, Seth… you really scared me, you looked so serious. I thought something was wrong…'

'So, you don't mind then?'

'Mind? Why on *earth* would I mind?' She shook her head, laughing.

'Because we're already so busy trying to organise the Christmas Eve party for the village and now there will be a whole heap of others things to do. I couldn't organise any of it because it was meant to be a surprise—'

'Hang on… run that by me again. Did you say it was all arranged?' She held her hands to her cheeks. 'When are we actually getting married, Seth?'

He put a hand over his eyes. 'The twenty-third of December… I didn't want it to be on the same day as the party – with us all at the wedding it would make organising it an impossibility. Besides, this way we can spread the celebrations out over two days; have something quieter and more intimate on the day of the wedding, and then a fabulous party for the whole village to share in our happiness the day after…'

It was quite possible the whole house heard Maddie's squeal. 'Oh my God, that's brilliant! Oh, I can't believe it… getting married at Christmas! How on earth did you pull that off?'

Seth rolled his eyes. 'I'm still not entirely sure,' he said. 'I think I had luck on my side. Or perhaps it was just that no one else is mad enough to get married two days before Christmas.'

She stared at him then. 'But that's in less than a month! And there's flowers, and a dress… and… a cake, and photographers, and… and…' She ground to a halt, suddenly struck by the enormity of trying to organise a wedding at such short notice. But not just any wedding… her wedding. To Seth. 'And it's still bloody brilliant!'

She clasped both hands around his face and gently drew him nearer. 'I love you, Mr Thomas,' she said. 'And nothing would make me happier than becoming your wife.'

He closed his eyes. 'Oh, thank heavens,' he murmured. 'I was terrified you were going to say no, or at the very least kill me for going ahead and organising it without asking you first.' He shook his head. 'At the time it seemed like the most romantic gesture, but now—'

'It still is. It's incredible. Getting married here at Christmas is a dream come true,' she said, firmly. 'Joy's Acre is our home, the village is our village, why would I want to get married anywhere else? It's honestly perfect.' She gave him a cheeky smile. 'And like you said, we have an army of people to help us, what could possibly go wrong?'

Seth chewed at his lip. 'There is just one other thing…'

She raised her eyebrows, watching in amusement as he pulled away from her, thrusting a hand into the pocket of his jeans and pulling out a cream coloured, small, square box.

She held her breath.

'I had this made for you.'

She reached out a hand that trembled as her fingers touched the lid of the box. 'I can't,' she whispered. 'You open it.'

He gently pulled back the lid.

Nestled inside was a gold band woven from intertwining leaves and flowers that curled this way and that. Scattered along their lengths were tiny diamonds and in the centre three roses bloomed, each with a diamond at their heart. It was the most beautiful thing she had ever seen.

She looked up into Seth's eyes, and saw there all the love, all the hope and all the promise that she could ever have wished for. The tears were running freely down her face as she took the ring from the box and held it out to Seth. His hands shook as he lifted her left hand and gently pushed the ring into place on her finger.

'Oh…' It fitted perfectly. In fact, it looked as if it had been there her whole life but she had just never seen it before.

She stared at her hand, and then at Seth as he held her look. Behind him the clock on the mantelpiece ticked softly as the flames danced in the fireplace, washing him with a golden glow. She looked across the room at the Christmas tree with its golden decorations and twinkling lights and then back again. Seth was still there, it was real, she wasn't dreaming after all.

And then something else occurred to her.

'So if we're definitely getting married on the twenty-third, that must mean that the vicar at least knows about this…? I'm just wondering who else knows…?' She trailed off, catching the sheepish look on Seth's face.

'Erm, pretty much everyone…'

'Define everyone.'

He grinned. 'Clara, Tom, Trixie—'

'Trixie? How on earth did she keep that a secret?'

'I don't know, but she has. And then there's Declan of course, Angus, Louise, the vicar's wife… and pretty much the whole village.'

Maddie stared at him for a moment, a slow smile spreading over her face. 'I was wondering why the house was so quiet.'

Seth nodded. 'They've all been banned for the evening.'

'Have they now?' she replied, grinning. 'That will mean we won't be interrupted then, won't it?'

He shook his head. 'No, we have the whole house to ourselves… all night.'

Maddie wound her fingers into the soft folds of his jumper, pulling him closer.

'It's awfully hot in here all of a sudden… I might have to take my jumper off…'

Chapter 3

'Jem, I'm leaving in five minutes, if you're not ready then—'

'Then what, Mum? You'll go without me?' he scoffed. 'Go ahead. I don't want to go to some dump in the middle of nowhere anyway.'

Ruby watched sadly as, despite his words, her son picked up his rucksack and stomped down the stairs. It was hard on her and little Darcie, but hardest on him most of all; Darcie was still too small to understand, but Jem was leaving everything that mattered to him, or so he thought anyway. He wasn't old enough to know what really mattered.

She looked around Jem's bedroom one last time, but like the rest of the house it was an empty shell; still full of furniture, but stripped of everything that gave it life and made it a home. Or at least pretended to. But it was now or never; if she didn't take this chance and leave today, nothing would ever change. And she would never be free. Perhaps one day her son would stop hating her for it.

The journey to Summersmeade took about two hours, but with every mile Ruby felt her spirits lift a little further. This was the new start she had been dreaming of for months and now she was on her way. She was under no illusion that what she faced next would all be plain sailing but, if nothing else, the last few years had taught her how to be resilient and resourceful.

Spotting the sign for the village, she turned left off the main road, letting a wry smile creep across her face. The day was bitterly cold and, despite the village's evocative name, the landscape had definitely cast off its summer clothing for the year, leaving behind a hauntingly beautiful sweep of dips and rises that rose up in front of her like a scene from a painting. Rows of rich brown furrows stretched away across the fields almost as far as she could see, and a low slanting sun glinted off the soil, turning the pale sky to orange.

She drove slowly, passing the line of unfamiliar houses until she rounded a sharp left-hand bend and, through the line of trees ahead of her, saw the church spire rising up. A part of her wanted to go and find her little cottage before taking the lane up to Joy's Acre but somehow it seemed as if this would be tempting fate. Her new home wasn't ready for her yet, and it would be well into January before the existing tenants moved out and she could prepare to move in. She must be patient.

Pulling in alongside the green opposite the church, Ruby checked her bearings against her map and the set of instructions she had written out for herself. By her reckoning, the village shop and post office should be just a little way further up the road, and although she had packed several bags of food, it wouldn't hurt to see what the village had to offer. She craned her neck around to the back seat.

Jem hadn't even looked up. His face was frowning in concentration, his lips pursed, finger jabbing at the screen of the tablet he held in front of him. Beside him Darcie slept on, her face flushed a little from the warmth of the car.

'We're almost there, Jem!'

Her son stared at her. 'When can we have lunch?' he said. 'I'm starving.'

She hadn't expected him to be excited, but she'd hoped he'd be at least a little curious. There was no expression on his face other than the usual half scowl he seemed to wear most days. She couldn't help her own expression though. She *was* excited. This was the start of their new life together, away from… She stopped herself. Now wasn't the time to be thinking about such things.

'We'll be at the cottage very soon, and lunch will be waiting for us when we get there.'

His head had bent back to the game he was playing. 'Can't I at least have another biscuit?'

Ruby eyed the half-eaten packet on the passenger seat beside her. He'd had plenty already.

'It really won't be long, I promise. Listen, can you wait here for a few minutes while I just pop to the shop? I'll be as quick as possible.'

There was no response, but then she hadn't expected one. She knew Jem had heard her though; he always did, even if he rarely responded. 'And keep an eye on your sister.'

She climbed from the car, reaching back inside for her handbag. She had only gone a few steps when she pulled out her phone automatically and checked it for messages. It was a habit she must try to break. She peered at the screen; there was no signal anyway, which was probably a good thing. Fishing in her pocket, she pulled out her gloves and put them on with a shiver.

The shop was only tiny, but had a surprising variety of things for sale, including fresh bread, and she picked up a crusty loaf that she knew Jem would like. She had booked meals for them at the holiday cottage for the rest of today and tomorrow to tide them over, but she couldn't afford to do so indefinitely. There would be a supermarket somewhere, but until she found out where, this little shop would be able to provide most of the things she might need.

Like most places at this time of year, the shop was already festooned with Christmas decorations, and a small area had been given over to festive treats. On impulse she picked up a couple of advent calendars which had been marked down in price. In the rush to get everything packed up to leave, it was something she hadn't yet got around to buying, and although it was already the second of December she didn't suppose that would matter too much. She smiled a greeting at another customer, pressing herself against the shelving so that he could pass, and went to pay for her things.

'Not a bad day,' said the young woman behind the till, taking hold of her loaf of bread. 'We've seen some sun at least.'

Ruby nodded. 'I've been stuck in the car for most of it… with the heating on full blast. It was bit of a shock getting out to be honest.'

'I love your gloves though… and your brooch, they're really pretty.'

Ruby looked down at her bright woolly hands, blushing slightly as she always did when someone complimented her on the things she had made. These pair were a combination of a fingerless glove and mitten so that, if she wanted, her fingers could still poke out the ends, leaving them free. It made life much easier in shops.

'Thank you,' she said. 'It's a hobby of mine.' It was on the tip of her tongue to say more, but she stopped herself. She'd only just arrived for goodness' sake, there would be plenty of time for all that.

The young woman looked on as Ruby took her purse from her bag.

'That's three pounds and fifty-six pence, please.'

Ruby handed her a five-pound note and waited for her change. She bit her lip a little nervously. 'Actually, could you help me with something?' she asked. 'I'm on my way to a holiday cottage near here, and I just wondered if it was easy to find. I've been told to take the lane up past the church, and then just drive for a couple of miles up the hill?'

The woman smiled, and leaned to one side so she was looking past Ruby. 'Where are you headed for? Joy's Acre, is it?'

'Oh, you know it?'

'There's not many places up that lane, least not until you get back down the other side of the hill.' She was still looking over Ruby's shoulder. 'Angus?' she called.

The space beside her was suddenly filled by the same enormous man she had made way for earlier.

'Are you headed back up to the farm when you're done here?' asked the woman.

'I can do,' he replied. 'I was on my home, but…' He suddenly smiled. 'Are you lost?'

'Not exactly,' answered Ruby. 'Well, not yet anyway. But I've been on the road for a while and I'm quite keen to get where I need to be. I'm not—'

There was a tinkling sound as the door to the shop opened and a sudden wailing sound filled the air. She turned around to see Jem marching towards her, a red-faced Darcie in his arms. He thrust his sister towards her.

'She woke up,' he said abruptly.

The wailing trailed off as Darcie clung to Ruby's neck, her pink cheeks puffy from sleep but now wet with tears.

'Oh Jem, couldn't you…' She tried to juggle her purse and bag so that she could hold her daughter more securely. 'It's okay, sweetheart,' she murmured.

'I tried, but she didn't want me… she never does.'

'Yes, but shouting—'

'I didn't shout. Do you think I'm stupid or what?'

And with that Jem marched back out of the shop.

Ruby turned back towards the till, her face now as red as her daughter's. 'Sorry, she was in the car and must have woken up… She got scared, I guess.' Darcie was still clinging to her desperately but her sobs had subsided to breathless hiccupping.

The young woman gave her a sympathetic smile. 'Shall I put your change away for you?' she asked, reaching forwards to take Ruby's purse, which was only just held in the tips of her fingers.

She flashed her a grateful smile. 'Yes, anywhere… thank you. In that zipped bit will be lovely.'

Angus reached past her and scooped up her bread and the advent calendars. 'You can follow me up to Joy's Acre,' he said. 'Probably best that way.'

Ruby looked up, horrified. 'I can't ask you to do that,' she said. 'You were on your way home.'

But the face in front of her simply smiled. 'I don't recall that you did ask me,' he said. 'I offered. Come on, let's get you all settled. You'll feel better then.' The arm not holding her shopping touched her sleeve gently. 'A cup of tea and one of Trixie's cakes is what you need.'

Who on earth was Trixie? But she managed a smile, suddenly longing to be out of the shop. The enormity of the day was just beginning to hit her, and the sudden kindness from complete strangers would be her total undoing if she wasn't careful.

'Thank you,' she said, offering the young woman a smile also. 'I don't normally…' But the woman was nodding in understanding. Ruby didn't need to say any more. She hitched Darcie further up her hip and followed the tall man out of the shop.

'I'm parked just opposite the church,' she said.

'And that's me,' he said, pointing to a pickup truck just beyond the shop. 'I'll turn around and then you can follow behind.'

She nodded and smiled gratefully, hurrying back to her car as fast as her daughter's weight would allow. She could feel her cheeks still burning in the cold air as she began to buckle Darcie back into her car seat. Jem had taken up his previous position, not even looking up as she opened the car door. She knew that she should say something about his rudeness but now that she was finally so close to her destination, the adrenaline that had been keeping her going all day evaporated and she suddenly felt overwhelmingly tired. All she wanted to do was get to the cottage. She hoped it was warm.

Pulling her seatbelt around her, she looked up to see the truck waiting patiently in front of her. She signalled that she was ready and took the turning, right behind him, immediately grateful, as the road narrowed to a single track almost straight away.

The road climbed for several minutes and then as they almost reached the brow of the hill, the truck indicated left and turned off the road through a tiny gap in the hedge. She registered a blue sign bearing the title 'Joy's Acre' as she drove past, but in all honesty she probably would have missed it had she been by herself. Moments later the road widened again and, a few seconds after that, Ruby pulled up behind the truck in a wide parking area. A red-brick house lay in front of her across a courtyard.

She glanced up at her rear-view mirror to see Jem look up and out of his window. A small smile played across his face for an instant before he turned his head resolutely away from the window. She looked away before she caught his eye.

The cab door to the pickup was opening and Ruby unclipped her seatbelt, climbing from the car and looking around her. They were here, but she was suddenly nervous. She would be staying here for over a month. What if she didn't like it? Or didn't like the people? The lady she had spoken with on the phone had sounded lovely, but that didn't mean anything. Ruby had dragged her children away from their home just before Christmas; it could be the worst mistake she had ever made. She suddenly shivered. Not the worst mistake; the worst mistake would have been to stay...

'So, welcome to Joy's Acre. What do you think?' Angus was walking over to her, a broad smile on his face. 'It's a handsome house, isn't it?'

It was. It looked inviting, friendly. The red front door was hung with a huge Christmas wreath, and a tree stood beside it covered in red bows. Silently Jem had come to stand by her side. His hand slid into hers.

'You'll be fine from here. Just knock on that door and ask for Maddie. She'll take care of you.'

Ruby nodded, remembering the name from her phone call.

He held out his hand. 'I'm Angus, by the way.'

'Ruby... and this is Jem.'

Angus dropped to his haunches. 'Pleased to meet you, young man.' He gave Jem a gentle smile, and held out his hand once more. 'And what's your sister's name?'

'Darcie, she's just a baby.'

Angus didn't seem the slightest bit offended that Jem didn't take his hand. 'Well, I know you'll do a fine job of looking after them both.' And with that he straightened back up to his full height, giving Ruby a look that she couldn't quite fathom.

'Shall I take your things inside for you?' he asked.

She blushed slightly, despite the cold air. 'No, I couldn't... Honestly, you've been very kind, but I can manage from here.'

He nodded. 'Then I will let you get settled. And if there's anything you need, just ask.'

'I will, thank you.' It sounded like he meant she should ask him, but she must have misunderstood, surely? In any case she smiled. She could hear Darcie protesting from the back of the car. It was time to make a move.

'It will be okay, Ruby. It might not seem like it now, but it will, in time...'

At first she wasn't sure that she had heard him right, but if she hadn't, what else could he possibly have said? He hadn't moved, but was standing, hands by his sides, a gentle expression on his face as he held her astonished look. And then he broke into another smile and with a slight wave turned away. She watched until he got back into his truck, a warmth inside her that simply hadn't been there before. *How did he know?*

'I'll see you tomorrow,' he called, as he drove off.

She returned his wave, only realising what he had said as she turned to fetch Darcie from the car. He had also driven off with her loaf of bread. She stared after him. What an extraordinary man...

Unclipping Darcie from her car seat, she pulled her daughter into her arms and then, fixing a bright smile on her face, she turned back to Jem. 'Come on, let's go and see what this place is like, and then we can have some lunch.'

*

Maddie appeared to be exactly as she had sounded on the phone: warm, friendly and full of energy. Despite the fact that Ruby was still holding Darcie in her arms, she bent to kiss her cheek as if greeting a long-lost friend. Moments later, a set of keys in her hand, Maddie led them around the side of the house.

Even Jem's face lit up at the sight in front of them. Despite holding Ruby's hand earlier, he was doing his level best to exude boredom and lack of interest from every pore, but there were some things that couldn't be ignored.

Ruby had seen pictures of the property from the farm's website, so she knew that the cottage they would be staying in must lie somewhere behind the main house, but nothing could prepare her for just how pretty everything was, or how festive. It reminded her of a scene from a Christmas card.

Four, thatched, whitewashed cottages were dotted around the edges of the most beautiful gardens, which were still full of colour even at this time of year. In their centre stood an enormous tree, covered in lights, which glowed with a golden hue. At night time they would truly come into their own, but even in the early afternoon they were still pretty. The eaves of each cottage were also hung with lights, as were the wrought-iron railings which enclosed their gardens.

Darcie reached out a hand as if to touch them, crowing with delight, and Ruby felt her heart lift, just a little. She hadn't been looking forward to Christmas at all, but here, just maybe, a little of its spirit might rub off on her, rub off on them all.

As they made their way across the gardens to the far side, Ruby realised that she hadn't taken in a word Maddie had been saying. She stopped suddenly, frowning, knowing that she had no idea how to answer the question that had just been asked of her. Maddie simply laughed.

'It gets you like that, this place, doesn't it? Don't worry, all will become clear. I was only rambling on about everyone here, but you'll get to meet us all soon. In fact, once I've shown you in, Seth can go fetch your luggage for you if you like. That way you can just have a rest and a cup of tea. Lunch is all laid out too.' She looked at Jem. 'How about you? Are you like most teenage boys I know and permanently hungry?'

'I'm only ten.'

'Are you? Gosh, you're very tall for your age… but I expect you get fed up of everyone telling you that, don't you?' She didn't wait for a reply. 'I bet you're still hungry though?'

Jem nodded at least, even if he didn't reply. He was often mistaken for someone older, and in some ways he was more mature than his peers; though sadly not in ways that Ruby was proud of. His maturity had been born out of necessity, rather than the process of simply getting older, and his last year at primary school hadn't started well either. He had been too big a fish in a small pond, and had pushed the boundaries, throwing his weight around with the younger children. She hadn't wanted to censor his friendships, knowing how difficult it was, but he had seemed to drop all his existing friends, preferring instead to hang around with a crowd of lads from the estate who were all at secondary school. Even though they were not the friends that Ruby would have chosen for him, she took no pleasure from the fact that he would probably never see them again; friends were friends, after all, and here he would have none.

'Here we are,' said Maddie. 'The Blacksmith's Cottage.'

Ruby followed her up the path to the cottage, holding open the gate for Jem to follow behind. A deep-red front door had been hung with a wreath made from holly, bright with berries and tartan ribbon. Slices of dried orange and cinnamon sticks bound with wool completed the decoration. To one side a smallish window glowed with light.

Maddie put the key in the door and pushed it open, turning to hand the keys back to Ruby. 'Yours now,' she said with a grin.

She led them down the hallway to a square kitchen, large enough to hold a table and four chairs, but small enough to retain a cosy charm. The table was covered in an assortment of plates and bowls – cloths protecting their contents, but still not thick enough to mask the heavenly smell coming from them.

There wasn't time to take it all in before Maddie had disappeared through a doorway to the right and, shifting Darcie to a more comfortable position on her hip, Ruby followed her through.

'Oh, Jem, look…' She turned to Maddie, her eyes bright, feeling suddenly quite emotional. 'Oh, this is beautiful…'

In the corner of the room stood yet another Christmas tree, lit with myriad twinkling lights and covered with tartan ribbons. From its branches, felted robins peeped out, alongside old-fashioned wooden ornaments; a train, a spinning top, a brightly coloured drum, too many for Ruby to take in all at once.

She smiled at Darcie's gurgling appreciation, looking at Jem to see his reaction. He was staring open-mouthed, not at the tree, but at the Victorian tiled fireplace which was ablaze with colour and dancing with flame, filling the room with a comforting warmth. A basket of logs sat on the hearth and either side of the chimney breast someone had hung a colourful felt stocking. A small label was pinned to each, bearing the names of her two children.

A sudden lump formed in her throat as she took in the rest of the room, small touches here and there which spoke of a thoughtfulness far beyond what she was paying for. Maybe Angus was right; maybe it *was* going to be okay, after all.

Chapter 4

Trixie giggled as she held the torch under her chin, casting a spooky shadow across her face. Beside her, Clara groaned.

'I was already beginning to think this was a mad idea, without you trying to give me nightmares as well,' she said.

'Spoilsport,' replied Trixie, but she was grinning. She reached over her head and flicked a switch back on, illuminating the lamp beside her. Its light shone out into the wide open space of the barn, nearly swallowed by the size of the darkness, but enough to cast a soft glow around them. She shut off the torch.

'So, what do you think?' she asked Clara.

Her reply was a broad grin. 'I can't blooming wait, can you?'

They were lying on two mattresses on the floor of the huge barn, snuggled into sleeping bags. Between them was an assortment of food in various stages of consumption: homemade sausage rolls, some tiny spiced pastries which Trixie had recently found the recipe for and now couldn't get enough of, some crisps, cheese straws and a tub of Quality Street. It wasn't quite midnight, but there was a feast going on nonetheless.

Trixie stared up at the wooden rafters towering above them. 'It doesn't seem possible that we'll be living here come the spring, does it? But Seth is adamant we will.'

She couldn't quite see into the furthest corners of the barn, but they had both stood in there this afternoon as Seth went through the final design with them. Central to the whole space would be a double-height atrium which would effectively become a dining and sitting area for everyone to use, with two smaller rooms either side from where they were hoping to run courses. Behind that would be a kitchen and store rooms, leaving the whole of the upper floor to provide accommodation for Clara and Trixie. It would be warm, comfortable and a real focal point for the wonderful food and hospitality for which Joy's Acre prided itself on. Whenever she pictured it in her mind, Trixie always saw it filled with a bustle of people, laughing mostly, and that was just the way she wanted it.

'The time will fly by,' said Clara. 'And we'll be in before we know it. And then things really will start to happen, won't they?'

'Did I mention my conversation with Noah?' Trixie asked.

'You were going to,' replied Clara, 'but I think we got interrupted. What did he say?'

Trixie inhaled a deep breath. 'Well…' She let the word out in a long rush of air. She was so excited, it was all she could do to stop from getting to her feet and jumping up and down in the air.

Clara took one look at her and grinned. 'Come on then, out with it. I can see that you're dying to tell me.'

'Let's just say I think he's almost as keen to get things going as we are. His business is really beginning to take off and this has come at just the right time for him too. It's the perfect opportunity for us both.'

Noah was the organising influence behind the popular farmers' market that took place in the local town. Clara had been selling surplus produce from the gardens there for some time now, but it hadn't been until Trixie had come to Joy's Acre that things had really taken off.

Not only did they now sell vegetables, but Trixie had started making bread on a regular basis and it had proved to be so popular that she couldn't keep up with demand. Then they had begun to experiment selling various cakes, as well as savoury pies, quiches and a selection of preserves. The flood of comments and requests for the recipes they had received had given rise to a handmade cookbook which, although still in its infancy, had already sold in sufficient quantity to make them consider having it professionally printed. Now there were several other plans in the pipeline.

'So is Noah really going to take over the shop in Penny Lane?'

Trixie nodded. 'Yes, from the new year. He'll continue to run the market, and hopefully find someone to keep his stall going, but the main emphasis of his business will shift to the shop. In some ways, though, it will make life easier for him as he'll be on hand rather than having to trek back and forth from his own farm.'

Clara picked up one of the cheese straws that Trixie had made and looked at it greedily, before shoving most of it into her mouth. 'The town's first specialist cheese shop,' she mused. 'It makes me hungry just thinking about it. But I'm so thrilled that he's finally seeing the rewards for all his hard work.'

'I think it's amazing what he's done. His dad would have been so proud of him.'

'I'm proud of *you*,' said Clara. 'I think what you've achieved is nothing short of miraculous. And Noah must be very grateful.'

Trixie hoped that the light in the barn was sufficiently dim that Clara couldn't see her blush. Noah had been *very* grateful, and although she knew that he'd been caught up in the excitement of his news, his hug and kiss had caught Trixie completely by surprise.

'But his cheese is soooo good! Anyone would have done the same.'

'No, they wouldn't,' replied Clara. 'They'd have just said his cheese was nice, and left it there, not gone around telling everyone how wonderful it was or devoting a whole chapter of their cookbook to him. They wouldn't have arranged for the details of his business to be added to the Joy's Acre website as an official supplier, or spoken to Seth about the possibility of running some courses with him from this very barn.'

'Possibly, possibly not, but it wouldn't have mattered one iota if what he produced was rubbish.'

'I guess not…' agreed Clara. 'But I'm still very proud of you.'

Trixie grinned. 'I'm proud of you too,' she countered.

Clara waved a hand towards the empty wine bottle which stood in between the two mattresses. 'Are we both a little bit drunk?' she asked, grinning.

'Probably,' replied Trixie, 'but I don't care. At least not at this precise moment. I might care a very great deal come the morning…'

'Indeed,' muttered Clara soberly. 'So, what are the plans for tomorrow anyway? Or perhaps I should rephrase that… What are we doing first?'

As usual there would be a massive list of things to be done, but with several extra projects on the go on top of their usual work, fitting everything in was going to require military-level planning.

Trixie groaned. 'Breakfast of course. No one around here thinks straight on an empty stomach.'

'Honestly… Do you ever think about anything other than food?' teased Clara.

'Not really… and I have a feeling I'm going to be dreaming about it too very soon. Noah is coming over mid-morning and we're going to have a brainstorming session with Maddie. If we don't nail the tricky question of catering for half the village soon then Maddie and

Seth's wedding reception is going to be a rather sorry affair. I think it's a fantastic idea to enlist as much help from the local community as we can, but it's going to take some organising. I need him to speak to everyone at the farmers' market as soon as possible.'

'Poor Maddie is going to be exhausted; I'm nabbing her later in the day to sort out how we're going to decorate this place.' Clara stared up at the rafters above her head. 'It's going to take several truckloads of flowers and foliage just to make a dent in it.' She sighed happily. 'I can't begin to think how we're going to achieve it all, there's so much to do I don't know where to start... So imagine how Maddie must be feeling? I still can't believe she didn't guess that Seth was going to pop the question, and I'm even more astonished that none of us gave the game away. I came so close on several occasions, and how on earth you managed to keep quiet, I'll never know.'

Trixie grinned. 'You and me both,' she said. 'It really is just like a fairytale, isn't it?'

'Getting married at Christmas...' Clara trailed off, peeping at Trixie from under her lashes. 'I can't help myself, I'm stupidly excited. I feel like a six-year-old on Christmas Eve.'

'I think we're all going to feel like six-year-olds this Christmas Eve,' Trixie replied. 'Maddie especially. It will be her first proper day as Mrs Thomas.'

'*And* there's a massive party to look forward to. She and Seth don't do things by halves, do they? But then I guess we wouldn't want it any other way.' Clara picked up a sausage roll and bit it in half.

Trixie nodded. 'We'll never be bored, that's for sure.' Taking Clara's lead, she helped herself to another snack. 'We should probably get some sleep, tomorrow's going to be another busy day.'

Clara nodded, but both of them knew they would talk for a while yet.

Chapter 5

Ruby loved this first hour or so of the day, when it was quiet and it was just her and Darcie. She knew she shouldn't feel like this, but somehow as soon as Jem was up and about things got more complicated. A glance at the kitchen clock confirmed that she could let him sleep a little while longer; the day was going to be tough enough for him as it was – there was no point in making it longer than it had to be.

Darcie pushed another piece of banana into her mouth, gurgling happily from her highchair. From where she was sitting in the kitchen she had a direct line of sight through to the living room where the Christmas tree stood. Ruby had already turned on the fairylights, and every now and again a twinkle would catch Darcie's eye and her face would light up. It was these moments that Ruby loved. Seeing the carefree joy on her daughter's face made her even more sure that the decision she had taken had been the right one.

She picked up a bundle of wool from the table and dropped it into her lap, pulling out two needles from within it. Within seconds she began to knit, the familiar, almost automatic movement soothing. Her knitting bag had been one of the first things she had unpacked and, as the line of stitches along the needle grew longer, her thoughts drifted towards the things she would need to sort out during the day. First on the list would be to find the local supermarket, and once their stock of food had been replenished, the second most important thing would be to find out where she could get more wool.

Having reached the end of the row, she swapped the needles around and carried on, scarcely even glancing at what she was doing. Her fingers were a blur as she knitted new stitch after stitch. It was another jacket, a riot of patchwork squares in sumptuous jewel-like colours, and she was almost finished. Her customer would receive it in about a week, giving her ample time before Christmas to wrap it up for her daughter and put it under the tree. More importantly, it would also mean that Ruby would receive payment before the big day too.

She glanced at the clock again; five more minutes and she would have to wake Jem. From tomorrow the school bus would collect him from the end of the lane, but she had promised to drive him today, and the last thing she wanted was for them to be late, not on his first day at a new school.

As she rose from the table, a gentle tap came at the door, and Ruby smiled, knowing exactly who would be standing there.

The morning hadn't yet woken behind her, but Trixie's hair still glowed a vivid pink as she stood on the doorstep holding a large square basket. Her cheeks were also flushed, either from the heat of her kitchen or the chill of the early morning air, Ruby couldn't tell, but her smile was just as warm as it had been the day before.

Trixie handed over the basket with a grin. 'Morning! It's going to be a beautiful day – well, according to the weather forecast it is anyway. Bit hard to tell just yet.'

Ruby nodded. 'It is. I love bright, crisp days, even if it does mean it's colder.'

Although still dark, there was enough light from the twinkle of the Christmas tree in the garden to see that everything had a beautiful white frosting to it this morning, and upon rising she had stood for several minutes just staring at it through the window. It was so pretty.

'Mind you, we'd better make the most of it,' Ruby went on. 'I heard on the news that there might be snow on the way.'

Trixie grinned. 'They say that every year. I think it's a ruse to make us all think we're going to have a white Christmas. We never do though. Anyway, make sure you eat that lot before it gets cold, it's a big day ahead,' she added. 'But at least Jem won't be hungry. I've popped a couple of extra treats in there as well, so if he doesn't fancy them now, perhaps he could take them for his lunch.'

Ruby peered into the basket, but everything was well wrapped. She didn't know quite what to say; gestures of kindness were not something she was used to.

'Enjoy your breakfast,' said Trixie, taking a step backwards. 'Got to dash, sorry.' She was already moving off down the path. 'But I'll see you later,' she called, giving a cheery wave.

Ruby stared after her before closing the door, already lost in thoughts of the day ahead.

Back inside the kitchen, her hunger was beginning to make itself known, but before she investigated the contents of the basket, she really needed to wake Jem. Perhaps the lure of a scrumptious breakfast would be enough to pull him from his bed. She moved through into the living room, and had one hand on the newel post of the stairs before she realised that Jem was sitting on the bottom step. She dropped to her haunches.

'Morning sweetheart,' she said to his bent head. 'I didn't realise you were up.'

'It's too quiet,' grumbled Jem, 'and too dark.'

Ruby had relished the change from the normal noise of the busy street where they had lived before. Even on the darkest of nights the rooms had been lit by the eerie orange glow from the street lights outside. But here, everything was still, and she had felt the peace it brought seep into her before drifting off to sleep. It hadn't occurred to her that Jem might feel differently about it.

'I could find you a night light,' she said. 'Just until you get used to it.'

His eyes looked jet-black as he looked up at her and for a moment she thought he might agree, but then he jumped up, causing her to almost lose her balance as she hastily moved out of the way. He pushed past her into the kitchen.

'Night lights are for babies,' he said.

Ruby's heart sank. It was such an awkward age for him, but no matter what she did he seemed to push her away. More so when he was feeling upset or unsure about something. She had expected it this morning, but it still hurt.

She followed him into the kitchen where he was already sitting at the table. She took out a couple of plates from a cupboard and placed them in front of him.

'Trixie's just been with breakfast,' she said. 'Shall we see what she's brought… She mentioned some special treats.'

As soon as she removed the cloth cover from the basket the most delicious smell wafted up. Warm bread, cinnamon and something smoky. She touched the first dish gingerly. She had made the mistake yesterday of diving in rather too eagerly and almost burnt her hand. The dishes were just as hot today. She lifted the first one out with a cloth and set it down, carefully removing the foil. Inside was a mini cooked breakfast, just for Jem: sausages, bacon, homemade potato rösti and some baked beans in a little ramekin. She transferred it all to his plate, trying not to smile as he clutched his knife and fork in anticipation.

A small platter came next, holding some toast fingers for Darcie, smeared in Marmite, together with a variety of fruit including some fresh figs which Ruby adored. A bowl lay underneath full of creamy Greek yoghurt swirled with honey. Finally, she lifted clear another cloth basket and revealed a selection of warm bread rolls, a couple of cinnamon swirls and some sticky flapjacks. Her stomach gurgled appreciatively as she laid it all out on the table. How they would eat it all she had no idea, but what they didn't use would certainly be saved for later. She handed a finger of toast to her daughter and took a bread roll for herself, holding it to her nose and sniffing the heavenly aroma. As breakfasts went, she didn't think it could be bettered.

Forty-five minutes later and the good start to the day had palled as she followed her morose son along the path through the gardens. Even the cheerful Christmas tree went unnoticed as he trudged past, head down, his virtually empty school bag bouncing on his back. She pulled the knitted blanket in which Darcie was wrapped closer around her and tried to remain cheerful.

She had already visited the local primary school before moving, a rather rushed visit given the circumstances, but the head teacher had taken one look at her and seemed to understand her predicament, assuring her that her son would be able to start with them at very short notice if that were necessary. Now, as she pulled up a little distance from the old Victorian building, she hoped that spirit of understanding would continue. There were only two weeks left in the term before the children finished for the Christmas holidays, but that was plenty of time for Jem to get into trouble.

It was only a small school – less than one hundred pupils so a quarter of the size of his old one – but, despite that, it had a huge playground that rang with the sound of excited voices. The lane was still busy with parents walking their children to school, a far cry from the vehicle-choked streets she was used to twice a day. She climbed from the car and opened the rear door, unclipping Darcie from her car seat.

'We're here, Jem,' she said gently. He was staring straight ahead.

Holding Darcie in her arms she smiled shyly at another mother passing by and walked around to open Jem's door. She held out her hand, praying that he would at least get out of the car. He had scarcely said two words the entire morning, but his body language spoke volumes. Jem was scared and it broke her heart to see him looking so vulnerable.

To her surprise, as she straightened, she realised that another boy was standing by her side, his mum hovering close by; the same woman she had just smiled at.

'Do you want to come in with me?' the boy said.

Ruby looked up gratefully, catching his mother's eye.

'This is William,' the woman said, smiling. 'We were told that someone new was starting today. The boys will be in the same class, you see.'

'Oh,' said Ruby. 'I really didn't expect… but thank you, that's very kind.' She waited until Jem was standing beside her.

'Say hello, Jem,' she said.

He managed a muttered reply, looking at the boy beside him with a mixture of horror and curiosity. He looked half Jem's age.

William swung his school bag onto his back. 'Do you want a game of kickabout?' he asked. 'We've still got ten minutes before we have to go in.'

Jem looked up and she nodded reassuringly. 'It's okay,' she said, 'I'll be there in a minute.'

William caught his arm. 'Come on!' he urged, and to her surprise Jem followed him, breaking into a run to keep up.

Ruby jiggled Darcie on her hip. 'Thank you,' she said again. 'He's a bit nervous.'

'Of course he is, but I'm sure he'll be fine. It's a lovely school. I'm Louise by the way, the vicar's wife.'

'Oh, I see,' replied Ruby, realising as soon as she said it how rude it sounded. But Louise just laughed.

'And you're right… I have been given my instructions,' she said. 'But that doesn't mean you're not very welcome to the village.' She smiled and held out her hand. 'And don't worry, my husband isn't about to try and get you to join his flock, although of course he'd be overjoyed if you wanted to. But it's his job to know who's coming into the village, it kind of goes with the territory.'

Ruby shook her hand. 'I'm so sorry… I didn't mean…' she trailed off, giving a rueful smile. 'Well, actually I probably did… although you look nothing like a vicar's wife—' She groaned. 'Oh God, I'm just making this worse.'

'And now you've blasphemed as well,' said Louise, giggling. 'But don't worry, I won't tell.' She smiled at Darcie. 'I'm also very pleased to hear I look nothing like a vicar's wife.'

'I'm Ruby… and I'm very pleased to meet you,' she said. 'Shall we start again?'

'No need,' replied Louise, grinning. 'I think that was a great start. I love your coat by the way.'

'I love yours!'

The two women smiled at one another and began to walk towards the school.

Ruby genuinely didn't think she had seen anyone who looked less like a vicar's wife than Louise did. She was wearing a very short stretchy skirt which was bright red in colour and had teamed it with thick black tights and biker boots. A leather jacket and multi-coloured scarf completed the outfit. She was, thought Ruby, extremely pretty. Her eyes were the most extraordinary colour, almost violet in hue, and they twinkled out from a heart-shaped face topped with jet-black hair cut into a short crop.

'And who's this little one?' Louise asked, reaching out a hand to touch Darcie's chubby leg which was peeking out from under the blanket. 'She's adorable.'

'Darcie,' Ruby replied. 'And I'm probably not supposed to say this, but she is, totally adorable. As good as gold…' She pulled a face. 'But then she is only eight months old. Time will tell, I suppose.'

'Oh yes, make the most of it. But she's beautiful… She has your colouring.'

Ruby felt herself blush slightly, but it was true. Darcie's eyes were the brightest blue, just like her own, and she had the same rosy brown hair, which was already beginning to curl.

'So I gather you're staying up at Joy's Acre for now?' said Louise. 'Sorry, Jenny in the shop mentioned you'd been in the other day. We did wonder, only I thought you were moving into the Fishers' place down by the Old Rectory?'

Ruby smiled to herself. So this was what village life was like.

'Yes, but the house won't be ready until the middle of January, so the cottage at the farm is just to tide me over until then. It's gorgeous though, I might not want to leave.'

Louise nodded. 'I haven't been up there in ages, but I hear good things about it. And now Seth and Maddie are getting married too. He was very sweet when he came to organise it with Peter… that's my husband. It was supposed to be a surprise because he hadn't even asked Maddie to marry him at the time, so we've all known about it for ages, but have been sworn to secrecy.'

'Oh, I didn't know... I've only met Seth briefly, and Maddie of course, but not surprisingly she didn't mention it. I mean, she wouldn't, would she? I'm a complete stranger.'

Louise laughed. 'Oh, don't bank on being that for long, not around here anyway.'

It was meant as a friendly comment, but Ruby couldn't help but feel a little nervous.

They paused by the school gate into the playground, where, after a quick scan of the area, she could see Jem running around, chasing after a football. She couldn't remember the last time she had seen him do that, and her heart lifted at the sight.

Louise slid a small drawstring bag from her shoulder. 'William!' she called, as he raced past her. 'Don't forget your PE kit!' She rolled her eyes at Ruby. 'What are they like?' she said, grinning.

As Ruby watched William run over, a tall woman began to make her way towards them. She was carrying a thermal mug and was muffled up against the cold.

'You must be Jem's mum?' she said. 'I'm Penny Robinson, the year five and six teacher, so Jem will be in my class.' She turned to look behind her. 'He doesn't look like he's going to have any bother settling in, does he?'

To Ruby's amazement, even though he must have seen her come over, Jem was still racing around the playground. It was on the tip of her tongue to disagree, but she was conscious of Louise still standing beside her, and given how happy Jem currently looked it would have seemed odd. And she certainly didn't want to come across as an overly anxious, neurotic mother.

'I hope not,' she replied instead. 'Although he was very nervous this morning... Not that you'd ever know it now,' she added.

'That's only to be expected, but I'm sure he'll be fine. I'll keep an eye on him in any case, I promise.' The teacher checked her watch, fishing a whistle out of her pocket. 'Will it be you picking him up this evening, or Dad? Just so that we know.' She was already looking back towards the playground, ready to marshal the children for the day ahead.

Ruby bit her lip. 'No, just me... Jem's dad's not around.'

Miss Robinson flashed her a smile. 'No problem. I'll see you later then... and don't worry, he'll be fine.' She turned away, leaving her and Louise still standing by the gate.

William rushed over as the whistle blew and grabbed his PE kit, hugging Louise tightly at the same time.

'Bye, Mum,' he panted and dashed off again. Ruby searched the line of children now filing into school for her son, but he was lost in the thick of them. She had wanted to say goodbye. To tell him everything would be okay. To have a kiss and hug from him just like William had given his mum, even if she knew that was very unlikely. But now Jem had gone and he hadn't even looked at her.

She felt a soft touch on her arm. 'It's tough, isn't it?' said Louise, a sympathetic expression on her face. 'You want them to be okay, to grow up and be independent, but you want them to need you as well... It's just like the song says really... they're slipping through your fingers all the while.'

Ruby stared at her. She had a horrible feeling that Jem had slipped through hers a long time ago.

Chapter 6

It had been all Ruby could do not to cry and, as such, Louise had offered her a cup of tea back at the vicarage, but she had politely declined. She had liked Louise instantly, but it felt too soon to be sharing things with someone else, and that was surely what would have happened if she had accepted her offer. She had pretended a list of things to do as long as your arm and promised to catch up with Louise another time, and she would, just not today.

She was only minutes away from Joy's Acre when she realised how silly she was being. She had been dreading this morning, and it had gone far better than she could ever have imagined. Jem had actually looked happy and the horrible scenes that she had envisaged had never materialised. More than that, even though by her own admission Louise had been sent as a welcoming committee, she had still been very kind and Ruby had felt a rare connection with her. Perhaps there would be a friendship in time, and that was more than she had dared to hope for. She drove back through the gates of Joy's Acre with a considerably lighter heart than when she had left.

Now that Jem was safely at school, the day stretched ahead of her. Although she had slightly misled Louise about the urgency of the things she needed to attend to, she hadn't lied about their existence in the first place. She had been on automatic pilot as she left the school, heading straight back to the cottage, but now she realised it would make far more sense to head back out again to do her shopping first, before she became involved in something else. What she needed was a set of instructions. Before she changed her mind, she made straight for the main house and knocked on the front door, popping a sleeping Darcie in her car seat down on the ground for a moment.

There was no reply straight away and, as the seconds clicked by, she wondered if she should knock again, only louder this time. She was just about to try when she heard Trixie's voice from the other side of the door.

'It's open… just turn the handle. Only if I try I'm going to cover everything in goo…'

Tentatively, Ruby did as she was asked. The door swung open and she came face-to-face with Trixie, whose hands were covered in a gloopy mess.

'Oh,' she said. 'Sorry, I could come back.'

'No, come in, come in.' Trixie smiled. 'It's an occupational hazard, I'm afraid. When I'm making bread it renders me quite incapable of anything else for a little while, not unless I want to cover the house in blobs of dough.'

Ruby hoisted the car seat and found herself in a welcoming hallway with original quarry tiles and the most delicious warmth enveloping her. Two bright paintings hung on the wall and, always drawn to colour, she peered at them for a moment.

'Lovely, aren't they?' said Trixie, standing back to allow Ruby the time to look at them properly.

'Beautiful… such a gorgeous use of colour.' She studied them again, and then looked up, thinking, a smile coming over her face as she realised their significance.

'They're here, aren't they? Paintings of the gardens?'

Trixie beamed. 'They are. Painted by Joy herself.'

Ruby gave her a puzzled look. 'Joy?'

'Yes. Joy Davenport. The farm is named after her.'

'Oh, of course... Joy's Acre! I remember reading about it on your website. It doesn't do justice to the real thing though, does it? The colours are so vibrant.'

Trixie smiled. 'I can see why you like them.' She was nodding towards Ruby's coat, a multi-coloured patchwork of knitted and fabric squares. 'Your jacket is amazing. You could never be gloomy in that, could you?'

Ruby didn't answer straight away. It was perfectly possible.

'It's kind of a thing I do,' she explained. 'I don't really work... not with Darcie, being on my own and all that.'

'You made that?' Trixie's voice had risen several octaves. She didn't seem the slightest bit concerned about Ruby's last statement. 'Oh my goodness, but that's incredible. It must have taken you ages.' She leaned in for a closer look, suddenly becoming aware of her sticky hands, and jumping back.

'I have some more, back at the cottage,' Ruby replied. 'You could come over and have a look if you like... One day, when you're not so busy...' She trailed off, biting her lip, but to her surprise, Trixie readily agreed.

'Oh, I'd love to. In fact, Maddie and Clara would probably want to come and have a look as well. Would that be all right? I know they'd love them too.'

Ruby nodded, beginning to feel a little overheated in the warm hallway.

'Anyway, come in,' said Trixie. 'If you can just give me a minute to finish bringing the dough together, I can clean my hands and make us some tea if you like.'

'No, honestly, it's fine. You carry on,' she replied. 'I don't want to interrupt you; I just came to ask for some directions actually.'

Trixie cocked her head to one side, glancing down and smiling at Darcie. 'Aw, bless her… It's no trouble, honestly. How did it go this morning anyway?'

Ruby thought for a moment, wondering just how much to say. 'It was good actually,' she said. 'Much better than I expected anyway, and amazingly Jem seemed quite happy. He was nervous on the way there, but then once we arrived another lad came and took him under his wing. That helped enormously.'

'And did you meet Louise?'

The question surprised her. 'The vicar's wife? Yes… actually it was her little boy who came over to play with Jem.'

Trixie laughed. 'I thought you might have. She's a one-woman welcoming committee, but don't let that put you off, Louise is one of the nicest people you could ever hope to meet.'

'Yes, she seemed lovely. In fact, she offered me a cup of tea as well. And it will be nice to know someone in the village for when I move on from here.'

'Well, I'm hoping she's going to give us a hand with the Christmas party we're having, although it's a joint celebration really, party on the one hand, wedding reception on the other. Anyway, you'll get to know her soon, I'm sure.' Trixie already had her hands plunged back into a huge mixing bowl, rhythmically pulling together the sticky dough. A warm yeasty smell filled the room.

'Yes, she mentioned that. It's for Maddie and Seth, isn't it?'

Trixie rubbed her forearm across her nose to satisfy an itch, and she nodded. 'I'm so excited… and it's not even me getting married.'

It was on the tip of Ruby's tongue to ask whether Trixie might need extra help, but she thought better of it. It sounded as if things were well under control.

'Anyway, I had better let you get on,' she said. 'But I just wondered if you could give me directions to the nearest supermarket. I really need to stock up a bit.'

Trixie smiled. 'No problem, it's dead easy to find, and not too far from the centre of town. Although we're lucky; amazingly, we still have a really good butcher and greengrocer in the town, and a fishmonger at the regular market.' She paused for a moment. 'And a specialist cheesemonger opening in the new year…'

Ruby's eyes lit up. 'Oh, no. I'm a bit of a pig when it comes to cheese. Jem is too.'

'Well, I'm not sure exactly when it's going to open, but I'll find out for you. I'm meeting the man who's opening it later on this morning. He supplies the farm at the minute.' She pulled off several great clumps of dough from her fingers and dropped them back into the bowl, before dumping out the whole lot onto the table.

'Anyway, Tesco is just on the roundabout before you get to the town, so when you get to the village, just go on past the school and you'll be on the right road. You can't miss it.'

Ruby thanked her and, picking up Darcie, headed for the door. 'I'll let myself out, don't worry.' A cloud of flour had just risen up around Trixie as she began to pound the dough. She grinned. 'And call in on your way back if you want to. There should be cake by then.'

★

Trixie was right, the supermarket wasn't difficult to find and, shopping completed, Ruby was soon out again and heading towards the town. There was only one thing she had to do out of necessity, but she was keen to see what else the town had to offer. Fifteen minutes later, she had parked and, deciding against the pushchair, strapped on her baby carrier and settled Darcie into it, who almost immediately began to kick her legs, gurgling with pleasure. She was getting heavy, but shopping trips were always far more enjoyable this way. Darcie loved being able to see everything, and although she often fell asleep, Ruby enjoyed feeling her close.

What with moving and Jem's first day at school, she had almost forgotten that it was quite so near to Christmas, but there was no escaping it here. The market square was dominated by a huge tree and every street seemed to be festooned with lights, dipping and swaying across the road. The individual shopfronts had made the most of their display space and everywhere Ruby looked either sparkled or was covered in fake snow. She began to feel a little of her old excitement at the season returning.

It was a pretty town, predominantly black and white timbered buildings and, despite the obvious trappings of modern-day life, it had a rather Dickensian feel to it that was just perfect for the time of year. She wandered up and down the streets for a little while soaking up the atmosphere and window shopping for the future. She found the butcher and the greengrocer that Trixie had mentioned, but there were also several other shops she would have loved to have lingered in if she'd had the money to do so; taking her time to choose a new book, or a colourful braided rug that she spotted in a fair-trade shop. As it was, she could scarcely afford to buy the new mobile phone she needed, but it was a necessity, and so she pushed open the door to the shop with some reluctance.

She hovered by the display for several minutes, trying to work out the relative costs of the phones on display, but the shop wasn't busy and after a polite period of time, a salesman approached her.

'I just need a very basic pay as you go phone,' she explained. 'The cheapest one you have.'

She watched as his face fell a little and she steeled herself for the hard sell. 'I'm not going to use it much, you see. It's just for back-up really in case anyone needs to get hold of me, or I need to make the odd call.'

He nodded, reaching towards the display for one of the handsets she had looked at previously.

'And I need a bit of data,' she added. 'Not much, but enough to check websites and email occasionally, that kind of thing.'

'I can do you two gigabytes for a tenner a month. The phone costs fifteen quid.' He thrust it at her with a blank expression.

'And do you have to spend that every month?'

'Yeah. They don't do rollovers any more. It renews every thirty days.' He stood waiting for her decision. 'Talk time is about an hour and a half with the two gig, but the talk time doubles if you only have one gig.'

She stared at him.

'It's a three-option pack, you see. Either more data, less talk time, less data and more talk time, or a bit of a mixture.'

It was tempting to ask him if he had any other tones of voice, but then she was bored with the whole thing too.

'I'll take it,' she said. 'And the option with the two gigs of data please.' She jiggled Darcie to one side slightly and fished about in her handbag. 'I'd also like the contract cancelling on this please.' She handed him one of the newer model iPhones. 'I won't be using it any more.'

His mouth dropped open slightly and it was all she could do not to giggle. It wasn't at all funny, but for some reason she found his reaction rather amusing. She could see the tussle on his face; he was dying to ask her why, but as she had no intention of telling him it didn't matter to her anyway. She held his look, and the question that began to form on his lips died.

'Sure, no problem. Would you like to come over to the desk?'

Twenty minutes later she left the shop, clutching a paper carrier. Her old phone was safely stashed back in her bag. It would work until the end of the month, she had been informed, and after then, nothing… That suited her just fine.

She was halfway down the road when she realised that her pace was not far off a march. She stopped and, turning, checked her reflection in the nearest shop window. She was scowling. She inhaled a deep breath and slowly stood up straight, pulling her shoulders back. The phone thing was done and dusted and she really didn't need to think about it any more. Or, more importantly, let it spoil what had otherwise been a very good day so far. She pushed it to the back of her mind and gave a little wave towards the window, knowing that Darcie would see it. Sure enough, her daughter's hand lifted as she attempted to copy Ruby, and her face broke into a smile.

'Come on, sweetheart,' she muttered. 'Let's go see the pretty lights.'

She retraced her steps back around to the market square and stood for a few minutes beside the Christmas tree, taking in the cold clear air as she let Darcie gently touch the ends of the branches. The lights moved gently in the sway of the wind and Darcie followed their dancing patterns with her eyes, gurgling with delight as she attempted to 'catch' them, even though they were some distance from her.

At the base of the tree a bright printed sign announced an evening of carols to be held right there in the square. Ruby bent to check the details. As a child she had loved singing from door to door in the village where she grew up; but sadly it was a tradition that seemed to have largely died out. Here though, a local choir would be visiting and everyone would be welcome to sing traditional carols around the tree, with mulled wine and mince pies served as refreshments. It would be lovely to come along, she thought, wondering whether she might be able to persuade Jem. Her head was already filling with how she imagined it would look: lots of rosy cheeks, heads bobbing with bright woolly hats, breath frosting in the cold air as they sang, and the swell of voices filling the starlit sky...

She sighed and after a few more moments moved off; there was no point getting ahead of herself. She followed a small lane to her right which she hadn't noticed at first, tiny as it was, not even big enough for cars to pass down. Overhead the leaning upper storeys of the timbered buildings almost touched and, at the far end, silhouetted against the brightness of the sky behind she could just make out a church spire. Lights glowed along the length of the passageway and Ruby felt like she had been transported into a scene from a bygone era. She had only taken a few steps when she realised that the enticing array of bay-fronted windows were, in fact, empty, and the shops themselves just shells. Intrigued, she moved closer.

It soon became clear that the whole row of buildings had just been renovated. The whitewash in between the dark wooden timbers on the front of the buildings was freshly painted and the beautiful mahogany woodwork of the doors and windows gleamed amid the twinkling lights. The pavement was divided into sections so that the centre of the lane was filled with flat cobblestones, a smooth pathway having been laid on either side. It was clean and free from the accumulated dirt of years of footsteps.

As she moved along she came to a slightly larger shop with a central doorway and two windows, one either side. The door was open and the sound of a radio playing Christmas music wafted from inside. A woman was standing behind a counter deep in conversation with a young man, while another woman was adding fresh poinsettias to each of the tables that filled the room. She looked up as Ruby hovered in the doorway.

'Sorry, love, we don't open until tomorrow, but it would be lovely if you could come back then.'

'Oh, I'm not… I was just being nosey, sorry. I've never been down here before.'

'Well, it's been all closed up for weeks, and they only just finished the footpath a couple of days ago, so you wouldn't have been able to even if you had wanted to.'

Ruby nodded. 'I've just moved to the area,' she explained. 'But this looks lovely…' She looked up to see if she could see a sign. 'What are you called?'

'Dotty Lottie's,' she replied, grinning. 'That's Lottie over there and she's completely crackers, never mind dotty…'

The other woman looked up. 'I heard that…' she said. 'Although it's all true, I'm afraid. I must be mad, opening a tearoom just weeks before Christmas.'

'Or very clever,' replied Ruby. 'I think people will enjoy having a break from all the Christmas shopping. I'll definitely try and come back. What sort of things will you have on the menu?'

'Well, Dotty Lotties for one…' The woman grinned and came out from behind the counter, picking up a jar that rested on its top. She took the lid off and tilted it forward so that Ruby could see.

'Would you like one for your daughter?' she asked. 'Well, you might want to share it, but…'

Ruby looked inside. The jar was filled with enormous cookies covered in brightly coloured chocolate beans. She laughed.

'That's a Dotty Lottie? Oh, I love it, what a brilliant name.'

'And the beans are made using only natural colourings as well, so no nasties.'

Ruby helped herself, swinging the biscuit out of the way of Darcie's eager hands. 'Thank you, that's very kind. I might save it for later though if you don't mind, otherwise I can foresee all kinds of mess!'

'I'll get you a bag and you can take it home with you. Just so long as you pop back to tell us what you thought.'

'It's a deal.'

She waited while the woman returned to the counter, placing the jar back down as she did so. The man still standing there watched with an amused expression on his face.

'Well, that's favouritism if ever I saw it. Here I am, one of your most favoured and reliable suppliers, not to mention favourite people, and I don't even get so much as a crumb.' He turned and smiled at Ruby.

'Oh go on with you, Noah, you're on your third cup of coffee at least this morning…' But Lottie took the lid off the jar again anyway and took out another cookie, popping it into a bag. 'Now go on, shoo, we've got work to do.'

The man pulled a face, before checking his watch. 'Crikey, is that the time? I'm going to be late.' He flashed a sheepish smile. 'Thanks, Lottie.'

Ruby stood to one side to let him pass before placing her biscuit into the proffered bag.

'I'd better get going too,' she said. 'But I'll come back soon. And, thanks again; it was lovely to meet you.'

'No problem.' Lottie grinned at Darcie, waving as she did so before giving her hand a tiny shake. 'And you can come back any time too, you're gorgeous…'

Ruby tucked the paper bag inside her coat pocket and left the tearoom with a smile still etched on her face. She gave a quick check of her own watch, before walking back down the lane. As she was about to rejoin the market square a man backed out of the last empty shop in the row, locking it behind him. He almost bumped straight into her.

'Oops, sorry… Oh, hello again!' It was the same man from the tearoom. 'More haste, less speed.'

Ruby smiled and peered past him. 'Is this your shop? Are you going to be opening one too?'

He grinned. 'I am,' he said proudly. 'Not until the new year though…' He trailed off. 'I'll give you a clue… *It's Gouda to meet you… To Brie or not to Brie, that is the question… Mind your step now, Caerphilly does it…*'

'Hah! It wouldn't be a *cheese* shop by any chance, would it?' she replied, her laughter cut short by a flash of something that Trixie had said that morning. 'Oh, wait a minute, are you the chap…? You must be, it would be too much of coincidence otherwise…'

His eyebrows raised in reply, an amused smirk on his face.

'Sorry… I was just trying to remember what someone had said this morning. I'm staying in a holiday cottage at the moment and the lady who cooks there mentioned there was a cheese shop opening in the town.'

'What, Trixie? It's got to be, hasn't it? Blimey, how weird is that? I'm on my way to meet her now as it happens. That was who you meant, was it? Pink spiky hair, gorgeous dimples, you can't miss her?'

Ruby nodded. 'One and the same. How funny…'

The man held out his hand. 'Noah Candlish,' he said. 'Purveyor of fine cheeses.'

'Pleased to meet you,' she said. What a day it was turning out to be. She looked up at the agent's 'To Let' board above their heads, now flashed with a big red banner proclaiming the shop taken.

'So are all these shops going to be opening soon? It's lovely down here.'

Noah squinted back up the lane. 'Most of them, I think. There's just one, more or less in the middle, that hasn't gone. It's a bit of a quirky shape, beautifully formed, but only tiny. I think that's the problem with it. Why? Are you interested?'

She felt her stomach give a little lurch. It had been a dream for as long as she could remember.

'No, not really…' she said, wondering how best to explain. Or whether she should explain at all. 'I mean, once upon a time I'd have given my teeth for the chance of something like this, but not now… I don't think I could.'

Noah cocked his head to one side. 'Well, if you're thinking about it at all, I would get down the agent's quick if I were you. The developer is probably quite keen to do a deal right now, otherwise he could well get stuck with that one.'

'Oh, I'm really not sure, I…' She trailed off. 'Sorry, I'm holding you up.'

He pulled a face. 'I probably should get going, but listen, it was nice meeting you, er…?'

'Ruby,' she supplied.

He nodded. 'And I'll probably see you around anyway as you're staying up at Joy's Acre. I have a feeling I might be there quite often, one way or another.'

He beamed a smile at her and took off across the market square, leaving her smiling in his wake. She kissed the top of her daughter's head.

'Well then, Darcie,' she said. 'What do you think to that?'

Chapter 7

Angus looked up at the sudden movement, and frowned as he saw Jem marching across the garden, his head down, dragging his rucksack along the ground behind him. His mum wasn't far behind, but there was no way she could keep up with her son, weighed down by a bag of shopping in one arm and her daughter in the other. Angus stopped what he was doing, put down his paintbrush and, without another thought, set off down the path that would intersect with hers.

Catching sight of him marching towards her, a look of alarm crossed her face and he slowed his pace, unconsciously dipping his head and hunching his shoulders to make himself appear smaller.

'May I carry your bag for you?' he asked, holding out his hand. Ruby looked flustered and, now that he was nearer, he could see two bright points of colour in her pale cheeks.

'Oh.' She stopped for a moment and looked around, almost as if Angus might be talking to someone else. Her eyes flicked anxiously towards her son. 'Sorry, it's just that…'

'I know,' he said gently.

Her eyes locked on his and he saw the faint look of surprise in them before recognition took over and she nodded.

'Thank you,' she said simply.

He took the bag from her and she used her free hand to help support the weight of her daughter, hitching her higher on her hip and looking relieved. They were like two peas in a pod, her and her baby. Both had the same bright blue eyes, chestnut hair curling around the same delicate heart-shaped face, and rosebud lips. Little Darcie would break a few hearts when she was older, that was for sure, just like someone had obviously broken her mother's…

He walked beside Ruby as she hurried to the cottage door, fishing in her pocket for the key. Jem stood to one side, still avoiding eye contact.

Ruby opened the door, intending to go first, but instead having to make way as Jem rudely pushed past her.

'Jem!'

He was through the door and down the hallway in a flash, and her remonstration fell on deaf ears. She flashed Angus an apologetic smile and left him standing in the doorway.

Her low, urgent voice came from the kitchen and, after a few moments, Angus heard the thump of heavy steps on the stairs and a thud above his head as something was dropped to the floor.

'You can come in, Angus! Please, don't stand on ceremony.' Her head poked around the kitchen door and he took a step forward, then another, encouraged by her smile.

Darcie was already sitting in her highchair by the time he entered the kitchen and he looked enquiringly at Ruby.

'Anywhere's fine,' she said.

He placed the bag of shopping carefully onto one of the chairs beside the table.

'Are there more?' he asked. 'I could fetch them for you.'

For a moment he thought she would refuse, but then he saw the slight sag in her shoulders as she accepted the tiredness she so obviously felt, and her face broke into a smile of gratitude.

'I have a boot load, I'm afraid,' she said, handing him back the same keys she had used to open the door with. 'I think you know which car is mine?'

He nodded and slipped back out into the garden.

Dusk was already on its way. Not quite with them yet, but years of working outdoors had given Angus a finely tuned sense of the seasons and the changes they brought. In another hour the light would be almost completely gone and he would need to continue with his work indoors. He should really be making the most of what little daylight there was left, but he knew that he wouldn't; the task he was engaged in would still be waiting for him tomorrow. This evening, or the early part of it at least, he knew he was needed elsewhere.

Something about Ruby struck a chord with him; perhaps it was the brightly coloured clothes she wore that were so joyful and confident although she seemed neither of things, or her deep blue eyes, that always seemed so wary and watchful. Whatever it was, he felt an overwhelming need to protect her.

It didn't take him long to fetch the bags from her car, and he carried all six of them easily, retracing his path through the garden. Maddie, or someone else, had switched on the fairylights along the side of the house and he guessed that shortly the occupants of the cottages would do the same. He hoped so, he loved the light.

Ruby had left the door of the cottage ajar, guessing quite rightly that he would have his hands full upon his return, and he nudged it gently with his hip, backing through the door, and using his boot to softly assist its closure. He could hear the kettle coming to the boil as he made his way down the hallway. Of Jem, there was still no sign, but Ruby had already unpacked the bag of shopping he had left with her.

'Would you like a cuppa?' she asked. 'Whichever you prefer.'

He nodded, placing the bags carefully on the floor beside the table before rubbing his hands together briskly. 'Tea would be lovely, thank you… if you have time.'

'Always.'

She added teabags to two cups and crossed to the table where she picked up her handbag and hung it in a tall cupboard. Finally, taking off her coat, she hung it over the back of a chair and took something from the pocket. She placed the paper bag down on the table.

'You might like that,' she said. 'I'm not sure my son deserves it.'

He eyed the bag for a moment before lifting one edge. Inside was a huge cookie, its sweet sugary smell wafting out at him. He smiled before letting the paper drop again.

'I'm tempted,' he said. 'I can't deny I'm a sucker for anything sweet, but I couldn't take it from Jem. He might deserve it later, perhaps when he's had the opportunity to calm down.'

Ruby assessed his comment but didn't reply, giving only the faintest of nods. Instead she took milk from the fridge, pouring a plastic sippy cup half full and giving it to Darcie before adding milk to another glass.

'First day at school, was it?' he asked. 'I take it things didn't go too well?'

Ruby regarded him quietly, obviously weighing up just how much she should confide. Then she sighed.

'I don't understand it,' she said. 'I know he wasn't looking forward to it, but when I left him in the playground this morning, he was running around with all the other boys playing football. Tonight when I picked him up, he said he'd had a horrible day. His teacher also told me that he'd been very sullen and withdrawn for most of it, despite her best efforts to draw him out. I suppose I should be grateful he didn't get into a fight with anyone. That would have gone down really well.'

Angus smiled sympathetically. 'Nerves make people behave awkwardly at the best of times,' he said.

'Yes, but still. You'd think he'd be relieved to be home if that were the case, but his mood doesn't seem to have improved at all.' She picked up the glass of milk. 'I'll just go and see if he'd like this,' she added. 'I won't be a moment.'

Angus watched her go, wondering whether he should finish making their tea. She looked like she could do with a cup. He glanced across at Darcie and smiled, rewarded as her face lit up.

'What do you think?' he said. 'Would Mummy mind if I made the tea?' He picked up the spoon from the side and began to prod the teabags, making faces at Darcie as he did so. The sound of voices could be heard from overhead.

He was just depositing the teabags into the bin when Ruby reappeared, her face a mixture of anger and despair.

'I don't care what kind of a day he's had,' she said. 'There's no excuse for rudeness.' She placed the still-full glass back down on the table and crossed to the other side of the kitchen where a small black box was plugged into the power. She flicked the switch to the off position. 'He can do without that for a while too,' she added before taking a seat at the table.

Angus placed a mug of tea beside her. Almost immediately, she jumped up. 'What am I doing? It's me that's supposed to be doing that… you're supposed to be sitting down and drinking it.'

He smiled. 'As are you,' he replied. 'If the end result is the same, does it matter who does what?'

She stared at him, slowly sinking back into her seat. 'Thank you,' she said. 'I'm not sure why you're doing this.'

'Perhaps simply because my day sounds like it's been slightly better than yours.'

She gave a rueful smile. 'That's the annoying thing,' she said. 'It's actually been rather a nice day but—' She was about to continue when there was a loud thump from upstairs and a scurry of feet.

'Mu-uuum!' came the wailing call through the doorway from the living room to the kitchen. 'The internet's gone off now. Why won't it work?'

Ruby calmly swivelled in her chair.

'It's gone off because I've turned it off, Jem.'

'But *whyyyy*?'

'Perhaps you might like to think about why,' she replied.

Angus looked at the boy's sulky face. 'Hi, Jem,' he said, smiling.

Jem looked over, but ignored Angus's greeting. 'I haven't done anything… That's not fair!'

'Neither have I, Jem,' said Ruby quietly. 'And yet you seem to think it's okay to be rude and uncaring, ungrateful even. We've had these conversations before. I know you've had a tough first day at your new school, but there is no excuse for behaving badly when someone is trying to help you. Nor is there any excuse for ignoring someone's greeting. Please say hello to Angus.'

Jem muttered something unintelligible under his breath, followed by, 'Well, I didn't ask him to come here!'

'No, neither did I. But Angus very kindly offered to help with the shopping bags, something which I asked you to do, but you refused. Therefore, we are now sharing a drink together because that's the polite way to behave when someone shows you a kindness.'

Angus stared at her, a warmth filling his insides. It was a simple sentiment, but so few people these days seemed to understand it, and he had never heard it put so eloquently.

'You're very welcome to sit and have your milk with us, Jem,' she added, nodding to the glass on the table.

'I don't want your stupid milk,' he said, tears welling up in his eyes. 'And I don't want you!'

Before either of them could stop him, he rushed past them both and into the hallway.

'Jem! Stop!'

But it was too late. The front door had been wrenched open and, as Angus reached the threshold, he could see the boy's figure running full pelt along the path towards the cottage which lay on the other side of the garden. From there, it was only a few more metres to the gate which led out into the fields.

He reached out a hand. 'I'll follow him, Ruby, don't worry.'

'But it's getting dark! He doesn't know his way around... and he hasn't even got his coat on.'

Her face was creased with anxiety and from the kitchen Angus could hear the first tentative cries from a startled Darcie.

'I know every inch of these fields like the back of my hand... and I promise you, he'll come to no harm. Look after Darcie.' He smiled. 'We'll be back soon.'

Despite his assurances, he was anxious to keep Jem within sight and, without waiting for a response, he took off after the lad. It was true, he did know every inch of the fields and the woodland that lay beyond, but he needed to be sure which way Jem would turn as he went through the gate.

Angus could easily outrun him, pick him up and bring him back if he wanted to. Small boys could run fast, but Angus's legs were long and strong and, despite his size, he was quick and agile. However, unless there was a danger of real harm befalling him, this was not Angus's intention. He sensed a very real need for release deep within Jem, and as long as he was safe, there was no better place to release it.

Angus reached the gate only moments behind Jem, but even so he only just spotted him running along the length of the hedgerow before he disappeared. The boy had no idea anyone was even behind him, and he suspected that he would continue running at the same pace until he could do so no longer. Keeping a measured distance behind, Angus gritted his teeth and began to follow him, slowing his pace once he was sure where Jem was headed.

In the open light of the fields, the dusk was not so obvious, but as soon as he entered the woodland, the light dimmed dramatically. It made no difference to Angus, but to a young, upset child, he imagined it would quickly become scary. He dropped his eyes to the woodland floor, scanning for signs that someone had passed, taking soundless steps until he picked up the trail. Several minutes later he spotted Jem up ahead of him, and slackened his pace still further, keeping Jem in his sights continually, and only stopping when he did. He leaned against a tree and watched as Jem stared around him, his movements now slow and hesitant.

It was bitterly cold, but at least under the cover provided by the trees the wind had dropped. Some day, if he got the chance, Angus could show him how to make a fire, or a shelter. How to navigate by looking around him and studying what he saw, or even by the sun or the stars. Now though, he simply watched.

After a few moments Jem kicked out at the ground with his foot in frustration, dislodging a branch that had fallen there. He picked it up, wiping his hands down his trousers, and picked at something on the branch before throwing it away dismissively. He kicked at the ground again, this time only disturbing a handful of rotting leaves.

Angus saw when his mood began to change, when Jem started to study the ground more intently and, after a few moments of looking around, found what he was looking for. It was a much larger branch this time, partly hidden in the undergrowth, and Jem reached down with both hands to pull it free. He lifted the log, testing its weight for a minute, raising it over his head experimentally before walking to the nearest tree and crashing the branch against it with all his might.

The first blow made Angus flinch, but not the second or the third. Or the dozen after that as Jem repeatedly vented his anger. Angus watched him calmly, feeling within his own body the satisfaction that the blows gave the boy. He knew exactly what they felt like because he had stood in very similar spots, raining down blows, just as he was.

He knew from his own experience that the all-consuming rage would pass just as quickly as it had arrived, leaving Jem feeling weak and perhaps at his most vulnerable; longing for comfort, familiarity and home. However, there were no guarantees that he would remember the way, and the lad could just as easily turn and run blindly in the wrong direction, shaken by the force of his own emotions. Even though he wanted to rush in and help, Angus forced himself to hold back until Jem's intentions were clear. If he knew Angus had witnessed his outburst Jem would feel hugely embarrassed, perhaps even ashamed. He might never allow himself to show his feelings again.

Eventually, Jem dropped the log, his arms hanging limply by his sides, exhausted. His chest was heaving from the physical exhaustion and his head hung low. He stayed that way for several minutes, his shoulders shaking with emotion, until finally he straightened and began to look around him. The dusk had fallen quickly since his outburst and, although he could still see the immediate area around him, Angus knew that the landmarks surrounding Jem would now be blurred and indistinct. Jem's head swivelled as he sought to make sense of where he was and, more importantly, where he needed to go, and his movements became quicker as panic rose within him. He took a few steps in one direction and then stopped, returning to his previous spot and looking around him once more. He moved forwards, head lifted to the sky, and set off again, this time in entirely the wrong direction. It was time for Angus to move.

He broke into a run, loudly crashing through the undergrowth, his movements exaggerated at first in order to make more noise until he was sure he had Jem's attention. He slowed then, waving, smiling and calmly stopping only a few metres from Jem.

'There you are, lad,' he said, moving no closer. ''Bout time we headed for home, I reckon…' He nodded his head over his shoulder to indicate the path Jem should take. It would be an awful lot quicker to pick the boy up, but he hadn't gained his trust yet. That was something he would need to earn. And robbing him of his dignity just now would be no way to go about it.

Jem narrowed his eyes but said nothing, looking nervously past Angus and beginning to shiver.

'You could follow me if you like?' said Angus. 'Just till we get out of the woodland. Then maybe you could find your own way home?'

He took a couple of small steps back towards Joy's Acre and then stopped again, his ears straining. When he heard Jem moving too, he took another few steps, then a few more, until he was happy the boy was following him at a distance. They continued that way until they reached the threshold of the wood where the path widened out into the wintry scrub of the meadow. It was almost fully dark now and Angus moved to one side so that Jem could walk beside him. Silently, and a little distance apart, the two of them walked home.

Chapter 8

Maddie looked up from her meal, suddenly aware that although the others were chatting readily around the table, the woodcutter seemed to be lost in his own thoughts.

'Is everything all right, Angus? Only you seem rather quiet.'

'Apologies,' he replied. 'I must admit to being a little preoccupied.' He gave her an engaging smile. 'But it's nothing to trouble you with… not when there is such fine food on the table.'

Trixie caught his words and dipped her head in acknowledgement. 'I may have been the cook on this occasion, but you have Clara to thank for the recipe.'

Maddie grinned. 'As do I. Because, in fact, this is the exact same dish that Clara taught me how to make on my second-ever day at Joy's Acre. I was utterly hopeless, trying to impress a certain chap sitting not too far from here, and this is what we made.' She smiled at Seth. 'I think it did the trick…'

'Oh, it wasn't your *cooking*…' fired back Seth. He gave Clara a hasty glance. 'Although this *is* lovely.'

Angus dipped his spoon back into the smoky vegetable and lentil casserole and took a reflective mouthful, nodding vigorously. Maddie pushed the plate of accompanying cheese scones towards him so that he could take another.

'You've been over with Ruby, haven't you?' she asked. 'Is everything all right?'

Angus looked rather uncomfortable for a moment, obviously deciding what, if anything, he should divulge.

'I think she's had rather a tough time of things lately,' he said.

Maddie nodded. 'I was in the kitchen when she got back with Jem earlier. I couldn't help but notice that things were a little… difficult. I don't think Jem was very happy after his first day at school.'

'No,' said Angus, chewing. 'He wasn't. He's not a happy young chap at all.' He picked up a piece of scone to dip in the juices from the stew. 'I think Ruby is doing her best under somewhat difficult circumstances. I didn't like to pry, but…'

'You can't help but notice things,' said Maddie, finishing his sentence. She looked around the table. 'I know she's a guest here, and it's really none of our business, but she can't move into her new house in the village until after Christmas…' Heads were nodding around the table, and both Clara and Trixie caught her eye. '… Which is a whole month or so away yet. If she needs some help I don't think we should ignore it, that's not really the way we do things here at Joy's Acre, is it? The move is obviously going to be a fresh start for her and her family, so why don't we see what we can do to make things a bit easier for her?'

'If she wants us to,' cautioned Seth.

'Well, yes of course,' she answered automatically, only just catching the look Seth gave to Tom.

'What?' she said.

Seth grinned. 'Nothing… just that not everyone might appreciate being "helped".'

'No, I know that.' She threw him a look that made it clear how ridiculous his last statement was. 'In any case, we wouldn't be interfering, we'd be offering our support, our friendship… and besides, sometimes the best way to help someone is by—'

'Getting them to help you!' Trixie flapped her hands in excitement. 'Of course it is. I was talking to her just this morning… Did you see her amazing coat by the way? She makes them herself… Anyway, she was popping into town to do some shopping and stopped by for directions. We got talking and I mentioned Louise to her and how she will probably be giving us a hand to organise the party here – she'd just met Louise outside the school, you see, and—'

Maddie held up her hand. 'You know how I hate to stop you when you're in full flow, Trixie, but…' She winked at Clara. 'Is there a point to this?'

'Bloody cheek!' said Trixie, not at all offended. 'There is, as a matter of fact…' She trailed off, looking expectantly at everyone around the table.

Tom leaned forward, clasping his hands together in front of his chest. 'Oh, do tell!'

Trixie stuck out her tongue. 'The point is, when Ruby and I were talking I also mentioned Noah, and by curious coincidence – or quirky twist of fate, whichever you want to call it – when he arrived here this morning for our chat, the very first thing he mentioned was that he had bumped into Ruby in town. She was looking at the new shops on Penny Lane, and he got the distinct impression that she was interested in one of them for herself.'

'To rent, do you mean?' asked Clara.

'I think so. It would make perfect sense for her to be interested in having a shop, given the wonderful things she makes. Anyway, the point is…' she broke off to look pointedly at Maddie, 'the point *is* that she is obviously a very creative person, and we're going to need an awful lot of help organising things here, decorations and the like. It struck me that Ruby might like to get involved. If she's having a tough time it could help to take her mind off things, but also, if Louise were to get involved too, it would give Ruby a chance to get to know her better as well. They're going to be neighbours soon, what could be more perfect?'

There was a moment of silence before Maddie burst out, 'Trixie, that's bloody genius! What a wonderful idea!'

Trixie gave a little bow. 'See, I don't talk rubbish *all* the time,' she said.

Angus gave a deep-throated chuckle. 'I'd heard folks say there was something a bit special about this place, and I thought they were just being fanciful.'

'And now you've come to join us as well,' replied Maddie, giving him a knowing look. 'And you're already helping Ruby, so whatever magic there is about this place, it would seem you've already picked it up.'

'Or had it in the first place,' said Seth. 'Agatha always used to tell me there was something about you she could never quite put her finger on.'

'She probably couldn't reach,' muttered Angus.

'*And*,' continued Seth, 'that she had never met a man who spoke so little, but managed to say so much.'

Trixie frowned. 'Well, what's that supposed to mean?'

'Enigmatic,' said Maddie. 'That's what you are.' She smiled at Angus. 'That's a compliment by the way.'

Angus beamed. 'I quite like the sound of that.' He paused for a moment. 'I've been meaning to go and see her, Agatha that is, and see how she is settling in to being waited on hand and foot.'

'Loving it,' replied Maddie. 'Moving into the village was the best thing she's ever done, she told me. She also admitted that although she had loved living at the Hall, she wished she'd had the courage to move years ago. The blacksmiths' competition in the autumn was like a wonderful swan song apparently, but now she'll be spending the winter warm and free from worry about the cost of heating the place… Oh, and enjoying all the village gossip. Her eyes lit up when she told me that bit, as you can imagine.'

Seth nodded. 'I think she's spreading quite a bit of it too by the sound of things.'

Maddie caught Clara's eye and smiled. 'You might not want to mention the bit about the cost of the heating bills to Declan.'

Clara was just about to take a bite of her scone, and waved an airy hand. 'I wouldn't worry,' she said. 'He's got pots of money.'

Trixie snorted. 'And their romance is still as strong as ever,' she said. 'I wonder why…'

Clara grinned.

'Don't knock it,' she said. 'Not when he's lending you the use of his kitchen, freezers, crockery, and seating for the wedding…'

'Fair point,' said Trixie. 'Did Agatha never throw anything away?' she asked.

'Oh no, she did,' said Maddie, 'but I think she always hoped that whoever took over ownership of the Hall would resurrect the tradition of hosting an annual village fete, and so anything that had ever been used to put on the event has been kept. Sorted, wrapped, stored, even catalogued. The fact that now there's going to be a Christmas party as well as a wedding is just icing on the cake. She couldn't possibly expect Declan to host it so soon after moving in though, so she's thrilled to bits that we're having it here this year, and even more so that Declan has already committed to holding the fete again in the summer.'

'Knowing Agatha, it was probably a condition of the sale,' said Tom.

'Quite possibly,' admitted Maddie. 'But it's still a good thing to do for the village. I think people are quite excited by the prospect.'

'I wonder why…' muttered Trixie with a coy look at Maddie.

She blushed. 'Well yes, obviously when I suggested we hold the Christmas party I had no idea that it was actually going to be my wedding reception as well…' And then a broad grin broke across her face. 'I'm getting married!' she squealed, unable to hold in her excitement any longer. 'At Christmas! And how you lot managed to keep it a secret I shall never know… you especially.' She directed a look at Trixie.

'I thought I'd blown it several times,' admitted Trixie, 'but by some miracle I managed to keep my mouth shut. Oh, but it was absolute *torture*…'

She caught hold of Maddie's hand, pulling it upwards and angling it towards the overhead light so that her ring sparkled.

Maddie stared at it herself, her face softening at the memory of the night that Seth had given it to her. She looked up at Trixie's grinning face.

'I was going to try to be professional here – and have a sensible conversation about where we were with all the plans – but bugger that, it can wait… There's something far more exciting coming up!' She couldn't hold back her news any longer and gave another high-pitched squeal.

'We're going wedding-dress shopping tomorrow!'

Seth's head shot up. 'Are you?' he said, giving her the look that made her knees feel fizzy. A slow smile broke over his face. 'That means it's real, doesn't it? It is actually happening and I don't have to keep pinching myself to check it's not all a dream.'

When he looked at her like that it was easy to forget that the room was full of other people.

'It is a dream,' she said. 'But I never thought that one day it would be *my* dream, or that it would come true. So these two gorgeous women here are coming with me tomorrow to make sure I get the most perfect wedding dress in the whole history of wedding dresses… ever.'

'Yep,' said Clara. 'We are.'

'And the best bridesmaids' dresses in the whole history of brides-maids' dresses, don't forget,' added Maddie.

'Yep, those too.'

'Well, *obviously…*' drawled Trixie.

Seth sat forward in his chair and looked around the table expectantly. 'Right,' he said in a business-like fashion. 'That's you three covered as far as tomorrow goes. What's everyone else up to?'

Clara picked up a piece of her scone which had broken off and threw it at him. 'Pig!' she said.

The laughter rippled around the table, but not before Maddie had caught a glimpse of the look in Seth's eye and seen three grown men turn to mush over the mention of a wedding.

Chapter 9

The shop was simply called 'Grace' and was tucked away on the corner of a small passageway in town that Maddie didn't think she'd ever been down before. From the outside, there was little to recommend it; a single small window held only one gown on display. The shop front was beautiful, elegantly dressed, but easy to overlook. However, a little careful research had revealed that it was certainly the place where she was most likely to find the dress of her dreams.

It was another bright blue-skied morning, and like all the others she had started early, when it was still dark and the night's frost was only visible under the twinkling lights of the tree in the garden. The kitchen was already busy by the time she arrived, and full of the enticing smells that always appeared whenever Trixie was hard at work.

She had tried to refuse the plate of scrambled eggs that Trixie had made for her, complaining that on today of all days her waistline didn't need any more inches, but Trixie was adamant that she eat. After all, it could be worse: she could have given her a full English breakfast instead of the somewhat lighter option she had prepared.

Now, as the three women walked side by side along the passage towards the shop, Maddie was grateful. Her stomach was turning somersaults, and she had a feeling it was only her breakfast keeping it in check. It was a mixture of nerves, anticipation and downright excitement, and the feel of Seth's lips on hers before they left the house had only added to the huge weight of importance that had attached itself to the day.

The shop opened by appointment only, so they would have the whole place to themselves. Maddie felt a little self-conscious at the thought of being the subject of so much attention, but she knew that Trixie at least could be relied upon to keep her feet very firmly on the ground.

She felt Clara's arm slip through hers as she reached forward to press the bell on the smart navy-blue door.

'I can't believe we're actually doing this,' she said.

'Well, you best get used to it,' replied Trixie. 'You're next.'

Clara blushed and pushed aside the comment, but Maddie could see by the look on her face that the thought of it pleased her. A summer wedding perhaps, now that *would* be something lovely to look forward to.

The door was opened almost immediately by a woman much older than Maddie had anticipated. She was simply dressed in pale blue jeans and a beautifully tailored shirt of an almost identical colour, but there was something about her that made even these everyday clothes look special. Softly curled grey hair tumbled halfway down her back.

She took one look at the three of them standing on the doorstep and immediately put out a hand towards Maddie.

'It's lovely to meet you,' she said. 'I'm Grace.' Her welcoming smile took them all in. 'And you must be Trixie?' she added, getting it right first time. 'Which of course means that you must be Clara.' She laughed at their simultaneously nodding heads. 'Come in, come in, and out of the cold.'

She opened the door wider and ushered them into a reception room, which surprisingly was rather dark, but so cosy and comforting after the icy chill of the day outside. A squishy sofa and two armchairs were arranged along one wall, and on the opposite side of the room a desk faced outwards. The third wall held an occasional table with an enormous vase full of deep red roses, glossy green holly and bursts of red berries. Dusky reds, heathery purples and soft blues lent colour to the room, while the mixture of tweed, leather and wool provided the texture. It was not what Maddie had expected to find at all, and neither was the open fire which burned brightly in front of them, the mantelpiece above festooned with gilded pine cones, giant church candles and trails of ivy.

'I thought we might all make ourselves comfortable in here,' said Grace, closing the door on the cold behind them. 'And then whenever you're ready I will show you through to see the gowns. Have a seat and throw off your coats, boots, scarves; whatever makes you feel most at home.' She waved a hand towards the sofa before slipping through a doorway behind the desk.

Maddie looked at both Trixie and Clara in turn and pulled a face that she hoped would convey surprise, slight confusion and delight all at the same time.

Trixie grinned. 'Is now a good time to mention that I think I might have a hole in my sock?'

Clara frowned. 'Oh Trixie, you haven't!' she whispered.

'Just kidding…' she answered, rolling her eyes. 'As if… Although I do think I have my Minnie Mouse knickers on…'

Maddie smothered a giggle. The topic of what to wear this morning had been discussed at length. When Maddie had first arrived at Joy's Acre, almost a year ago, her wardrobe had been as uptight as she was; tailored suits and dresses, all designer and incredibly expensive. Now though, she favoured jeans or leggings which were practical, comfortable and suited her new way of life. These were usually teamed with boots and socks in this weather, and Maddie had cringed at the thought of trying on sumptuous gowns with her bright striped feet peeking out from underneath. Similarly, the rest of her underwear could only be described as functional, well-washed and a little tired-looking. But it was all she had, and the nightmarish description of each other's undergarments the night before had had them all in stitches.

She was just about to make further comment when Grace reappeared carrying a tea tray laden with cups, saucers, a huge teapot, milk, sugar and a plate of tiny shortbread biscuits shaped like stars.

'Not compulsory,' she said, 'but sometimes it helps. And don't worry, I've seen no end of cups upturned or clashed together, tea spilled and dribbled, and biscuits shattered into tiny pieces. It's quite amazing what the human body can do when it's nervous or excited, so please don't worry about any of it.' She placed the tray down on the desk. 'Now, would anyone like a cup?'

Maddie felt relief wash over her, and her nerves began to settle. It was going to be okay after all.

'I'll give it a go,' she said. 'That would be lovely, thank you.'

Five minutes later they were all chatting as if they had known one another for years.

'And you had no clue that's what Seth had planned?' asked Grace. 'That's so romantic… I love summer weddings, but there is something so special about winter ones. We might even get a sprinkling of snow, I hear. Now wouldn't that be magical?'

Maddie smiled and breathed in deeply, feeling a rush of happiness sweep over her. 'And Joy's Acre is so pretty, imagine what it would look like all covered in white…' She sighed. 'The whole thing is magical,' she said. 'That's the thing about Christmas – proper Christmas, that is, not what the shops try to sell you – it's the spirit, that feeling of hope and joy, of giving and kindness, that somehow the whole world remembers what it is to be human.'

'Light amongst the darkness…' breathed Clara.

'Yes,' said Maddie, staring at her. 'That's exactly what it is!'

'Well, it sounds absolutely perfect,' said Grace. 'And the party for all the villagers is a wonderful idea. I can tell it's going to be a very special time.' She put down her cup. 'And on that note, would now be the right moment to go and find that very special dress?'

Maddie looked at the others and grinned. 'I think it might be,' she said. 'Although I still haven't the faintest idea what I'd like.'

'Even better,' said Grace. 'I much prefer a bride who is open to ideas, and we have as much time as you need. You can try the whole lot on if you like.' She rose from her chair and gestured to the door behind the desk. 'Before I show you through, however, I do just want to say one thing, and that's that, in all my time as the owner of this shop, I have seen every size and shape of boobs, bums, thighs and tums… big ones, small ones, wobbly ones and perfectly toned taut ones, and it matters not one jot which type you have. There is a dress somewhere in the next room that will love every inch of you…' Her face lit up with a beaming smile. 'Ladies, shall we?'

She pulled open the door and ushered them along a corridor to a set of double doors at the end. She then paused, a hand on each doorknob, before simultaneously and theatrically throwing them wide open. The minute Maddie glimpsed the room she could understand why, and her mouth hung open in awe and surprise.

The contrast from the cosy, warm, but dimly lit sitting room to this shining, ethereal hall of light was rather magical. From the deep pile of the pale gold carpet and matching chaises longues, to the polished crystal droplets that hung from the series of chandeliers lighting the room, the whole impression was one of grandeur and opulence, and in among it all stood rows and rows of dresses. From the frothy to the sleek, the highly decorated to the understated, and all of them in a palette of white through to the richest of creams.

Directly in front of them stood a ten-foot-high gold-frosted Christmas tree, which glowed with sparkling lights from top to bottom. It was dressed with huge raw-silk bows ranging in colour from the palest wintry sunrise to the rosy hues of a blushing sunset, so beautiful it needed no other decoration.

Even Trixie was speechless.

But perhaps the biggest surprise of all was the sudden peal of laughter that came from Grace's lips.

'Isn't it all so wonderfully over the top,' she said. 'I never tire of seeing people's reactions to it.'

'I've never seen anything like it,' muttered Maddie, wandering over to the tree. 'It's stunning…' She reached out a hand to touch one of the bows, just lightly, enough to confirm that the whole thing wasn't a figment of her imagination.

She stood back a little, her eyes roaming from one bow to another, taking in their crystal centres which at first she had taken for more lights. Her mind was already conjuring up images of how they could transform their own tree. It wouldn't look exactly like this of course, because it was a real tree, but they could follow the same principle and—

Her thoughts came to a sudden stop as she realised that no one else was speaking. In fact, there seemed to be rather an odd hush in the room. She turned around to find the three other women staring at her.

'Erm, Maddie…? I don't think Grace was actually referring to the tree…'

She looked across at their host, suddenly realising her mistake.

'Oh God, you weren't, were you? I'm so sorry… It's just that we have this huge barn, you see, and we need some ideas as to how we're going to decorate it… This would be absolutely perfect, so simple and yet stunning, a real centrepiece.' She turned to Trixie and Clara. 'We could do this, couldn't we? I don't know how many bows we would need, but if everyone made a few then—' She broke off again, blushing furiously. 'Sorry…' she repeated.

Clara was standing with her hands on her hips, shaking her head in amusement.

'Maddie Porter,' she said. 'Only you could come to choose a dress for arguably the most memorable day in your life and get side-tracked with work…'

'Yes, but it's not really work, is it? I mean, I'm thinking about this for the party, which is my wedding reception as well.' She looked at Clara's face, and then Trixie's. 'Okay,' she said. 'I'll shut up now.' She moved to stand so that her back was turned on the tree. 'Right.' She grinned, looking around her. 'Where on earth do we start?'

Grace stepped forward. 'Well, first of all, you're a size ten if I'm not very much mistaken, possibly a size twelve up top, so you need to be looking to start on that side of the room. I'm not going to interfere, and I'd like your friends to hold back too, just for starters, to see what you're naturally drawn towards. Take your time to browse and then maybe pick out four or five gowns that take your eye the most.'

She nodded encouragingly.

Maddie's heart began to beat a little faster, and a bubble of excitement burst inside her. She was actually about to choose her wedding dress…

She walked forwards, scanning the rows of dresses, not knowing quite where to start, but deciding that the beginning was as good a place as any. She didn't want to miss a thing. It took her ten full minutes to get to the last dress on the rack, almost overwhelmed by the assault on her senses, the nuance of colours, the competing forms of decoration, and the sheer amount of choice, and she took a step back for a moment, thinking about what she had just seen. And then she stepped forward once more.

Perhaps sensing that the time was right, Grace crossed the room to a curtained area at the far end, and drew back the heavy drapes, arranging them artfully behind a pair of heavily gilded holdbacks. Behind the curtains was a smaller anteroom, mirrored and flooded with light. A series of hooks hung around the room and, as Maddie withdrew a dress from the rack, Grace seemed to glide across to her, carefully receiving each dress and removing it to hang on display. By the time Maddie had again reached the end of the row, five dresses had been ferried in turn.

Grace beckoned them all to stand so that they could view Maddie's choices.

'Now, tell us what appeals to you about these.'

Maddie looked again at each of the dresses in turn.

'That's so difficult…' she said, screwing up her face. 'This one I love because it's so simple… truly elegant.' She bit her lip. 'It's probably how I think I'd like to look, but I'm not really sure it would actually suit me.' She pointed to one on the end of the row. 'That one because the material is just heavenly. The weight of it for one, and all the beadwork; I just think you'd feel like royalty.' She took a step forward. 'And I love this… utterly dreamy…'

Grace nodded her head, smiling. 'Then let's try them on, shall we?'

Maddie looked confused for a moment. 'Oh…'

'Is that okay…?'

'Yes… it's just that… well, I thought you would try and steer me to the one you think would be best, that's all.'

Grace grinned, looking warmly at Maddie. 'Oh, I already know which one is perfect for you. It's the one you're going to pick, but you need to work that out for yourself.'

'But, what if I don't pick the right one?'

'You will…'

Clara came forward. 'Faith, Maddie,' she said. 'All you need is faith…' She winked at Grace. 'And a little sprinkling of Christmas magic… Now, go on, go… try them on. I need to see you!'

Grace gently took Maddie's arm, and led her behind the curtains, lifting them off their holdbacks so that they fell free. 'One moment, ladies,' she said.

And then Maddie was on her own.

'Which would you like to try first?' asked Grace.

'This one please,' said Maddie, pointing to the very simply styled gown.

'Then let's get going,' said Grace, her face a picture of excitement too. She crossed to a small chest of drawers in the corner that Maddie hadn't even noticed, and took out a flat package wrapped in cellophane. 'Much as I love your socks,' she said, pointing at Maddie's feet, 'I think perhaps you might look more the part in these.' She handed her a pair of white silky tights.

It took Maddie a few minutes to remove her clothes and put on the tights, but then she stood, feeling very self-conscious as Grace lifted the first of the dresses from its hanger and brought it over.

'Now there's a definite knack to putting these on,' she said, 'which is basically for you to stand still and I will fit it around you. Otherwise we end up a tangle of arms, legs and material... So, arms up for me?'

Maddie nodded, feeling the slither of cool fabric glide over her skin.

Grace moved around her with practised ease, a deft touch here and there, until the dress had settled on her like a second skin.

'I daren't look...' Maddie kept her eyes on the ground, holding off the moment when she would look in the mirrors for the first time.

'Right, stand still for just a minute longer while I find you some shoes to pop on, just to lift your height a little for this particular dress.' She cocked her head at Maddie. 'And just one more thing... are you planning on wearing your hair up or down?'

'Up... I think.'

The drawer opened again and Maddie felt the other woman's hands in her hair, gently twisting and pinning her curls away from her shoulders. When Grace was done she took Maddie's hand and held it while she stepped into the shoes. She stood back, an experienced eye running over the dress, checking the detail, assessing what she saw there. She looked up and gave a wide, warm smile.

'I think you're ready to have a look now...'

Maddie's heart fluttered in her chest.

The dress fitted like a glove. Smooth satin clung to her arms in long slender sleeves, wrapping around her bust and waist, skirting her hips before dropping to the floor in a sheath of creamy material. But it was wrong. Maddie was so disappointed she could cry.

What had looked sophisticated and elegant with nothing underneath it, when on, accentuated every lump, bump and imperfection. The fabric was too shiny, too restrictive. She felt trussed up rather than graceful.

'Come on!' came Trixie's voice from the other side of the curtain. 'We're having kittens out here waiting…'

Maddie looked at Grace, but her face gave nothing away. 'Shall we show them?' she suggested.

Maddie turned around while Grace placed the curtains back behind their holders. She saw Trixie's eyes widen and Clara's hand go to her chest, but neither of them said anything immediately.

'What do you think?' whispered Clara after a moment. 'It's stunning…'

'Blimey,' said Trixie. 'Folks would be able to see what you had for dinner.'

Clara looked shocked. 'Trixie, you can't say that!'

But Maddie burst out laughing. 'Oh, bless you!' she said. 'It's awful, isn't it? I feel like an oven-ready turkey. I'd never be able to relax in this.'

'You have a beautiful figure, Maddie,' said Clara, still not comfortable with the idea of being critical.

'Aw, thank you,' she answered, 'but I wouldn't know where to put myself in this. I'd have to stand in one position all day so that it looked perfect.' She turned and looked at Grace. 'Nope,' she said. 'Not for me.'

Grace dipped her head, but still didn't comment, moving instead to swing the curtains closed again.

The second dress was beautiful and so was the third. Both had a similar shape with a fitted bodice and full tulle skirt and Maddie felt her heart lift at the sight of herself. Her head filled with images of the expression on Seth's face the first time he saw her in it, and it was more than she could ever have dreamed of. But how was she ever going to choose?

'If it helps to mention,' said Grace, 'I am a seamstress too, so if you wanted any alterations to a particular dress, I'm always happy to see what I could do. The last dress you tried on, for example, was absolutely delightful, but the amount of embellishment on it has pushed the price up rather. I'm not sure if that's of concern, but if it is I could achieve something similar for you on the previous dress, but without such a hefty price tag.' She hung the dress in question back on the hook.

Maddie nodded. 'It's heavier too, which might be quite nice as it's going to be cold.' She looked back at the others. 'I don't know, what do you think?'

Trixie pursed her lips. 'I like the beading… but there was something about the shape of the other one I preferred. I think it gave you a bit more…' She motioned, pushing her boobs up. 'Well, just a bit more…' She giggled. 'Although having said that, it wouldn't be a good idea for the groom to be seen drooling in public, would it?'

'Trixie!' exclaimed Clara, exasperated.

'What? It was a compliment!'

Maddie exchanged a look with Grace. 'I think I'd better try the next one on,' she said.

She waited while Grace lifted the dress clear over her head, gathering the folds and wisps of material until there was a space for Maddie to slip her arms through. She looked at the two other dresses while the fabric was draped as had been intended, imagining herself walking down the aisle, the notes of Isobel's violin floating out into the air around them… and then, without thinking, she glanced back at the mirror…

Her breath caught in her throat as she took in the reflection of the woman who stood there. A woman with creamy skin, and a figure softly revealed… Her hand went to her cheek as she looked over at Grace, her eyes widening as if to seek assurance that what she had seen was real.

'Is this it?' she whispered.

Grace nodded, a gentle smile slipping over her face, her eyes filled with emotion.

'Yes, Maddie, this is it.' She swung the curtain back one last time as Maddie turned to show her friends the dress that made her feel like the woman she never thought she could be.

Chapter 10

Ruby stared at the phone, torn. She knew she shouldn't look, it would only do damage, but it was like a horror movie you watched through closed fingers, where you couldn't bring yourself to shut your eyes completely.

The phone was still fully charged. She had placed it under her bed last night, and connected it to the power so that it could lie there undiscovered until she had time alone this morning to pull it back out. Now the last of the contacts she still wished to keep had been transferred to her new phone and she was about to put her old one away, for good this time.

She had heard the messages and texts arrive during the night, and could only assume that a stream of them had been delivered in the time since she had arrived at Joy's Acre at the weekend. Her finger hovered for a moment. If she deleted the messages and texts they would no longer be there to haunt her, but to do so would mean she would have to access them first and she was sure to see what they said. She doubted she was ready for that. Besides, she already knew what they would say.

Her thoughts were interrupted by a knock on the door downstairs and, as if someone else had decided her fate for her, she pushed the phone under a pile of jumpers with a resolute nod of her head and shut the drawer.

She opened the door and was surprised to find Maddie, Clara and Trixie all standing on the doorstep looking like a bunch of carol singers about to burst into song.

Clara held out a plate full of mince pies. 'We thought you might like some of these for later,' she said.

'No, we didn't,' argued Trixie, grinning. 'They're a bribe, because we wanted to come see your jackets and thought this would give us a good excuse for arriving mob-handed.'

Ruby laughed and, taking the plate, stood back to make space for them. 'You'd better come in then,' she said.

Maddie rolled her eyes at Trixie's comment. 'Only if it's an okay time though. We haven't interrupted Darcie's nap, have we?'

'She *is* asleep, but no one wakes that child unless she wants to be woken, don't worry. It's a perfect time.'

And it was, it would put paid to dwelling any longer on the life she had left behind.

She led them through into the kitchen, placing the plate down on the table. Beside it lay a jacket, neatly folded and ready for posting. All she had to do was write one of her labels and she could send it on its way.

'You could have a look at this one, if you like,' she said. 'I've made it to order, but I've got a few more upstairs… Actually there's some other things in the living room as well.'

In fact, they were all over the cottage, which was generally what happened when Ruby was around; her woolly projects seemed to expand to fill the space available.

Trixie was the first to come forward, laying her fingers gently against the riot of coloured shapes.

'You can unfold it,' said Ruby. 'I don't mind.'

Trixie did so, her face full of wonder at what Ruby had created. 'I can't believe you made this,' she said. 'How long must something like that take…? And all the different colours as well. I bet you have the most enormous stock of wool.'

'Not as much as you'd think actually,' replied Ruby moving to stand beside her. 'This is a recycled piece, so all the elements came from charity shops mostly…' She paused, wondering how much to say. 'I can't really afford to buy all the wool, so in a way these are better for everyone; better for me financially, better for the environment as I reuse things people no longer want, and it benefits the charities too.'

'I had no idea you could even recycle wool,' said Clara. 'How on earth do you do that, you can't unravel it all, surely?'

Ruby pulled a face. 'Well, you do if you want to knit it again, yes…' She smiled at their amused faces. 'Yes, I know, it sounds like madness, but it's actually quite therapeutic, especially on long dark winter evenings sitting beside the fire. This jacket hasn't been knitted though, not as such. I've simply reused woollen squares – it's a little quicker, and it suited what my customer had in mind.'

'But don't they fray?' asked Trixie. 'If you just cut them up, I mean?'

Ruby smiled. 'I have some magic gumption,' she said. 'It stops all that.'

Trixie turned the jacket over so that she could see the full expanse of the design. 'Did you say you have more of these?' she asked. 'Only I'm a firm believer in buying myself a Christmas present, and I think I may have just found the perfect thing…'

'I have a few here… but I could make you something if you like? That way you could specify the design and colours you wanted…' She looked at the expression on Trixie's face. 'Or I could show you how to make them… We could even make one together, I'm sure there's time.'

Trixie's eyes lit up. 'Could we really? Oh my God, I'd love that…'

Ruby saw Maddie exchange a swift glance with Clara. It was a *told you so* look if ever she saw one.

'Would you like some tea? Hot chocolate, even? We could have them with the mince pies.' They had obviously come for a reason, and while it was lovely that Trixie was so taken with her work, Ruby had a feeling that wasn't why they had come en-masse.

There were enthusiastic nods of heads as all three declared that hot chocolate would be just the thing, and a few minutes later they were seated at the table, a steaming mug each in front of them. Ruby swirled a little cream into the top.

'I always have this handy,' she admitted. 'It's one of the only ways I can successfully bribe Jem when he's in a bad mood. He's a sucker for squirty cream and marshmallows.'

Maddie dipped her finger into the froth, before popping it into her mouth and sighing. 'Who isn't? I think it's what winter was made for,' she said, helping herself to a mince pie. 'How's he getting on anyway?' she asked. 'It's a lovely time of year to be joining the school, but I guess it's tough at any time.'

Ruby pulled a face. 'I think it's probably fair to say the jury's still out,' she said. She really didn't want to talk about it, not when the conversation she'd had with the head teacher yesterday evening was still ringing in her ears. 'He doesn't find change particularly easy,' she added.

'Blimey, who does?' said Trixie. 'I've moved far too many times for my liking, I'm not doing it again.' She gave Maddie a furtive look. 'I don't think I've mentioned this before, but I'm afraid I'm staying at Joy's Acre forever. I hope that's all right?'

Maddie laughed. 'I think you'll find we're all banking on it,' she said, waving her mince pie as proof of her sincerity. 'How about you,

Ruby, are you hoping this is going to be a permanent move for you? I expect it will be good to have the children settled through school.'

'I don't know, we'll have to see,' she said quickly. 'I mean, I'd like to, but... not everything's certain in life, is it?' She took a sip of her chocolate to hide her panic. There was only one reason she'd be moving on again, and if that happened, well... who knew where she'd end up.

Clara was watching her, but she smiled as Ruby caught her eye. 'So what made you choose our little corner of Shropshire then?' she asked. 'You're not from around here, are you?'

Ruby shook her head. 'No, Surrey originally. My parents still live there but I... we don't really keep in touch any more.' She gave a rueful smile. 'They didn't approve when I got pregnant with Jem, or rather, they didn't approve of my relationship with his father.' She lifted her head a little. 'As it happens, they were right... but, well, it's too late now. Water under the bridge and all that.'

'Oh, I'm sorry, Ruby. That must be hard.' Clara looked anxious that she had spoiled the mood. 'I didn't mean to pry.'

Ruby forced a smile onto her face. 'It's no problem,' she said. 'It was all a while ago now, and I'm definitely better off without him. So, I thought the new year was the perfect time for a fresh start, and even though I never knew where Shropshire was until I saw it on a farming programme, it all looked so beautiful I thought what better place to raise a family? I was so lucky to get the cottage in the village, and coming here just fitted in nicely with my plans.'

'Well, we're very glad that you are here,' said Maddie firmly. She paused for a moment, and judging by the hesitant expression on her face, Ruby was certain she was trying to decide whether to spill the beans. 'In fact, we had something we wanted to ask you,' she admitted.

'Trixie was right, the mince pies were a bribe, but not just because we wanted to see your jackets.'

Ruby smiled. 'I guessed as much,' she said. 'But it's fine, ask away.'

'Well, you know I'm getting married at Christmas,' she began.

Trixie rolled her eyes. 'And if you didn't, what planet have you been living on?'

Maddie nudged her arm. 'And we wondered if you might be able to help with one or two things,' she continued, completely ignoring her. 'That is, if you'd like to, of course.'

'What kind of things?' Ruby asked.

She watched as Maddie pulled her phone from out of her pocket.

'We went to get my wedding dress yesterday, and in the shop they had this wonderfully decorated Christmas tree… None of us are any good at sewing things, but seeing as you knit, we wondered if you might be. I took a load of photos – here, have a look.'

Ruby peered at the screen, taking the phone for a better view. She scrolled back and forth between the shots, some in close-up, others from a distance.

'Wow!' she said. 'That's pretty impressive.' She looked back at the photos, flipping through them until she found one which captured the whole tree in the frame. She started to count. 'And how big was this?' she asked.

'About ten foot, I think,' said Maddie. 'But the one we're going to have will be half that again. It's going in the barn.'

Ruby nodded, redoing her sums. She grimaced. 'I reckon you're going to need about a hundred bows,' she said. 'Give or take a few. That's a lot of sewing.'

Maddie's face fell. 'Oh… I didn't really think of that.' She glanced at Clara. 'Ah well, never mind. It was just a thought.'

Ruby held up her hand. 'No, wait a minute. I didn't say it wasn't possible, just that it would take rather a lot of work... But it would look absolutely amazing.' She was certain that the photos hadn't done it justice, and she could only imagine what it would look like in the barn, at night, all lit up for the party...

'Who else do you know who can sew?' Ruby asked. 'They needn't be massively skilled, in fact, if I made a template for the bows, I'm sure all of you would be able to make them.' She thought for a moment. 'We'd need the material of course... and if you wanted the bows decorated like they are in the photos, a selection of beads and crystals, but you can glue them on, we wouldn't need to sew them...' She got up abruptly. 'Hang on, let me just go and fetch something.'

She went into the living room and picked up a big wicker hamper that was sitting on the floor beside the armchair. It was her treasure trove. She brought it back into the kitchen and, moving her chair away from the table, hefted it onto the seat. She lifted the lid of the hamper and took out a large plastic box that sat on top of the contents beneath. Moving the plate of mince pies to one side, she slid the box onto the table.

inside the box were lots of compartments, and each was filled with something different; odd buttons, ribbon, and in one, something sparkling. Ruby scooped out a handful of beads, putting them carefully on the table. They were differing sizes and colours, some clear, some opaque, but they were just the kind of thing they would need.

'I picked these off an old top I took apart once,' she said. 'But you can buy this kind of thing online. It wouldn't take many to give each bow a finishing touch.'

Maddie rolled one between her fingers. 'Oh yes, these would be brilliant.' Her face was a picture. 'Do you really think we could do all this? Wouldn't it take too long?'

'Not if we had enough people. Maybe eight or so, that way we'd only need to make a dozen each. That's doable, surely? And there's four of us here for starters.'

Trixie leaned forward. 'I wonder if Louise could help,' she said. 'And she is the vicar's wife so if she can't then she must know people who can. She's on first-name terms with pretty much everyone in the village.'

'I can ask her at the school gate in the morning if you like,' said Ruby, the first faint stirrings of proper excitement bubbling inside her. This was just the sort of thing she loved doing, and if she ever had the chance to fulfil her dream, then some testimonies from people like Maddie would stand her in good stead... She stopped herself then. *What on earth was she thinking?* There was no way anything like that was ever going to happen. She looked again at Maddie's delighted face. It would still be worth doing though, if only for the fact that it would keep her busy through the days ahead.

She stared at the pile of beads on the table as another idea popped into her head. Carefully, she separated several small round crystals from the pile and placed them a little distance away from the others. Then she rummaged back in the hamper, pulling out a pair of knitting needles and a ball of fine white baby wool.

'Let me just show you something quickly,' she said. 'I made some of these for the Christmas fayre at Jem's old school one year, and even I was surprised by how well they turned out. They were really effective.'

She cast on a row of stitches, her fingers moving so fast they were a blur. 'It's much better if you see them rather than have me just describe them. They sound a bit naff otherwise.' She smiled up at them all. 'Tell me about this dress then, Maddie,' she said. 'Only if you want to, of course...'

Trixie snorted. 'Yeah right...'

Ruby's fingers flew as she listened to Maddie describe her dress. It had been something she had dreamed of for herself once upon a time, but it was clear now that it wasn't meant to be. It didn't mean she couldn't enjoy someone else's excitement though, and Ruby smiled as she watched a softness come over not just Maddie's face, but Trixie and Clara's too. The dress sounded absolutely beautiful and, with Maddie's lovely peaches-and-cream complexion and gleaming curls, Ruby knew she would look stunning.

'Where on earth did you learn to knit like that?' asked Clara, after a few minutes. 'You're not even looking at what you're doing,' she added.

'My grandma taught me,' replied Ruby. 'When I was very, very young. I used to knit endless scarves as a child, which drove my family up the wall, but since then, I've branched out a bit. I've done it for so long it's just second nature to me now,' she said. 'I don't really have to think about it and it relaxes me. I find I think better when I knit.'

Trixie nodded. 'Hmm. Peeling potatoes does it for me,' she said. 'My brain just sort of free-wheels…'

Ruby grinned. 'That's exactly it,' she said, picking up the last of the beads. She finished the row she was working on and then laid the knitting down on the table.

'There,' she said. 'What do you think?'

It wasn't a massive square, but it was big enough to see what Ruby had done. Here and there, dotted among the stitches, individual beads had been added to the knitting. Random in pattern, they nonetheless caught the light, sparkling like tiny dew drops caught in a cobweb.

Maddie shook her head in amazement. 'I have absolutely no idea how you just did that, but it's beautiful! So pretty… just think how it could look at night, then it would really twinkle.'

'I'm not sure what other decoration you'll be having, for the tables and so on,' said Ruby, 'but when I made these before they were actually designed as jam jar covers. You just slip the jar inside, and then you can use it for anything, even put night lights in, I suppose. Or you could have some others lined up on the tables and filled with flowers?'

Clara stared at Maddie. 'Oh my God,' she said. 'She's right. Oh, Maddie, wouldn't they look stunning? A line of these right down the middle of the long trestle tables, some with candles and others filled with the same varieties of flowers that are going in your bouquet. However we dress it up, the barn is still going to look rustic and these would be the perfect foil, especially if we could do the tree as well…'

'And it would look so much better than any of the awful ideas we came up with before. No offence, Clara, but apart from the flower garlands we really didn't have anything to go with, did we?' She took a mouthful of hot chocolate, looking at Ruby over the rim of her mug. 'Clara and I met up the other day to discuss how we were going to transform the barn for the party, but our ideas were a bit lacklustre, shall we say. We obviously should have come to see you first. I can't thank you enough.' She grinned cheekily. 'And if you have any other brilliant notions, please let us know.' She gave a satisfied sigh. 'Oh, I'm so excited now…'

'So what do we need to do first?' asked Trixie. 'Order stuff, I guess?'

Ruby nodded. 'It would be really useful to have some material by the weekend if we could. I know a fair few websites which are really good. We ought to have a look for the beads and crystals too. Once we get those ordered, I can have a think about the best way to make up the bows, get a template sorted out, and then we'd be able to make a start as soon as possible.'

'I could bring my laptop over,' said Maddie, 'but only if you've got time. You must have things of your own you need to do.'

Ruby shook her head. There wasn't anything that couldn't wait, and the prospect of spending a day doing the kinds of things she loved best was far better than trying to keep busy so that unwelcome thoughts didn't start to accumulate.

Trixie glanced at her watch. 'Crikey, is that the time? I need to get on with lunch… You'll join us though, Ruby, won't you? And bring Darcie as well, obviously. I'm sure I can rustle up something for her too.' She drained her mug and got up from the table. 'See you soon,' she said as she headed towards the door.

'I have a man to see about a tree,' said Clara, also getting to her feet. 'So, I best be off too, but I'll catch up with you later.'

And then there were just the two of them left. Ruby smiled, feeling more hopeful than she had for a very long time.

'Right,' said Maddie, 'I'll go and fetch my laptop while you think up even more amazing ideas!'

Chapter 11

Trixie sat down with a satisfied smile. She was tired after another busy day but everyone at Joy's Acre had been fed and watered and, if the clean plates were anything to go by, including those of Ruby, Jem and Darcie, then everyone had enjoyed their meals. She had been going to suggest herself that Joy's Acre provide meals for Ruby and her family. Given the huge amount of help that Ruby would be giving, it seemed only right under the circumstances, so she was inordinately pleased when Maddie had wandered into the kitchen during the early afternoon and asked her to do just that. Now though, the washing-up was done, the kitchen was tidy for another day tomorrow, and Trixie had a lovely evening ahead of her. What could be better?

Her phone suddenly pinged into life beside her and she glanced at the screen as it lit up with a text message.

How do you eat cheese in Wales?

Trixie's smile broadened into a wide grin.

Caerphilly! she typed back, pressing send, and then fired off another. *Hah! You'll have to do better than that…*

Almost immediately a reply came back.

What cheese is made backwards?

She thought for a moment, stumped, until it suddenly came to her.

Edam!

Bugger…

She typed again. *Noah, is there any point to this or are you just trying to impress me with your witty repartee?*

She stared at the screen, waiting for a reply, an amused expression on her face.

Who is Noah? Am insanely jealous.

She laughed out loud, shaking her head. *Idiot*, she thought. Her phone suddenly trilled into life, making her jump, and she snatched it up to answer the call.

'You are a complete lunatic, you know that!'

'I shall take that as a compliment,' said Noah, pausing for a moment. 'How's tricks, Trixie?'

She groaned. 'Will you stop…' she said. 'Honestly, what are you like?'

'Got your attention though, didn't I?'

'You did, but Noah, you could have just rung me, you know.'

'I know, but that's not half as much fun… Anyway, I just rang because I'm going to be running a bit late tomorrow, so I wondered whether I could come about eleven instead of ten? Would that be okay?'

'Noah, it's fine, I'll be here. You can come any time.'

'Great. How are things going?'

'Good, I think. Although that rather depends on how you're getting on.'

'Well, I do have one or two things I could update you with. I tell you what, if you've got time tomorrow, I could stay a little longer and we could have a catch-up.'

'That sounds like a plan. I'll see you at eleven then, shall I?'

'Absolutely, great… I'll look forward to it.'

'Night, Noah.'

'Oh… yeah, night, Trixie.'

She smiled. *Noah Candlish*, she thought to herself. *What are you like?*

★

'Brrr, it's cold out here,' said Trixie as Ruby opened her door a few minutes later. She held up a flask in her hand. 'I hope you like mulled wine? It's non-alcoholic, but still as good, I reckon. I brought some cookies too.'

'Do you know, I'm not really sure,' Ruby replied. 'I may have had it once or twice, but that would have been a long time ago… I don't drink, you know, with the children, and I never really…' She beckoned Trixie to come in, her face brightening. 'I'll certainly give it a try though.' She held out her hands for the goodies.

Trixie followed her down the hallway and back into the kitchen where they had sat earlier that day.

'Goodness!' The table was piled high with knitwear of every conceivable colour.

'I mentioned earlier that I don't have a huge stock of wool,' said Ruby, 'but what I neglected to say was that I do have a very bad habit of collecting jumpers…'

'I'll say.' Trixie crossed to the table and picked up a bright blue sweater. 'Blimey, I can see why someone would have passed this over. You'd look like a peacock.'

'It is a bit eye-watering, isn't it? I bet someone's granny knitted it for them. That's the beauty about reusing wool though – taking something hideous to start with and turning it into something lovely…' she trailed off. 'At least I think that's what I do.'

'Oh you do, definitely…'

Trixie bent down to coo at Darcie who was sitting in a bouncy chair on the floor. She held a bright coloured cloth toy and was energetically trying to stuff it in her mouth.

'I'll need to pop her to bed in a minute,' said Ruby. 'Or she'll start to grizzle.'

'She's such a happy soul though, or she seems to be,' replied Trixie. 'I don't think I've ever heard her cry.'

Ruby looked fondly at her daughter. 'She has her moments, believe me, and I think she's about to start teething, but you're right, generally she's a contented little thing. It makes life so much easier.' She shot Trixie a look and the unspoken comparison between Darcie and Jem dangled in the air between them.

'Should I go and say hello to Jem?' asked Trixie. 'I thought he might like a biscuit.'

'I'm sure he would,' said Ruby. 'He's through in the other room, watching television.'

Trixie nodded and took back the bag of biscuits she had brought with her. Jem was staring at the screen in the corner of the room, exactly as Ruby had said. He was lying on his stomach in front of the fire, both legs bent at the knee, one lazily bending and straightening as he watched. His elbows were bent, hands cupping his chin.

'Hi, Jem,' she said, brightly.

Almost immediately, he shot up from his position on the floor, scooting backwards until his back was against the nearest armchair. He bent his legs up in front of him, folding his arms around them protectively.

'Hey, sorry. I didn't mean to make you jump.' She bent down to his level, holding out the paper bag in front of her. 'I made some biscuits,' she said. 'Would you like one?'

Jem regarded her warily, his eyes flicking to the bag.

'They're chocolate chip…'

From the kitchen came the sound of voices. Trixie hadn't heard anyone knock at the door, but was certain she could hear a man's voice. Jem's eyes darted towards the doorway just as it filled with Angus's huge bulk, and he shot to his feet, leaving Trixie still crouching, her arm outstretched. She got up slowly, feeling a complete fool.

Angus was carrying a basket full of logs and he crossed to place them beside the hearth. Moving the fire guard away, he picked up a poker from a set standing there. He hadn't said a word and neither had Jem but, as she watched, Jem moved to his side and plucked a log from the basket, automatically looking to Angus for approval.

The woodcutter nodded and waited while Jem carefully placed the log onto the fire, before settling it with a prod of the poker.

'How about another?' Angus said. 'It's a cold night out there.'

Jem did as Angus suggested, giving him a shy look, and then he took the fire guard and moved it back into position.

Angus hung up the poker and straightened.

'Evening, Trixie,' he said, giving her an enormous smile. 'Got myself a great assistant here.'

'So I see,' she replied. 'I could make use of one of those.'

Angus shook his head. 'No can do, I'm afraid. I got here first.' His gaze switched to the bag in her hand. 'Oh Lord, are those what I think they are? Here Jem, have a cookie. You haven't tasted cookies until you've had one of Trixie's.'

Trixie smiled encouragingly and held out the bag again. This time Jem took one, looking up at her with big brown eyes.

'Thank you,' he said.

Angus nodded. 'Good lad.' He took a biscuit for himself, winking at Trixie, before taking a huge bite. 'Right, so you were first on my list of log topping up for this evening, but I'd get round the other cottages a lot quicker if I had help. How about coming to give me a hand, Jem, provided I ask Mum and she says it's all right?'

Jem shrugged.

'Suit yourself,' said Angus. 'But I wouldn't ask just anyone, you know. In fact, I don't recall ever having asked anyone to help me before. Fancy that… it must mean I like you.' He turned to walk back towards the door, stopping just as he was about to pass through it.

'Sure you don't want to change your mind?'

Jem was at his side in an instant.

Angus raised a huge hand in farewell. 'Night, Trixie,' he said.

She stared after them, smiling to herself. The more she saw of Angus, the more she liked him.

After giving Ruby and Angus a few moments to have the required conversation, Trixie returned to the kitchen, placing the cookies back down on top of the pile of jumpers.

'He's a nice man,' she said.

'I don't really know him,' replied Ruby, frowning slightly and picking up one of the sweaters. She peered at it as if she had never seen it before.

'Sorry,' said Trixie, 'I think that came across a bit wrong. I wasn't trying to, well, you know, make out that you should like him or anything, just that…'

Ruby looked up and dropped the jumper back down. 'No, *I'm* sorry,' she said. 'I'm just a bit touchy about things like that… being a single parent. Sometimes it can seem as if the whole world thinks you should be part of a couple. Angus *is* lovely, a bit scary to look at, but he's been very kind, especially with Jem. It's been a big help actually.'

'He's worked at the estate next door for years, but now that it's been sold and the woodland transferred to Joy's Acre's ownership, he's come on board with us. I don't think any of us know him that well – Seth and Clara maybe more than the rest of us – but I'm sure he'll look after Jem. He might be huge, but from what I've seen, he's one of the gentlest men I know.'

Ruby smoothed the sleeve of the jumper closest to her, and opened her mouth to speak, but then she closed it again and stared into the distance as if what she wanted to say was written on the wall. Almost abruptly she turned away.

'I tell you what, why don't I pour us a drink and then we can make a start… There's a bit of preparation to be got through before we can knit.' Ruby cocked her head to one side. 'Although, I'll confess, I enjoy this bit just as much.' She indicated the chairs. 'Have a seat.'

Trixie began to look through the heaps of knitwear while she waited for Ruby to join her. Intermittently she pulled faces at Darcie and was rewarded by a gurgling smile.

'Pull out any you particularly like the colour of,' said Ruby, 'and we can have a look.'

She joined Trixie moments later, handing her a glass while at the same time taking a sip of her own drink.

'Ooooh, this *is* good,' she commented. 'Are you sure this isn't going to get me drunk?' she asked. 'It tastes as if it should do…'

Trixie shook her head. 'Cross my heart,' she replied. 'There's not a drop of alcohol in it, although it does taste as if there is, I agree.'

Ruby unceremoniously pushed the woolly heap to one side so that she could put her glass down.

'Do you think that Jem's the way he is because his dad isn't around all the time?'

The question came out of the blue and Trixie had no idea how to answer it. After all, she wasn't the best person to ask.

'He seems a bit shy around people, a little bit…' she searched for a word that wouldn't give offence, '… sullen, sometimes perhaps. But I think that might just be his age. Isn't that how boys of his age are supposed to be?'

Ruby sighed. 'I don't know what I think any more. He's so difficult at times, so angry, and I can't help but think that's my fault, I…'

'Why would it be your fault?'

'Because I…' Ruby looked up, anguish plain to see on her face. 'My relationship with his father is… difficult,' she said. 'And I wonder if that's at the heart of it, let alone the fact that we're no longer together. I've taken Jem's dad away from him.'

Trixie studied her for a minute. 'And what about you?' she said eventually. 'What about what the relationship was doing to you? Isn't that just as important…? Aren't you just as important?' She gave her an encouraging smile. 'I think that Jem will be just fine. It might take a little time, but I honestly think that having a happy mum is far better for him than being around two unhappy parents who just argue all the time.'

Ruby gave a weak smile. 'That's what I try to convince myself. It doesn't always work of course.'

'And having a mum who obviously cares about her children a very great deal makes a huge difference,' Trixie added. 'Don't forget that. Before I moved down here I used to work in one of those so-called "family" pubs, you know, the ones with a token climbing frame in the garden. I saw no end of regular customers at the weekends, and I mean *every* weekend, especially in the summer, who stayed virtually the whole day, drinking steadily, getting progressively louder and more obnoxious as the day went on. It wasn't unusual for arguments to break out either and all this was in front of their children; setting a wonderful example for how to behave. I don't think so.' She broke off and rolled her eyes. 'The poor kids were just left to their own devices, and woe betide any child who wanted anything; they got very short shrift, I can tell you. That kind of parenting isn't parenting at all in my book.'

Ruby smiled. 'You're very kind.'

'No, I'm not,' answered Trixie. 'I'm just honest.' She took a sip of her drink. 'Plus, if Angus is the man I think he is, then it won't do Jem any harm at all to spend time with him.'

She could see that Ruby was reflecting on her words and she hoped it had gone some way to making her feel a little better. The practicalities alone of life as a single parent must be tough enough without feeling that you had somehow failed. She picked up a couple of items from the table, wondering whether she should try and change the subject or let Ruby talk. She didn't suppose she had many opportunities to talk over her concerns with anyone, but she was also conscious that Ruby might feel she was prying and she had no wish to look like she was interfering.

'Right,' said Ruby decisively, and it was obvious that the same consideration had been running through her head as well. It was time to change the subject. 'Let's get going, shall we? Pick a colour you like and we'll go from there.'

Trixie immediately selected the blue jumper that she had spotted earlier. She held it up against her. 'Having bright pink hair doesn't always make wardrobe choices easy.' She grinned. 'So, I've tended to go with the "anything goes" philosophy and just hope for the best.'

'No, I love what you wear,' said Ruby. 'And you're right. There's so much lovely colour in the world to wear only beige or grey. Mix it up, I say.' She pulled an orange cardigan from the pile. 'Is that what you want to go for then, a real mixture of bright colours?'

'I think so,' replied Trixie. 'I think it will make it more individual somehow. It might suit me better.'

Ruby took the cardigan and turned it inside out, peering at the seams. 'What we need are seams like this, do you see? Where there are what look like two rows of braids sewn together. We need to unpick these, otherwise when we unravel the wool all we'll get are short rows of wool which are really hard to do anything with.' She pushed her hand underneath the pile of knitting, searching for something and, after a second, triumphantly removing two pairs of scissors.

'Don't worry about the very bottom, just snip through it, but then after that pull the two bits of the seam apart so that you can cut through the threads that are holding them. See?' She showed Trixie what she meant. 'Why don't you have a go with the blue one and I'll do this?'

Trixie picked up her scissors and tried to copy what Ruby had just shown her. She held it out for inspection.

'Yep, that's right. Just keep going until you get to the neck seam.'

There was a companionable silence for a few minutes while both women concentrated on their task.

'So, are children on the cards for you at some point then?' asked Ruby.

Trixie snorted. 'Hardly,' she said. 'I mean, I don't even have a boy-friend, or any sign of one on the horizon. Besides, I have too many other things I want to do right now. I'm not sure I'm ready for any of that.'

Ruby pulled at a stray thread and nodded. 'There seems to be a lot going on here still, is that what you mean?'

'Here yes, that's where the focus will be, but also out there in the local community so that we get the two things working together. We've already begun to lay some of the groundwork, with the local farmers' market for one. We had no idea that would prove to be the success it's been and it's provided a stepping stone to a few other ideas as well.'

'Hmm?'

'Well, we have a cookbook for one. Nothing professional...' She smiled. 'But it has a sort of rustic authenticity which I like, and it's great for bringing in comment from people. That's how I got to know Noah really, and he's introduced us to more local suppliers like him. Obviously, much of what we serve here comes from Clara's garden, but as far as possible I'd like everything else we use to come from the local area. It makes sound business sense, but it feels right too.'

Ruby thought for a moment. 'I like that. It's what I missed about where I was living before. It will feel nice to be a part of something again.' She glanced at Darcie who was just beginning to fidget. 'I met Noah, did he tell you? I bumped into him when I went into town the other day. He was chatting up the woman from the new tearoom.'

'Which one?'

Ruby pursed her lips together. 'It had a really cute name... I know, Dotty Lottie's.'

Trixie shook her head. 'No, I meant, which woman?'

Ruby raised her eyebrows.

'No, it's nothing like that,' said Trixie hastily. 'Noah is just a friend…
I asked which one because the owner, Lottie, is actually his sister. Small
world.' She grinned.

'Oh, I see… Well, that makes sense.'

Trixie smiled. 'Noah did mention you. In fact, it was pretty much
the very first thing he said.' She gave a teasing smile. 'It wasn't the only
thing he mentioned though…'

'Why, what did he say?' said Ruby, looking up sharply and taking
the bait.

Trixie slugged her drink. 'Only that you seemed interested in the
shops that are up for rent. Are you thinking of taking one?'

Ruby blew out a breath. 'Oh, I wish,' she said. She stopped what she
was doing for a moment and searched Trixie's face. 'I've wanted a shop
of my own ever since I was a little girl,' she admitted. 'My grandparents
used to have a post office and newsagents when I was little. Back then,
places didn't open on a Sunday so whenever we visited them I used to
play for hours, pretending I was the shopkeeper.'

'So, what's stopping you?' asked Trixie.

'Money, time, circumstances… the children,' said Ruby, pulling
a face. 'There are quite a lot of reasons actually. It's just bad timing.'

'But put like that it doesn't sound like there would ever be a right
time,' said Trixie. 'I know the children are only young, but Jem is at
school all day, and Darcie's an absolute dream, you could take her with
you for now. It would be your shop after all, you could do whatever
you wanted.'

Ruby shook her head. 'It's a nice idea, but not really very practical.
And where would I get the money for one? I have a little bit saved,
but not enough to take on something like that.'

'Then get a bank loan, that's what everyone else does.'

'But I'd need a business plan and… stuff like that, and I—'

'Noah would help you, I know he would. In fact, we'd all help you.'

Ruby looked at her, a confused expression on her face. 'But why would you even do something like that? You don't really know me.'

Trixie didn't know exactly why, but then she didn't have a reason for why they wouldn't help her either, which was just as important. She shrugged. 'Why wouldn't we?'

Ruby just stared at her, and a slow smile broke over her face. 'Oh my God…' she said. And then she burst into tears.

Chapter 12

'I didn't quite know what to do. I mean, they were happy tears, but I don't know who was more embarrassed, me or Ruby, and then Angus came back with Jem, and oh, you should have seen the look on his face.'

Noah regarded her from across the table with an amused expression. 'It sounds as if you had quite an eventful evening.'

Trixie groaned. 'Sorry,' she said, realising that she had been talking at double her usual speed. She was a little bit nervous for some reason. 'I'm rabbiting.'

'Don't apologise,' he replied. 'I rather like it. It's quite endearing really…'

She slapped his arm. 'Oh, stop it,' she said. 'You're making me blush… Anyway, I am sorry because, apart from not needing to know that Angus has the hots for Ruby, I've landed you in it as well.'

'Has he?' asked Noah.

'Has he, what?'

'Got the hots for Ruby?'

'What?' Trixie was distracted for a moment. 'Well, no, not exactly…' She thought for a second or two. 'Actually I don't really know, he might have… It's just that he always seems to be round there, and he's so thoughtful and considerate towards her. I mean, when he saw she was in tears last night I really thought for a minute that he was going to pick her up and carry her off to his cave.'

Noah roared with laughter. 'You really are priceless, Trixie, do you know that?'

She shook her head at him, confused. 'But he did!' she protested. 'Honest to goodness, that's what it looked like.'

'I'll take your word for it,' said Noah. 'But to get back to the other part of your earlier sentence for a moment, just why exactly have you landed me in it?'

Trixie bit her lip. 'Oh,' she said. 'Well, it kind of slipped out, but I sort of offered your services in helping Ruby to get a business loan, so she might take on one of the shops…'

Noah sat up a little straighter. 'Did you now…' he said.

'Yes, I know,' said Trixie, screwing up her face. 'It was in the heat of the moment and I know I shouldn't have but I—'

'No, I think that's a brilliant idea!'

Trixie stared at him. 'You do?'

'Well yes, Jake's desperate to get someone to take on that middle shop. Of course, I didn't let on to Ruby that he's my brother-in-law when I first saw her. I just suggested that the owner might be willing to do a good deal on the price, after all he is trying to run a business. But I really liked Ruby and, if she is serious about having the shop, it would do quite a few people a favour…'

Trixie arched her eyebrows. 'Nothing like a spot of well-placed nepotism, is there?'

'Nope. Nothing at all.' Noah grinned. 'But Jake's all right. I know he's family, kind of, but believe me, if I didn't like the bloke there's no way I'd be taking a shop from him. Lottie's finally got what she wants, I'll have something I never even thought would be possible and, if

Ruby comes on board, Jake will be cock-a-hoop. It will earn me a few brownie points and, more importantly, your lovely new guest here will get the shop of her dreams.'

He sat back with a satisfied sigh. 'It's a total win-win situation, Trixie. I think you're a bloody genius.'

Trixie cleared her throat and looked at the plate of cheese samples in front of her. 'I thought we were supposed to be discussing this lot,' she said. 'And having a general catch-up about the food for the wedding. Maddie and Clara should be back soon.'

Noah lifted both hands in the air. 'You brought up the subject of Ruby, not me,' he replied, grinning. 'In lengthy and extravagant detail…'

She narrowed her eyes at him. 'Right, well, I think we can park that particular discussion for a moment. Let me get my notebook and we can go through this lot again. I really liked the new blue cheese, but it packs rather a punch. I'm not sure it will appeal to everyone.'

Moving across to the place beside the cooker where she kept her notebook, Trixie was well aware that Noah was watching her, probably trying to come up with some ribald comment about the size of her bum. She had a good mind to turn around and stick her tongue out; she was a cook for goodness' sake, it was in the job description to be a little… comfortable. Just because Noah had the body of a… She drew herself up short. *Well, really Trixie, that is quite enough of that.*

She averted her eyes as she sat back down. 'So run those names and prices by me again,' she said, 'and I'll write them down this time.'

Noah did as she asked and when she had finished she tapped her pen against the paper. 'I'll have a think and let you know what I need, is that okay?'

He gave a lazy smile. 'That's what you usually do…'

'Yes, I *know*…' God he was infuriating sometimes. She picked up another chunk of cheese and popped it in her mouth. 'So, come on then, tell me where you're up to and what miracles you've worked.'

His manner changed in an instant as he sat up straight once more. 'I need a biscuit first.'

'Oh, for heaven's sake…'

However, once she had fetched the tin and slid it across the table at him, he took a deep breath. 'Let me have a look at that list we made the last time. I think better when I'm looking at something.'

Without warning he swapped chairs, moving around the table so that he was sitting next to her. He leaned across and rested one arm on the table, right next to hers. He scanned the list quickly.

'Okay, bread first. Michelle is very definitely going to help. We discussed the roll option; cottage are fine, but more expensive obviously, so she suggested plain or seeded baguettes might be easier. They slice better apart from anything.' He looked up for a moment. 'Oh, and she won't need to use the freezers, you can have the whole lot fresh on the day, so all she'll need is a final order in the next couple of weeks and the job's a good un.'

He ran his finger down the list on the page, stopping after a few more lines. 'I'm still working on Geoff. He's playing hardball because he's a tight bugger, but he'll come round. He's not the only fishmonger around here, and really he shouldn't have a stall at the farmers' market at all, and he knows it. It's only 'cause he's been in from the beginning that I humour him.'

'So, what do we do if he says no then?'

'He won't.'

Trixie gave him a quizzical look.

'Trust me, he'll come around… And whatever happens you'll still have your salmon, dressed to perfection, it's only the price we're haggling over. It's good business and he knows it, but Geoff doesn't like to give in without a fight.' He checked the list. 'Now then, darling Henry says you can have all the sausage you need – make of that what you will! – and has also agreed that his pies and sausage rolls are yours for the taking.'

Trixie rolled her eyes.

'He has also promised you several turkeys which he will cook with his own fair hands and personally deliver, along with everything else ready sliced… just so long as he can have a kiss under the mistletoe.' His eyes twinkled as he watched for her reaction. 'And then last on the list for now is Mel, whose quiches, salads and other delicatessen dishes are also at your disposal. She's going to bring me over a list of what's available and I'll pop it up to you, hopefully before the weekend. Will that be okay?'

'Noah, you really don't have to go to so much trouble, I can just as easily go down and get it.'

'Yes, but what's the point in having me as your gofer if you're the one who's going for…' He was watching her with an amused expression on his face. 'You don't get it, do you?'

'Get what?'

'*Trixie*,' he said in a firm voice as if talking to a child. 'When I first met you I was a dairy farmer with a passion for making cheese and aspirations that seemed so far out of my reach that it would have been easier to fly to the moon. Now, not only do I have a growing business with established customers, I'm opening a shop, which even in my wildest dreams I thought was several years down the line…'

'All of which you would have got anyway…'

'No, I wouldn't.' He sat further forward in his seat. 'Would you just shut up and listen to me for a minute… I'm trying to wax lyrical about the positive influence you've had on Candlish Cheeses and you keep interrupting me! I might have got somewhere eventually, but not in such a short space of time, or with as much success as I'm having at the moment, and all of that is down to you.'

Trixie could feel herself colouring up. Noah looked so earnest; he obviously believed what he was saying but he was far too modest for his own good. She pulled a face. 'I spoke to a few people, that's all. You make bloody good cheese, Noah, all I did was tell the truth.'

'Yes, but the people you told it to spoke to other people, who in turn spoke to other people. The upshot of which is that I now have firm repeat orders for several local hotels, and enquiries from several other avenues.'

'Oh…'

He grinned at her. 'There now, now you're beginning to understand… *finally*.' He dropped his head a moment, contemplating his biscuit, which he still had not eaten. Then he looked back up at her, eyes full of sudden emotion. 'I just wanted to say thank you, Trixie… a really big thank you. I'm not sure you know quite how much this means to me.'

She could only hold his look for a moment before having to look away herself, otherwise her own welling emotions threatened to get the better of her. She took hold of his hand and gave it a quick squeeze. 'I do, and your dad would be so proud of you… Now eat your biscuit and tell me what you think. Those are a new recipe.'

Having declared that he couldn't possibly make a judgement based on a single sampling, Noah was just sinking his teeth into a second biscuit when the sound of laughter and running feet made them both look up and turn towards the window.

'Oh my God, Noah, look!'

Trixie stared in astonishment at the steady fall of thick white flakes outside the window. 'It's snowing!'

As she spoke, Maddie and Clara ran past the window, their hair and the tops of their shoulders already speckled white. They burst in through the front door, tumbling into the hallway, and laughing like excited school children.

'Oooh, it's all gone down the back of my neck!' cried Maddie, wriggling her arms as she shrugged off her coat to shake off the snow. She stamped her feet to do the same to her boots, grimacing at the rapidly melting ice on the floor.

'Where on earth did this come from?' she asked as she came into the kitchen. 'The sky was clear when we went into the florist, now look at it!'

Clara followed close behind, trying to catch the melted snow as it dripped from the ends of her long hair.

'Oh, hi Noah,' said Maddie.

He was standing by the window, peering out at the sky. 'Looks like the forecasters got it slightly wrong,' he replied, turning to receive Maddie's hug of greeting.

Maddie stood by his side looking out. 'Oh, but isn't it pretty? It's already sticking, look.'

All four of them stood in a line, looking out.

'Of course you know what this means, don't you?' said Trixie, an impish grin on her face. 'Time for a snowball fight!'

'Oh, trust you,' said Clara. 'Snowman building more like…'

'Oh, yes! Even better. With a prize for the biggest one.' She caught Noah's eye. 'Not that I'm competitive or anything…'

'No… really?' He looked at Maddie and Clara for confirmation. 'I'd have thought you were the worst…'

Clara snorted. 'Hah! He's got you sussed.'

Noah turned back to the window. 'Well, sadly ladies, I think we need a bit more snow before we can do either of those things, but you never know, maybe we will have a white Christmas after all.'

Maddie's face lit up. 'Do you really think so?' she asked, looking at Clara. 'Oh, wouldn't it look amazing if it is… The flowers will make a perfect contrast against a snowy backdrop.'

Clara nodded. 'Let's get the kettle on, and I can show you what I mean. I took some photos of what we've decided on; so beautiful. It's going to look absolutely amazing… Maddie's going to look absolutely amazing.'

Noah glanced at his watch. 'I really should get going,' he said, pulling a face. 'Sorry. But Trixie can fill you in with where we are with everything food-wise, Maddie, and once I get the menu from the deli I'll pop back and we can make some firm choices on everything. How does that sound?'

'Fantastic,' replied Maddie, looking fit to burst with excitement.

Trixie walked Noah out to the door, touching his arm for a moment as he took his coat down from the row of pegs. She gave a backward glance towards the kitchen and leaned a little closer to him.

'What do you think?' she whispered, anxiety clouding her face.

He shook his head. 'Don't let's worry just yet. There's plenty of snow left up there to come down today, but hopefully that will be all. The long-range forecast still looks okay, and that's what counts. There's snow coming, but further north. We'll be okay.'

He rubbed Trixie's arm before turning and pulling on his coat. 'I'll give you a ring later, okay?'

She nodded and then frowned. 'What for?' she asked.

Noah held her look for a moment. 'I don't know,' he said, 'but I'll think of something.' And with that he dropped a kiss on her cheek and disappeared through the door.

Trixie was still blushing as she re-entered the kitchen, but fortunately Maddie was busy making drinks while Clara was hacking into a fruit cake, one of the many that Trixie had made while trying to perfect the perfect wedding cake recipe. Clara looked up as Trixie came in.

'Crikey, I'm starving, sorry.'

Trixie waved a hand. 'No, go ahead. I'll be making more tomorrow… and the day after, and probably the day after that as well.' She flashed a grin at Maddie. 'Right, come on then, what flowers did you choose? I'm dying to know.'

Maddie gave a dramatic sigh and fanned her face. 'I'm not sure how much more excitement I can stand, but honestly, how do people *choose*…? Everything was wonderful. I don't know what I would have done without Clara; if she hadn't been there I'd have just said yes to everything.'

Maddie picked up the tray of drinks and carried it over to the table, glancing out of the window as she did so, grinning. 'You never really get proper snow in London, or it never felt like that anyway. This is something else I have to look forward to.'

She handed around the mugs of tea. 'So, we've gone for a really loose look for the bouquet, nothing tight and uniform, it's going to look like someone just gathered a bunch of gorgeousness straight from the fields.' She fished her phone from out of her pocket and began scrolling through the images. 'There'll be huge anemones, glorious white ones and deep purple, then dark magenta peonies, and the deepest red roses you've ever seen. They look just like velvet. Then there's berries, I forget the name of them, fronds of eucalyptus and these other silvery things, oh and trailing ivy too. The contrast between the light and dark is so beautiful.'

'And it will complement Maddie's colouring no end,' added Clara. 'Her dark hair and lips against the creaminess of the dress will be echoed in the colour scheme, and if we do still have a drop of snow on the ground the contrast will be even more vivid.'

'The church is going to be decorated as well,' continued Maddie. 'A wreath on the lych gate, and then a huge garland of similar flowers in an arch over the porch door. The pew ends are going to have little posies, probably just with the anemones and something trailing, ribbons too, and then up by the altar will be a replica of my bouquet on a stand, only much bigger.'

Clara nodded. 'We thought about more of the same for the barn, but because the main feature will be the tree with its golden bows, we're going to keep to a white and gold theme in there, with some greenery, which should complement it beautifully.'

Trixie stared at the photos and then back up at Maddie's face shining with happiness. The flowers would look stunning, but that wasn't what was making ribbons of excitement thread through Trixie's stomach. This was the final piece of the jigsaw that she had been waiting for, and as soon as she'd seen the images she'd known that what she had in mind for the wedding cake would work beautifully.

'What's the matter, Trixie? Don't you like them?'

It took a second for Clara's question to penetrate her brain. 'Oh, no, it's not that, I think the flowers are perfect,' she replied, grinning at Maddie. 'But they've just given me the answers to the questions I had about the design for the wedding cake. I wasn't sure whether what I was thinking would work, but now… I'm absolutely convinced it will.' She gave Clara an excited look. 'So, come on, Maddie, either drink up or, better still, take it somewhere else. Clara and I have things to discuss… in private.'

Chapter 13

Clara pressed her ear against the closed kitchen door for a minute or so after Maddie left to make sure she wasn't lurking behind it trying to earwig. As soon as she was satisfied that the coast was clear, she returned to the table. In the meantime, Trixie had fetched her laptop from the dresser and was waiting for it to boot up.

'I'm not sure I'm skilled enough to pull this off,' she said. 'I've never really used icing this way before, but here's what I had in mind for the cake. See what you think. If I practise enough and I can achieve the same look, I think it will look amazing.'

Clara peered over her shoulder as Trixie navigated her way to the page she had bookmarked several weeks ago. 'There are loads of these videos, but this seemed one of the simplest to follow.' She pressed a button and let it play, sitting back in her chair so that Clara could have a better look.

Trixie had watched this video, and others like it, what felt like a million times over. Just as she had trawled through hundreds of photos and stared at any number of websites that showed the 'perfect' wedding cake. There were so many new and exciting looks, from the traditional iced three-tiered cake to creations that were truly imaginative and gravity-defying. It had been almost impossible to choose but, for some reason, it was the ruffle-iced cakes that she had kept coming back to. They echoed the beautiful draped and feminine lines of Maddie's dress, and Trixie was sure that she and Seth would love the design too.

Trixie watched Clara's expression as the video played for the final couple of minutes. She was concentrating on the images in front of her, frowning slightly, but her face was also tinged with wonder, and as the screen grew dark, she turned to Trixie, her eyes shining.

'They look stunning,' she said. 'When you first see them, they look incredibly difficult, it's hard to work out how it's done at all, but once you see how the technique works, it looks almost easy.' She paused for a moment. 'I'm sure it isn't, at all, but it's very effective... and it will match Maddie's dress perfectly.' She stared back at the screen. 'Oh, Trixie, I love these designs; they're so elegant, and you could even add some flowers here and there.'

Trixie nodded. 'That's what I was thinking. As soon as I saw the flowers you'd picked for the bouquet, I realised that the ruffles of the peonies would match the look, wouldn't they?' She touched a key on the laptop so that the screen sprang back to life showing the last image from the video and the fully decorated cake in all its glory. 'See, if we put them here, they'd look stunning.' She pointed to the join where the first smaller cake met the bottom larger one. 'They could nestle in the ruffles...'

Clara's eyes were wide. 'Oh yes...' she breathed. 'Oh, do it, Trixie, this is the one.' She waggled her hand at the screen. 'Play it again so I can see it one more time.'

Trixie was just about to do as she was asked when there was a rapid knock on the door. A second later, Tom's head appeared around it.

'Only me,' he said. 'But your presence is required outside, ladies... So grab your coats, hats, scarves and mittens.' He was grinning like a Cheshire cat, his face flushed from the cold. 'Oh, and Trixie, could we have a couple of carrots please...?'

Trixie's head swivelled towards Clara. 'Snowmen!' she cried. 'It's got to be.' She slammed down the lid of her laptop. 'Come on! Last one outside's a…'

★

Moments later, Trixie skidded to a halt as she rounded the corner of the courtyard into the garden. Her hand flew to her mouth as she inhaled a sharp breath.

'Oh, my God, just look at it! It's beautiful…'

Maddie was standing on the path, just a few feet from her, the same awed expression on her face. Tom was grinning at them both.

Joy's Acre looked like something from the pages of a glossy magazine; an artfully arranged display of the perfect Christmas-card scene. Except this was no artificial photo shoot, this was the real thing. Trixie felt as if she needed to pinch herself.

The sky was still heavy with snow, grey tinged with a little pink, against which the cottages with their snow-capped thatched roofs stood out in stark relief. Twinkling with lights, their vivid red doors adorned with wreaths, they looked so cosy and inviting. There was even, noticed Trixie, a robin perched on the handle of Clara's fork in the middle of one of the gardens.

In front of the cottages lay an expanse of snow across the lawn, perfect, untouched, like the softest cashmere blanket and, of course, right in the centre of it all, the huge Christmas tree, the tips of its branches now dipped in white.

As she watched, Ruby came down the path from her cottage, wearing nearly every colour of the rainbow, from her multi-coloured coat down to her bright red wellies. Little Darcie was strapped to her chest, almost invisible under a huge woolly hat. Jem came running out after them, a long scarf trailing behind him as he ran over to Seth and Angus by the barn.

'Rumour has it there's going to be a boys versus girls competition,' said Tom, as they walked to join the others. 'We're pretty even in number… Me, Seth, Angus and Jem against you two plus Clara and Ruby.'

'Sounds fair enough,' said Trixie with a look at Maddie. 'We'll win, obviously… but at least if the numbers are the same on each team we won't be accused of having an unfair advantage. It will just be down to our natural talent…'

Tom caught the look in her eye.

'Challenge accepted,' he said with a grin.

'I can't believe it settled so fast,' said Maddie. 'It's already quite thick.'

'We've had no rain recently,' replied Tom. 'But plenty of frosts, so the ground was already cold and dry.' He blinked rapidly, laughing as a swirling snowflake landed on his eyelashes. 'Plus, it doesn't take long when it's coming down fast like this.'

He ducked as they caught up with the others, dodging a snowball that Jem had thrown at Angus but in his excitement was very far wide of the mark. It caught Seth just above his left ear.

Seconds later, childish shrieks filled the air as Jem took off across the garden followed by Seth in hot pursuit.

Ruby was grinning from ear to ear. 'I can't remember the last time we had snow like this,' she said. 'I'm not sure who's the bigger kid…' she added, watching the antics of her son and Seth.

'No, you have a point there,' agreed Maddie. She called out to Seth, who stopped to reply, turning towards her and immediately taking a snowball in the back of the neck as punishment for his lack of attention. He held up his hands to Jem, signalling a truce, and waited until he caught up before rejoining the others.

'So, are we having rules, or is this a no-holds-barred competition?' he asked, as he reached them.

Clara came forward. 'Well, it has to look like a snowman,' she said, directing a look at Angus. 'I know what you're like. Just because you're at least a foot taller than the rest of us doesn't mean you can get away with making the biggest pile of snow imaginable and thinking that will win.'

Angus held his hand over his heart. 'I can do pretty,' he said, pretending to be hurt by the comment, but he winked at Jem, who giggled.

'I think we should set a time limit though,' said Tom. 'Otherwise you girls will be there for hours, curling its hair and trying to get the make-up right.'

Trixie slapped his arm. 'One hour,' she said. 'Are we ready, ladies?'

There were nods all round. Maddie solemnly handed Seth one of the carrots she was holding. 'May the best team win,' she said.

Half an hour later, Trixie collapsed dramatically to the ground, lying flat on her back for a moment. 'I'd forgotten how much hard work this was,' she groaned. 'And my hands are frozen solid. I haven't been able to feel them for the last twenty minutes.'

She moved her arms and legs up and down to leave the classic snow angel shape on the ground before waggling a hand at Clara who laughed and hauled her to her feet.

'Don't you give up on us now,' she said. 'Because if we let the men win, we will never hear the last of it, from Tom in particular, you know what he's like.'

She stood back to assess their snowman, which was currently a rather round and portly figure with a very small head. 'I think he still needs a bit of work,' she said.

'He... or she?' asked Ruby. 'The men all seem to think we're only capable of making a "girly" snowman, so why don't we make a snowwoman? Slim it down a bit and add a few details.' She cocked her head to one side. 'Hang on, I've had an idea…' She took off at a pace towards her cottage.

Trixie looked at Maddie. 'Do you know, that's not a bad idea. We could give her hair and eyelashes, make her a skirt even…'

'I think you might be overestimating our skills,' she replied with a grin. 'Although… I wonder if Ruby might just be our secret weapon…'

'You may well be right.'

They waited until Ruby reappeared a couple of minutes later. She was still carrying Darcie, but now also a bag which she was doing her best to hide from the men by pulling her coat around it.

'Right, first of all,' she said as she reached them. 'I've brought some replacement mittens. Here, put these on, there's a pair for everyone.' She handed them around.

Trixie took hold of the pair offered to her. They were bright orange, yellow and red stripes. She peeled of her own sodden gloves and, rubbing her hands dry as best she could, thrust a hand inside one of the mittens. Almost immediately, she pulled it out again, her mouth a round 'O' of surprise. She peered inside.

'They're called thrums,' said Ruby, taking in her delighted expression. 'Small wisps of unspun fleece which you knit in every now and again. It makes the insides of the mittens all soft and fuzzy, and because it's natural fleece, incredibly warm. I do it with blankets sometimes too.'

Trixie turned the tops of the mittens over to better see what Ruby meant, the soft fluff apparent as she did so.

'I've never seen that done before,' she exclaimed. 'It's gorgeous…'

Ruby grinned. 'Well, all these have thrumming in them, I thought it might help us beat the competition.' She rummaged in the bag. 'As will these…'

She held out several balls of wool. 'Hair, and possibly eyelashes,' she said.

The women all grinned at one another. 'Right then, let's get to work,' said Trixie, putting the mittens back on again.

As the final few minutes of the hour approached, a cackle of laughter rang out. Seth and Tom were standing back to admire their handiwork, while Angus lifted Jem to add a detail to their snowman's head. Ruby too was just adding the finishing touches to their snow woman's hair. She looked up moments later as her son came running over.

'Did you have fun?' she asked. 'It looked like you were.'

Jem's head bobbed up and down several times, his cheeks and nose flushed pink with the cold. 'Brilliant! Come and see our snowman, Mum, it's huge!'

He tugged at her arm and pulled her across to where it was standing.

Trixie looked at the other two. It was so lovely to see Jem enjoying himself, and Ruby more relaxed than she had been. It was tough moving to somewhere new, especially for a boy of Jem's age and just before Christmas too, but at least the snow had provided a little magic, right when they needed it.

The snow had slowed to a few intermittent flurries now, but the flakes were tiny and already the sky was beginning to lighten.

'Well, it's big, I'll say that much,' said Trixie, looking up at the mountain of snow in front of her which passed for the men's effort. The lawn all around it had been well and truly cleared.

'We went for impressive rather than aesthetic in the end,' said Seth. 'Because Jem was amazing at collecting snow.'

The figure in front of them was nearly six foot high, with no real difference between its head and body, although a bright blue scarf had been tied around where its neck might be. Other than that, a carrot was its only other adornment, stuck somewhere in the centre of its 'face'.

Angus laughed. 'In fact, if we'd had a ladder I dread to think how much taller it would have got. But it's a real beauty, don't you think?'

'It certainly is,' agreed Ruby. 'Well done, Jem!'

Trixie caught a look between Seth and Maddie and smiled to herself. Its meaning was clear, and she hoped that one day they would have children of their own.

'Well, I don't know how we're ever going to choose a winner,' she said. 'Because our snowman, actually she's a snow-lady, is very small by comparison.' She grinned at Tom. 'Although she is very pretty…'

'Well, we had better go and take a look,' he replied. 'Come on, Jem, let's go and see; as head judge, I think you should be the one to decide which one is the winner.'

Jem trotted over quite happily, pleased with his position of responsibility. Trixie was pretty certain that she knew who was going to win, but was astonished when Jem shouted with excitement.

'Aw, Mum, she's even got *eyelashes*…' He grabbed Angus's hand, pulling him in a circle around their creation. 'Ours is taller, but this is way better, look…'

Tom came to stand in between Trixie and Clara, putting his arm around them both. 'Well, I have to hand it to you ladies, she's a stunner and no mistake.'

Their 'lady' had a nipped-in waist, a full wide skirt, moulded so that it seemed to hang in folds, the merest suggestion of a bust so as not to embarrass Jem, bright-blue button eyes, huge spidery woollen eyelashes and a mass of black 'hair' which was currently being held in place, a little crookedly, by a scarlet beret set at a jaunty angle. They may have cheated a little with their use of props, but she was still undeniably a lady.

'Well, gentlemen,' said Seth, moving to stand beside Maddie, 'I hate to say it, but I think we've been outplayed. What do you think, Jem, is your mum's team the winners?'

Jem stood for a moment contemplating the question with a serious look on his face. He looked backwards and forwards between the two creations and then nodded his head. 'I still think ours is brilliant,' he said. 'I mean, it's *way* bigger than theirs, but this one is cleverer, so I think it should win.'

Angus held out his hand for Jem to shake. 'Excellent judging,' he said. 'A very fair decision, I reckon… and one that calls for a celebration, don't you think?' He straightened up, looking at Trixie.

'Of course!' agreed Trixie, taking the hint. 'I think the very least we all deserve is the biggest, gooiest piece of chocolate cake in the world… and fortunately I happen to know where there is such a thing.' She grinned at Jem. 'Does that sound like a good idea? And something warm to drink. I don't know about you, but I think something with cream and marshmallows on the top would go down very well indeed.'

Jem nodded. 'My hands are freezing!' he said, each breath puffing out a little white cloud into the air.

His cheeks were flushed pink and his eyes shining, whether from the cold or excitement, Trixie couldn't tell, but judging by the similar looks on everyone's faces, they were all ready for a warm-up. The last hour had been huge fun, but suddenly the thought of the comforting fug of the cosy kitchen was very welcome indeed.

The hallway was soon filled with a multi-coloured assortment of wellies which gently oozed melted snow onto the floor around them and, as everyone shed their outdoor clothes, the doorknobs along the corridor became hung with hats while several scarves were draped along the bannisters. A woolly collection of mittens and gloves were also laid to dry on the huge cast-iron radiator at the foot of the stairs. Trixie felt a rush of happiness as she led the way into the kitchen.

She glanced out of the window as she went to fetch the cake, suddenly stopping in her tracks.

'Oh…' Her note of disappointment echoed around the kitchen.

'What is it?' asked Maddie, following her line of sight. 'Oh, that's sad…' she said, staring at the bright blue patch of sky outside. 'Well, I guess that's it then,' she sighed. 'No white Christmas for us, after all.'

'The wedding will still be fairytale, Maddie, snow or no snow. Besides, I know it's impossibly romantic, but it's also very cold, wet and makes getting around difficult. Wedding dresses in the snow look beautiful in photo shoots, but not so good in real life…'

'I know,' replied Maddie, and although she was smiling, she still couldn't quite hide the slightly wistful note in her voice.

A sudden whistling noise brought Trixie to the table as her mobile phone lit up. She studied the screen for a minute, looking first at Maddie and then at Ruby, a smile breaking over her face as she read the text message.

'That was from Noah,' she said. 'He mentioned earlier that he would bring the menu over from the delicatessen for us to look at. He was going to pop it up before the weekend, but is now wondering if we can wait until he sees me on Monday? Or rather sees me and Ruby…'

She looked up, her smile breaking into a grin. 'Are you free on Monday?' she asked Ruby. 'And please say you are because it's all arranged…'

Ruby looked bemused. 'Well, apart from taking Jem to school, I've nothing else on… or rather nowhere I need to be. Why?'

Trixie felt a burble of excitement begin to well up.

'Because we're going to look around the empty shop on Penny Lane, that's why.'

Ruby looked startled. 'What?'

'I know I mentioned that Noah's sister is Lottie of Dotty Lottie's fame, but I don't think I mentioned that it's his brother-in-law who has redeveloped all those shops – he's the landlord. They're all meeting for a family lunch on Sunday and Noah has arranged to get the keys. Now what do you think of *that*?'

Chapter 14

'You'll need to put on something a bit warmer,' said Angus. 'It's a beautiful day, but bitter this morning and we're going to be outside for quite a while.'

'I've got my coat on.'

Ruby glanced at her son in exasperation but Angus just smiled. 'Don't you want to come then?'

Jem just shrugged.

'Oh well, never mind, it was just a thought. You'll have to stay with your mum and all those women, sewing stuff. It will probably be quite good fun, and at least you'll be in the warm...' He zipped his own jacket up slightly. 'I'll see you later, Ruby, have fun.'

Angus had almost reached the cottage door by the time Jem's plaintive voice reached him.

'Mu-uum, I can't find my scarf.'

He smiled to himself, and slowed his steps. 'Get your gloves too, Jem,' he shouted back down the hallway.

Moments later Jem joined him, muffled up against the cold, and he opened the door. 'Okay?' he asked.

There was a slight smile in reply, but it was good enough for Angus. Small steps. He beamed one back in reply. 'Come on then, let's go and make a start.'

He led the way down the path and away from the cottage.

'I had thought that we might take the truck over to the Hall to collect the wood, but then I realised it might be a better idea to walk through the woods to get there.' He half glanced at Jem. 'It isn't far, but the woodland is a great place to go, once you know your way through the paths of course. If I show you, then as long as your mum knows where you're going, you could come out here any time you wanted to… safely, without getting lost or scared.'

Jem stayed silent beside him.

'Did you go for walks where you lived before?'

'No.'

Angus smiled to himself. He had a feeling this was going to be a rather one-sided conversation.

'What, not at all? How come?'

'Jus' houses and stuff.'

'A park then? Or when you went on holiday maybe?'

Jem shrugged. 'The park was just for babies… or the… big lads.'

Angus took in the hesitancy in his voice. 'Yeah, best to stay out of their way. When I was your age the big lads where I grew up never seemed to understand how to play fair. I don't suppose it's changed much, has it? Did they give you a lot of grief?'

'Some. It was boring anyway, and a long way to walk. My mum didn't like me going there sometimes.'

Angus could imagine exactly why that was. 'So where did you play then?'

Jem scuffed at a stone on the path. 'In my bedroom mostly. On my PlayStation.'

Angus nodded as he opened the gate to the field at the back of the Gardener's Cottage. 'Well then, by the sounds of it, you're in for a treat.' He motioned for Jem to go through.

He was very conscious that the last time Jem and he had been standing here was the day when the boy had run off, hurtling across the field, neither knowing nor caring where he had been going. It wouldn't be kind to remind him of it, but if Jem was to be safe he needed to know the lie of the land. In front of them the field sloped down the hill towards the village. It was bare and wintry-looking, the odd pocket of snow still lying on the ground and the outline of the trees stark against the skyline. It was beautiful. Angus inhaled a deep breath.

'Have you ever done that?' he asked suddenly.

Jem looked up at him.

'Just stood and taken a really deep breath? There's nothing quite like it.' He chuckled, noting the expression on Jem's face.

'I know, you probably think I'm mad, but why don't you try it?' He looked around him. 'There's no one else here. No one to say you look stupid or to call you names… I'll do it with you if you like.'

There was no reply, but Jem was still watching him.

'Shall we do it on three then? A really deep breath through our noses until we can't take in any more and then we can let it out again slowly.' He nodded at Jem. 'I'll count, shall I…? One… two… three…' He motioned with his hand, holding Jem's look all the while.

There was a splutter as Jem began to cough. He burst out laughing. 'It's cold!'

'Aye, it is. It can take you a bit unawares, can't it? Shall we do it again? Only this time don't breathe in quite so far, you looked like you were going to go pop.' He held up fingers this time, one, two… three.

Jem closed his eyes, drawing the still air deep inside him. 'It tastes funny,' he said.

Angus cocked his head to one side. 'I suppose it does, although I think I quite like it. What does it taste of to you?'

Jem thought for a moment. 'It tastes of the cold… but the outdoors too. Like if you eat grass or something.'

It was Angus's turn to laugh. 'Eat grass often, do you?'

'No, but…'

Angus smiled. 'I know what you mean. That's a really good description. It does taste of the grass, and maybe the trees too, and the soil. I bet you didn't know you could taste the cold, did you?'

Jem shook his head.

'You can hear it too. I bet you didn't know that either.' He grinned.

Jem gave him a look. One of the ones he reserved for 'silly' grown-ups.

'It's true, honestly… Close your eyes a minute.' He waited until Jem had done as he asked. 'Now, no talking… and just listen. I'll tell you when to stop.'

Angus stood, raising his face to the sky and letting the sounds around him fill him up. They were as familiar to him as the nose on his face and yet subtly different too, just as they were every day he stopped to listen. He let the seconds tick by until he reckoned a full minute had passed. He touched a hand to Jem's sleeve, not wishing his voice to sound suddenly harsh.

'Well, what did you hear?'

Jem blinked and looked around him. 'The birds, a car, or a tractor maybe… the wind I think, because something was rustling.'

'Did you hear the stillness?' asked Angus, knowing that it might be beyond Jem's comprehension. 'How big it was?'

The boy's eyes widened as he searched Angus's face for clues to what he had just heard. He frowned, thinking, and then his face cleared as a thought came to him. 'It sounded like it went right down the hill, all the way across the field… Is that what you mean?'

Angus beamed at him. 'The very thing! You know, I didn't think you'd be half as clever at this as you are. If you stand here in summer, the sound is very different. It sort of hums, on a really hot day, like it's fizzing with energy, but the sound always seems much closer. I think it's because there's leaf on the trees and the grass here gets really tall. It traps the sound somehow, and that's amazing too, but when it's cold, the sound doesn't seem to get stuck so much, it flows away from you. On a frosty morning, like today, it's as if it bounces off all the hard things around, the ground, the bare trees, the blades of frozen grass, a bit like an echo.'

Jem nodded, a look of excitement on his face. 'But when it snows, like it did the other day, everything seems so quiet, even where there's lots of houses. Is that the same sort of thing?'

'I like to think so. Almost as if there's a big blanket over everything, keeping all the sound beneath it.' He stared out across the fields. 'Do you know the other really great thing about the sound out here?'

'No.'

'Well, you know those times when your head is really full of stuff? Often stuff that you wish wasn't there in the first place… It makes it hard to think, and I don't like that. It makes me feel…' he searched for the right word, '…scratchy? Does that make sense?' He didn't wait for a reply. 'When I come out here, and I listen to all the other stuff, like we just have, somehow it chases away all the things in my head I wish weren't there, and just leaves nice things behind.' He smiled at Jem. 'Shall we carry on?'

There was still an awful lot to do. Jem fell into step beside him.

'You know where you are of course though, don't you?' He pointed down the slope. 'See, that's the village down there; Summersmeade. And you can spot the church spire clear as anything. That's where your mum parked when you first got here.'

He waited until he was sure that Jem had made the connection. 'I walk into the village from here sometimes. It's not quicker than going by car of course, but if you ever needed to get there and you didn't have one, it's by far the best way. Right in the corner of that bottom field is a stile, and if you climb over that you get to another field that meets the edge of the churchyard. Just walk towards the spire, then you know where you are. Of course, once you're down there, if you look back up the hill you can see Joy's Acre too so you can always find your way home again. Easy peasy.' He gave a slight shiver. 'Right, let's march it out a bit, shall we, so we don't get cold.'

They both fell silent for a few minutes, Angus's long legs setting the pace across the fields towards the wood. From time to time he risked a furtive glance towards Jem, but he seemed happy enough. It wouldn't do for him to think he was being checked up on though. They had made good progress so far, and Angus was conscious that it wouldn't take much to destroy it.

After ten minutes or so they reached the edge of the woodland, and Angus put out his hand to stop Jem.

'Shh,' he whispered, motioning that Jem should crouch down. He followed suit, sitting on his haunches. 'We might be a bit late to see them, and they're also quite skittish so if we make a noise we'll never see one. They are used to having me around, but I make sure not to ever get really close; they're wild animals, after all.'

Jem's eyes widened, a flicker of anxiety passing through them. 'What are?' he whispered.

'The deer.'

The boy's eyes darted back to the thicket of trees. Angus would lay money on him never having seen a deer before in his life. It was very unlikely that they would see one now, but he wanted to plant the suggestion nonetheless. His own eyes scanned the trees in front of them, lingering in the places he knew they tended to favour. There was more snow still on the ground here, but there were no signs of any tracks, or movement either.

After a few more minutes he straightened again. 'Ah well, maybe we'll see them another time.' He motioned for them to start walking once more.

'Are there really deer here?' asked Jem. 'Proper ones?'

Angus smiled, wondering what an improper deer would look like, but he knew exactly what Jem meant. He could still vividly recall the thrill of first seeing them.

'There are. And we're very lucky to have them. I don't think you've met Agatha, the lady who used to live at the Hall, but before she moved, she lived there a very long time, and she says they were here before she was. How amazing is that?'

'Cool.'

'I need to ask you to pay attention now though, Jem,' he said. 'Because woodland can be a tricky business, and it's easy to get lost if you don't know how to pinpoint where you are. It always looks different, you see, in summer, winter, rain or sunshine, and it can be confusing. I know every inch of this place, but even I get a bit disorientated sometimes and I have to stop and work out where I am.'

He smiled warmly. 'But we're very lucky because Mother Nature has given us some brilliant clues.' He pointed straight ahead of them. 'Like this for example, isn't she a beauty?'

Jem looked confused until Angus led him on a little further to stand at the base of an enormous tree.

'I think this is one of the oldest trees in this woodland. It's a horse chestnut, you know, the ones you get conkers from.'

He rested a hand on the gnarled bark. 'There's probably still a few around if you have a look. The deer will have had most of them, and some of the boys from the village no doubt, but…' He scuffed at the leaf litter at his feet, sure enough turning over one of the prickly seed pods. It was brown and a little chewed. He picked it up and passed it Jem. 'There you go.'

The pod practically fell apart as Jem took it, revealing the shiny seed inside. He pulled it out, rubbing a finger over the glossy skin, before grinning and putting it in his pocket.

'Can I look for some more?' he said, throwing away the empty casing.

'If you want,' said Angus easily.

He waited until Jem had collected a few more and then he pointed to the tree itself. 'This tree's important because it's where the path splits,' said Angus. 'If you go this way,' he pointed to the right, 'it takes you down the hill and away from the Hall. But if you go the other way, then you'll stay on the right side.'

It was also the path that Jem had instinctively taken the other day, but Angus made no mention of it.

'Come on.'

Shortly they would arrive at the clearing where it was always tricky to know which path to take. He would need Jem to pay attention, but he didn't want to make a big deal of it. The light would grow more dim as they walked beyond it and deeper into the woodland and, although while Jem was with him that was not a problem, if he ever came to this spot again on his own, it would be easy to become spooked. He wondered if Jem would recognise his surroundings.

'Oh, I've been here before!' he exclaimed, running forward down the slope into the slight dip.

'Have you?' asked Angus carefully.

'Yes, the other day…' Jem trailed off as if suddenly realising what he was saying. He looked at Angus anxiously. 'I ran off 'cause I was angry, and you came and found me.'

Angus made a show of tapping his head. 'I remember! I don't think you ever said what had upset you though, did you?' He smiled.

'It was my first day at school.'

'That's right, it was, wasn't it? I thought you'd had a good day though, playing with the other boys and so on.'

Jem bowed his head. 'I did have a good day. It was heaps better than my old school. But I got cross… with Mum.'

Angus bent down to pick up a leaf. The green had gone and all that was left was its skeleton. He ran his fingers over it, leaving a space for Jem to continue talking.

'She said I was rude and so she turned the internet off.' His face had taken on the sulky demeanour it had worn previously.

'I remember,' said Angus slowly. 'I think perhaps you were rude, but it's odd, isn't it, because sometimes when we're angry or upset we don't do the thing we should do, which is talk about what's made us feel that way. Instead we pretend it doesn't matter, or we lash out at the person who is trying to make us feel better. I used to do that all the time until I learned that it wasn't the right way to go about things.'

He smiled reassuringly. 'Don't worry, I'm sure your mum understands that too… In fact, I'm sure she knows that her turning the internet off wasn't the real reason you got angry with her in the first place, but something else…' He frowned. 'But then if you'd had a good day at school I'm not sure what else it could have been… Sorry, Jem, I think I'm a bit confused now.'

Jem picked up a stick and began to poke at the ground. 'Why can't things just stay the same? Why do they have to change all the time?' He stared at Angus, a challenging look on his face.

'Well now, that's a very good question.' He rubbed at his chin for a moment. 'Although, I suppose it depends what kind of things you mean…'

'I didn't ask to come to this stupid place. Why couldn't we have just stayed where we were? It's only because Mum hates Dad so much that we had to move in the first place. And then it wasn't even a year later that we had to move again, just before Darcie was born.'

Angus nodded. 'And now you've moved again. That must be hard.' He watched while Jem continued poking at the ground. 'But then, I guess, your mum probably wished she didn't have to move again either. She must have had a really good reason for doing so,' he said softly. He would need to tread carefully; he was on very dangerous ground. 'I wonder why your mum doesn't like your dad. Did they have an argument?'

Jem screwed up his face. 'All the time. And I know Dad shouts a lot but then Mum cries a lot too, and I don't like that. I guess he probably doesn't either. It always seems to make him more cross.'

Angus licked his lips, feeling his mouth go suddenly dry. He had no wish to pry, for Ruby's sake as much as for his own. There were things he had no desire to be reminded of.

He thought for a moment. 'Adults can be very hard to understand sometimes, Jem, but I do know your mum loves you a great deal, so I'm sure she wouldn't have brought you and Darcie here unless she really thought it was the best thing for you both. And I'm sure that once you settle into school and make some new friends you'll feel a lot better about things.'

Jem suddenly threw down the stick. 'I'm not making any friends,' he shouted, his face contorted in misery. 'Because we'll only leave, just like we did before, and then I'll have to say goodbye to everyone again!'

Jem looked as if he was on the verge of tears, and Angus felt his heart go out to the frightened boy as he finally admitted what was at the root of his anger. Angus looked down at the leaf, still in his hands.

'Look at this,' he said. 'Isn't it lovely?' He held the leaf out for Jem to see. 'The leaf has died, but there's still something beautiful about it. That's good old Mother Nature at work again. She does that a lot; changes things all the time, but even then all she really does is give us something else wonderful instead.'

Jem sniffed, but he took the leaf, tracing a finger down the spine.

'Earlier in the spring this leaf was still on the tree, the brightest freshest green, catching the sunlight this way and that as it grew. The summer sun made it bigger so that it could help make food for the tree, but after a while as the autumn sun turned it a rich rusty brown it fell to the ground. But its story doesn't end there.' He gazed around the clearing. 'When you look around here, what can you see, Jem?'

He followed Jem's eyes as they swept the clearing, taking in the rotted wood, the trees, stark without their greenery, the decaying leaf litter on the floor.

'Nothing,' he said. 'It's all dead.' A tear spilled over onto his cheek. 'There's nothing here.'

He was about to turn away when Angus caught a gentle hold of his sleeve.

'No,' he said. 'It isn't, look…' And he reached above his head to pull down a slender branch. Swiftly withdrawing his penknife from his pocket, he pared away a little of the bark, revealing what lay inside. It was bright green.

'See, it's only sleeping, not dead. Just waiting for the spring.' He knelt down and pushed aside the covering of leaves until he found what he was looking for. A woodlouse and a shiny black beetle scuttled from their hiding places. 'And the leaves, when they die, give food and shelter to all the wee beasties that live down here. Not only that but when the leaves fall from the trees, the light can return to the woodland floor and something else magical happens.'

He scooted a little further away into the clearing so that he was out from under the tree's canopy. Moving aside the leaves, he prayed he would find what he was looking for. A slow smile slid over his face.

'These are snowdrops,' he said. 'Still just the teeniest of shoots at the moment, but in a few weeks, just after Christmas, there will be carpets of them here, bright green, with delicate white bell-shaped flowers. They come even before the trees are waking up, in fact, that's why they come.'

He fished in his pocket again, this time pulling out a handkerchief and handing it to Jem. 'Change is never easy,' he said. 'But it's part of life, and if you look, there is always something good to be found in it… always.'

Chapter 15

Angus glanced up at the sky. The temperature was dropping and he was beginning to feel a chill. The last thing he wanted was for Jem to get cold.

'Right, come on then,' he said. 'I thought we were supposed to be getting firewood. At this rate, by the time we get back, it will be time to go out and collect more.' He grinned at Jem. 'That made sense in my head,' he said, smiling.

Jem scrubbed at his nose with the hanky Angus had given him, and held it back for him to take.

'Perhaps you'd better keep it,' he said. 'I've got another one.' He looked around the clearing. 'I was really pleased to hear that you recognised this space because there are lots of landmarks from here to the Hall, so we'll just concentrate on those today. That way you'll always be able to find your way. And the first one we need to look for is the tree with the hollow at the bottom.'

He watched as Jem ran across to it, pleased that his earlier emotion seemed to have passed.

'Good stuff. So now we follow the path again, with the tree on our right. Got that?'

Jem nodded.

'And I'm going to let you find the next clue, so let's see if you can. We need to find a tree that looks like a letter of the alphabet…'

They continued for a few moments, Jem's head darting from side to side, before he suddenly dashed off to the left, careering into a tree and throwing his arms around the trunk. 'This one!' he yelled.

A storm several years ago had torn a huge branch from the tree so that now all that remained was a central trunk, with branches forking to either side. It did indeed resemble a huge 'Y' in the ground.

'Brilliant, well done, Jem. Now look for a huge holly bush because that's the direction we need to go.'

He followed, letting Jem have the lead as he strode out confidently onto a curving path that stretched for some distance. 'That's it, keep going. This is the hardest bit because you just have to stay on this path and there's not much else to look out for, but in a few more minutes I think you might realise where you are.'

Only Angus knew that all the while they were skirting the very edge of the woodland, following in fact the boundary line between the Hall and Joy's Acre. To their right lay the largest expanse of trees that stretched in thick lines from the Hall right the way down to the road that led into the village. If Jem kept walking in pretty much any direction he would eventually come to the road, but it was easy to become confused and Angus was anxious that he should know the quickest route through the wood. If he ever ran off again, it was likely he would come this way. He would feel safe, but it would also mean that Angus could find him all the more quickly too, should he ever need to.

'Look!' shouted Jem suddenly, and Angus knew that he had spotted the tall chimneys of the Hall. Moments later they came to a stile beside another enormous horse chestnut.

'And just in case you ever feel the need,' said Angus. 'That is absolutely the best tree for climbing around here. I probably shouldn't be telling you this, but when I was about your age I used to come up here all the time. There used to be a hole in the fence at the bottom of the Hall gardens and I used to sneak through, run across the lawn and dash around the courtyard at the back. That's where we're headed. You can see the road up to the farm from there and so if anyone came past I pretended that I was a spy and that they were the villains after me. I used to climb the tree to hide from them and lie in wait. In the autumn I used to pick the conkers and throw them down, pretending they were stun grenades.' He laughed, smiling fondly at the memory. 'I'd stay up there for hours sometimes.'

Jem was staring up at the branches overhead, but Angus shook his head. 'Nuh-uh, your mum would have my guts for garters. Anyway, we've got work to do…' He paused, his head on one side. 'Or are you too tired?'

'No way,' Jem snorted. 'I'll race you.'

★

It took another hour to load up the truck with logs that Angus had already chopped, and ten minutes after that they were back at Joy's Acre. Jem had worked hard, helping him to fill each barrow load before emptying it once they reached the truck, throwing the logs onto the flatbed at the back. It would take a while to move them all to their new homes, but such was the nature of the task and Angus had always found it strangely comforting. There was nothing he liked to see more at this time of year than a fireplace dancing with flame, and the cottages, all decorated for Christmas, were the perfect setting.

He climbed down from the cab and went around to the other side of the truck to let Jem out.

'Do you want to have a break first?' he asked, looking at his watch. It was early afternoon, and he was beginning to feel rather hungry. To his surprise Jem shook his head.

'Will all those women still be there?' he asked. 'Because I don't want to go home if they are.'

Angus smiled. He couldn't blame the boy. He liked Louise and her friends from the village but they could talk the hind leg off a donkey. He glanced up at the main house.

'I tell you what,' he said. 'We could go and find Trixie. I'm sure she'll have some sandwiches or something in the kitchen, maybe even a hot chocolate for us both. What do you think? I know a place we can eat them as well.'

Jem nodded rapidly. 'Could we have cake?'

'Let's go and find out, shall we?' He held out his hand so that Jem could jump down.

Trixie was in the kitchen and waved a greeting at them as they passed by the window. Angus motioned for her to let them in.

'Did you two smell the gingerbread men, or what?' she said, as she greeted them. 'I've honestly just this minute taken them out of the oven. Come in and have a look.'

She led them through into the kitchen where Angus could smell the most amazing aroma. 'I thought they might be quite fun to have with lunch.' She looked at Jem. 'What do you think?'

Jem looked at Angus. 'Would that be all right?' he asked.

'If Trixie says it is, then I'm sure it's fine,' he replied.

She smiled. 'I've made some sandwiches as well,' she added. 'I was going to make cheese on toast but as everyone is up to their eyeballs in all that gorgeous fabric I wasn't sure greasy fingers would be such a good idea.'

Angus could feel his stomach begin to gurgle at the thought.

Trixie laughed. 'On second thoughts, judging by the look on your face, I think the cheese on toast is going to go down better.' She winked at Jem. 'How about you, would you like some too?'

Jem nodded shyly.

'Do you want to go and wash your hands then, and I'll make a start. The cloakroom is just down the hall.'

She waited until Jem was out of the room. 'How have things been?' she asked. 'I think Ruby has been rather anxious on your behalf in case Jem gave you a hard time.' She pulled a face. 'Even though he thinks the world of you.'

Angus was rather taken aback. 'Does he?' he asked. 'Who said that?'

Trixie pursed her lips. 'Well Ruby did. Apparently he never stops talking about you. And she's incredibly grateful for all your help.'

Well, that was news to him. Ruby was always polite and friendly, but that was about as far as their conversations went. She had obviously opened up to some of her new friends at Joy's Acre, so perhaps it was just men she kept at a distance. He was beginning to understand why.

He nodded. 'Jem's a good lad. Just had a tough time of things, that's all.'

'They both have, I reckon.'

Angus just smiled. 'I probably ought to go and wash my hands too,' he said, excusing himself.

A few minutes later, he carried a loaded tray out through the back door and across the courtyard to where a row of outbuildings adjoined the main house. One of these was already being used by Clara for her gardening tools, but the other two had served as storage in the past and, before Angus's arrival, had accumulated a ton of junk.

He had spent several days clearing and cleaning them out, with the result that the interconnecting doors between all three buildings were now usable, thus opening up the space. As he had sorted through many years' worth of rubbish, he had been astonished to find an old cast-iron pot-bellied stove propped in one corner. Moving an wooden cupboard with broken shelves had revealed the flue, unused but still largely intact. It had taken a couple more days' work to clean the stove and make remedial repairs to the flue, with the end result that it had now been put to very good use. Clara had managed to scavenge a couple of old armchairs and a low table from Declan that were no longer required at the Hall and now the space provided somewhere for she and Angus to go when they took their breaks. Somewhere out of the wind and the wet and now, thanks to the stove, somewhere a little warmer.

Angus motioned for Jem to open the door and, once inside, he set the tray down on the table. He peeled off the foil from the two plates it held and passed one to Jem. 'Go on, get stuck in,' he said, picking up his own plate.

He settled himself into one of the chairs and took a huge bite of his lunch. The toast was oozing with molten cheese, and butter dripped from its edge. Trixie had added a little mustard to his bread as well and the tang of it hit his tongue in a pleasurable burst. He glanced at Jem who was nodding with a look of bliss on his face.

'There's nothing better, is there?' asked Angus. 'Especially when you've worked up an appetite. And gingerbread men for afters. I don't know, I think we're being spoilt rotten.' He grinned at Jem. 'I'm not complaining though.'

He was about to say something else when there was a strange noise from the corner of the room. He cocked his head to listen but there was nothing, just the sound of Jem slurping his hot chocolate.

'My mum always puts lots of cream on these, just like Trixie does,' said Jem, flicking out his tongue to lick the foamy surface of his drink.

'Aye, she mentioned you liked them. And now that Trixie knows, there'll be no shortage of them coming in your direction I dare say, particularly if you're going to be my helper on a regular basis.'

Jem's eyes widened. 'Oh, do you think I could be?'

'I don't see why not. We'd have to ask your mum, mind, and if it's on a school night, only after your homework was done…'

He took another bite of his toast, smiling as Jem did likewise.

The second time it happened they both heard it, eyes locking as they queried the source of the noise. It was only soft, a tiny squeak, but then it came again, a little stronger.

Jem dropped to his hands and knees and peered under the side of Angus's chair. He sat back, astonished, his eyes wide as he looked back up at Angus.

'It's a cat,' he said breathily. 'Kittens.'

Angus hastily replaced his plate on the table and copied Jem's stance. Sure enough, right at the back nearest the wall was a fat ginger cat, and one… two, three… four, wriggling kittens. There was a sudden plaintive cry.

'Oh, she must be starving!' said Jem. He glanced back at his plate.

'No, not that,' said Angus. 'Do you want to go and see if you can find Trixie. Tell her what's happened and see if she has any fish, tuna, that sort of thing. Or chicken. And some water, not milk…'

Jem was already heading for the door, sliding it open, slipping through and closing it firmly behind him.

Angus peered back under the chair. 'Well, well, well,' he said. 'How long have you been in here then, Rumpus?' he muttered. 'You silly girl. You didn't tell anyone you were going to have babies. It's a good job we came in here when we did.' He shook his head, knowing full well that that was the way little miracles always worked.

The cat had done the best she could and scrunched up a piece of old sacking onto which she had delivered her kittens, but it was far from ideal. He gently stretched a hand under the chair to see if he could tempt Rumpus out, but all that happened was that the cries became louder. He got back to his feet and went through to the next room where Clara kept most of her tools. He soon found what he was looking for and, retracing his steps, laid the box he had collected on the floor beside the stove, hoping that Clara wouldn't begrudge the loss of the old fleece he had found there either. It would make a good warm lining. Carefully he began to rip away part of one side of the cardboard, until he had made an entrance with a step low enough for Mum to climb over but high enough that the kittens wouldn't get through, not until they were old enough, that was.

Almost as soon as he had finished he heard muffled voices from outside and the door was cautiously opened again. Jem had only been gone a minute. He must have run the whole way. He beckoned Trixie inside.

'Quick, shut the door. Look, she's over here.' Jem pulled at Trixie's arm. 'I reckon she's starving…'

Trixie flashed Angus a grin. 'I only had time to grab a couple of bowls, a tin of tuna and the can opener,' she said. 'Jem was rather anxious that we get back here.' She put the things down on the table. 'Poor little thing. I bet she is desperate for something to eat too. Do you know how long she's been in here?'

Angus shook her head. 'Clara is in and out all the time, so it could perhaps have been any day this last week. I can't really get a look at the kittens yet, but they're tiny, only a day or two old, I would think.'

'Well, then it's quite possible you've saved her life, Jem. And her babies. How many has she got?'

'Four, as far as I could tell.'

Trixie nodded, and picked up the can of tuna. She handed one of the bowls to Jem. 'There's a tap in the end room. Would you like to go and get Rumpus some water?' She spooned some of the fish out into the bowl. 'We need to get the kittens off the cold floor,' she said to Angus. 'Let's hope this does the trick.'

She placed the bowl down on the floor a little way in front of the armchair and then beside it set the bowl of water that Jem had fetched.

'What do we do now?' whispered Jem.

'We wait,' replied Angus. 'Rumpus is usually a friendly cat but she'll be very protective of her babies so we need to let her know that she can trust us before we try to move the kittens. We need to give her a bit of time to get used to us, and hopefully have something to eat. She'll need to keep her strength up to be able to feed them, and we need to keep them all warm as well.'

'Is that what the box is for?'

Angus nodded. 'I've put one of Clara's old fleeces in the bottom for them to snuggle into, but at some point we need to fetch something a bit bigger, a nice warm blanket maybe. They'll be fine there beside the stove.'

The mewling had continued, faint and intermittent, but then it suddenly increased and Angus pointed to the chair. A small pink nose could just be seen poking out from underneath. It twitched expectantly. Gradually bit by bit, a paw appeared, followed by a head, until finally Rumpus slunk out and cautiously approached the bowl.

'Go on, sweetheart,' muttered Angus. 'It's okay…'

They held their collective breath until the cat began to eat, grinning at each other as she took her first mouthful, followed by another and then another.

'I think I'll need to go and buy some more tuna,' said Trixie.

Jem looked up at Angus. 'Can I stroke her?' he asked. 'If I'm gentle?'

Angus nodded. 'Move slowly, so you don't startle her, but I'm sure she'd like that.'

Jem did as Angus said, watching Rumpus carefully for any sign that he was frightening her, but she seemed oblivious to his movement, intent on eating her way steadily through the bowl of food. Jem laid a gentle hand on her head and smoothed it down her neck onto her back. Almost immediately a low rumbling noise rose up and Jem's face creased into a wide smile.

'Oh, she likes it!' he said, beaming. And from the continuous purring that vibrated around them it was clear that she did, almost as much as Jem in fact.

'I tell you what, Jem. Do you think you could continue to stroke Rumpus for a bit while we just check to see that her kittens are okay? And then I think we can pop them in the box without too much bother.'

Jem nodded and settled himself on the floor, cross-legged and completely oblivious to the dust and cold. He kept up a continuous stream of endearments in a low voice as he rhythmically smoothed Rumpus's silky fur.

The kittens were wedged right up against the wall and it was hard to know quite the best way to get at them. Eventually, after deciding that lifting the chair away would only startle Mum, Trixie declared that there was nothing for it and gamely wriggled her way under the chair, flat on her belly. There was no way that Angus's bulk would have allowed him to get anywhere near them, but Trixie, with her petite frame, just managed to hook a couple of fingers around the sacking that the kittens were lying on and slid it very gently forwards.

Rumpus, very sensibly deciding that her brood were in safe hands, didn't even move and, after a few minutes, Trixie was able to pull the sacking clear from under the chair. Four tiny balls of fluff were heaped on top of one another, eyes shut tight, their fur the colour of rich, amber honey. Trixie looked up at Angus and he could see she felt just as he did. There was relief that they were all alive and wriggling, pride that they had been able to help, but more than anything two hearts turned to utter mush at the unbearably adorable sight before them.

'Jem,' whispered Angus. 'Look…'

When Jem looked up, his face was wreathed with emotion and full of wonder. 'I've never seen a kitten before,' he said.

'Me neither,' said Trixie. 'Aren't they beautiful?'

Jem feasted his eyes for a few more minutes. 'Can we give them names?' he asked.

Angus caught Trixie's glance. He had no idea what to say.

'Jem,' he said gently. 'I'm not sure who will be looking after them. Rumpus is a farm cat, she doesn't really belong to anyone, and it wouldn't be right to have five cats all wandering about the place.'

Jem caught the tone in his voice. 'But what will happen to them? Where will they go?'

Trixie cleared her throat. 'I think we might have to find new owners for them, Jem. But we'll make sure it's someone who really wants a cat. Someone who will look after them properly and will love and care for them.'

Jem looked close to tears. 'But I could look after them. I would… I'd come every day and feed them and…' He trailed off, knowing that this could never be, but still searching Angus's eyes for any sign that he might be wrong.

'I know you'd do a fantastic job but… well, let's just wait and see, shall we.'

Angus looked at Trixie for help. Jem's hand was still stroking Rumpus's back, but his head hung and Angus fully expected to see a tear drop from his cheek at any moment. It was breaking his heart.

Trixie laid a gentle hand on the head of one of the kittens. 'You know, even if we do find new owners for the kittens, we can't do it yet, not until they're able to fend for themselves and that won't be for a good few weeks yet, not until well past Christmas. They're going to need someone to look after them for all that time. Do you think you could still do that?'

Jem inhaled a sharp breath. 'Could I?'

Angus smiled gratefully at Trixie. 'I'm sure you could. We'd have to check with your mum of course, but I don't mind you coming in here and I know Clara won't.'

For the first time since starting her food, Rumpus lifted her head and looked around her, sniffing the air.

'Right, time to get these babies into the box and see if Rumpus likes her new home,' said Angus. 'And then we'd better go and see your mum and let her know what's been going on.' He grinned at Jem. 'Plus we have our lunch to finish and an awful lot of logs still to fetch and carry.'

He'd never considered having a pet before but, as Angus watched Jem's face as he helped Trixie settle the kittens into the box, he knew without a shadow of a doubt that he'd have all four of them if it meant the smile would stay on Jem's face.

Chapter 16

Ruby glanced at the clock on the kitchen wall. She wasn't worried as such – Angus had warned her that they might be out some time – but lunch had been and gone and there was still no sign of Jem. What concerned her was more that Jem could be a real handful at times and she would feel awful if that had been the case.

She'd been astonished when Angus had suggested that he take Jem out for the day. Astonished, and extremely grateful. Her house was currently a hive of activity and friendly chatter and adding Jem into that mix would most likely have been an utter disaster. As it was, she couldn't remember a time when she had enjoyed herself more, well not in recent months anyway. And, if she had been astonished by Angus's generosity, she was even more astonished by the way that her life seemed to have changed in such a short space of time.

When she had got up this morning, she had crossed to the window, as was her habit, to stand and ponder the day ahead. The view was familiar to her now and never failed to bring a smile to her lips, but it wasn't until she began to make her way downstairs to make the first cup of tea of the day that she realised with a start that she had been at Joy's Acre for only a little over a week. It felt as if she had been here for months and, although she knew that it was only temporary, already she could see possibilities in her future that she had never dreamed of.

Louise had been good to her word and, after a quick discussion with Ruby at the school gates earlier in the week, had immediately offered her services, together with those of two of her friends, Daisy and Sophia. They were currently sitting at her kitchen table, along with Maddie and Clara. There was fabric everywhere, some folded, some hanging, some spilling onto the floor and some already transformed into shimmery, crystal-encrusted bows.

As Ruby had suspected, Louise was a dab hand with a sewing machine, as was Daisy, while their other friend, Sophia, had immediately opted to cut out the fabric shapes using the template that Ruby had designed. She was also nearest the kettle and cheerfully provided a steady stream of refreshments for them all.

The women had arrived about half past ten, Louise casually announcing that she usually hated Sundays. Although she had already attended the early morning service, she was happy to be away from home on a day when she always felt obligated to do 'good works'.

'But you're doing good works now,' argued Daisy, and Louise had pulled a face.

'Yes, but these are good works I'm actually going to enjoy as opposed to talking with elderly parishioners, or visiting sick villagers. Not that I mind, not really, but Sundays have a flavour all of their own and if I do anything different I feel the most ridiculous amounts of guilt. This is such a wonderful excuse, I'm beginning to think that we should invent more and more reasons to do stuff like this. And, let's face it, what self-respecting village isn't made better by the addition of bunting.'

Daisy groaned. 'Oh, please not more Cath Kidston, I couldn't bear it…'

The conversation had flowed around the room ever since and now they were just beginning to find their stride again after lunch. So far that morning, Clara and Sophia had cut out thirty-two pieces of the golden taffeta silk that Ruby had found online. She, Daisy and Louise had sewn together thirty-two bows, and Maddie had glued a handful of beads and crystals to thirty-two lengths of ribbon which formed the central decoration to each. They had a way to go yet but already Trixie could see that Maddie's dreams were beginning to take shape.

'What time are you expecting Jem back, Ruby?' asked Maddie, seeing her glance towards the clock.

She stilled the machine for a moment. 'No particular time, I just wondered how they were getting on, that's all. It can be quite a challenge keeping Jem occupied when he doesn't want to be.'

Daisy looked up. 'I wouldn't mind keeping Angus occupied, that's for sure.'

'Daisy Hamilton! That's a scandalous thing to say.' Louise grinned. 'Not only are you a married woman, but a stalwart of the WI to boot, how could you say such a thing?'

Daisy took a pin from out of her mouth. 'Oh, come on, don't tell me you haven't thought about it. That man is six-foot-five-inches of solid phwoar!'

'Is he really that tall?' asked Maddie.

Daisy grinned. 'Why are you asking how tall he is? It's the *phwoar* that counts. You're well in there, Ruby, although quite how you've managed it, I don't know. He's never taken any notice of the female species before, no matter how hard they bat their eyelashes.'

Ruby looked at Maddie helplessly. Neither of those things had occurred to her, and she wasn't at all sure she wanted to get into a conversation about them either.

'Perhaps it's because I'm *not* batting my eyelashes?' she said, but smiled so that they wouldn't think her pompous.

'That's what they all say,' muttered Daisy drily, but then she glanced at Clara. 'Seriously though, I think it's lovely that you're friends. Moving somewhere new isn't easy, is it? And Angus is as good as they come. He has an air of mystery about him that us salacious gossipy types like to talk about, that's all, and that's only because he's so quiet.'

'I'm just so grateful to him,' said Ruby. 'My son doesn't always find relationships easy and for some reason or another he seems to have taken quite a shine to Angus.'

'And the other way around it would seem…' added Sophia. 'But don't you go worrying yourself on that score. Angus is as straight as a die and what happened before was just speculation really, it was never proven. Plus, the woman concerned was completely off her head of course. In any case it was a long time ago now.'

Clara looked up sharply and darted a look at Sophia who immediately put a hand over her mouth.

'Oh, crap. I'm so sorry. I really shouldn't have said anything. I have such a big mouth at times.' She smiled reassuringly at Ruby. 'Please, just ignore me.'

But the trouble was that however much Sophia wished she could take her words back, they were out there, floating in the air above their heads, settling onto Ruby's shoulders where they could whisper in her ear.

'What happened?' she asked.

'I really don't—'

'That's probably not—'

Louise and Clara both spoke together, and smiled apologetically at each other. Louise motioned for Clara to speak.

'I'm not sure that's particularly helpful,' she said. 'Like Sophia said, it's a very old story and repeating it isn't going to help anyone.'

'Except that the only way for me to put it to one side and forget about it is to make my own mind up,' said Ruby. 'I can't unhear what Sophia said, and this is my son we're taking about.'

An uneasy jangling had started in the pit of her stomach. It was a feeling that she knew only too well and reminded her of things she had no wish to be reminded of, ever again.

Clara sighed and looked at the others. 'About five years ago a new couple moved into the village so that the guy, David, could take up the new doctor's job when the bigger surgery opened in town. David was lovely, but his wife, Tiffany, was a total nightmare from the minute they moved in. I'm not sure where she thought she was, but she obviously felt that her husband's career entitled her to some sort of special status. She antagonised all the local mums by insisting that she take over the running of various things at the school and kicked up a huge fuss at the local shop because they wouldn't deliver her shopping. All in all, she got herself a bit of a reputation.' Clara paused for a moment, looking at the others to check that they agreed with her version of events. 'And then she made an allegation against Angus.'

Ruby swallowed, feeling suddenly hot. 'What was the allegation?' she asked.

Clara fidgeted, grimacing. 'It hardly seems fair to even say it…' She took a deep breath. 'Angus spent quite a few weeks fitting new decking and fencing in their garden. It was the summer holidays and very hot. Her girls were constantly in the garden, playing in the paddling pool… you get the picture. At the end of the holidays when they went back to school, she told everyone that Angus had… you know, enjoyed looking at them a bit too much. She painted him to be some sort of pervert.'

Ruby felt sick.

'But the whole thing was utterly, utterly ridiculous,' added Clara, rubbing Ruby's arm. 'In fact, on several of the occasions when all this was supposed to have happened, David was actually in the garden with the girls the whole time and he stuck up for Angus. It made me so angry, because even though people didn't like Tiffany they still took her word, joining in the type of small-minded hysteria that can happen in close communities. Of course, it all died a death two weeks later when David found Tiffany in bed with the local plumber and all hell broke loose. It quickly became clear then that Angus was indeed a perfect gent, and Tiffany was a total slapper who'd obviously had her advances towards him spurned.'

'Oh my God,' said Ruby, shocked. 'How could somebody *do* such a thing?'

'What? Sleep around? Or try and trash somebody's reputation?' said Daisy. 'I don't think she cared about either. She really was rather a nasty piece of work.'

'So you see, you don't need to give the thing another thought. Just be grateful that you have someone as honourable as Angus looking out for Jem,' said Clara.

Maddie looked around her. 'Blimey, I never knew any of that,' she said.

'And please don't let it go any further than this room,' said Clara in reply. 'It's been more or less forgotten and Angus has been a good friend to me over the years. It was a truly awful time for him and I'd hate him to have to live through all this again.'

Sophia got slowly to her feet. 'I'll make a drink, shall I?' she said, smiling apologetically. 'Before I say anything else stupid.'

Ruby nodded, but she smiled too. 'I appreciate your honesty, actually,' she said. 'Imagine how I would feel if I'd just heard this from someone in the village, out of context, and without the full story. I'd say you've done me a huge favour.' And then she looked at the array of wonderful finished bows that lay on the kitchen counter tops. 'Several huge favours…'

'Hear, hear,' echoed Maddie.

Ruby heaved a sigh of relief. The awkwardness had passed and in a way she was pleased that this whole sorry matter was out in the open. She picked up another piece of silk and began to smooth it out ready for sewing. It was just unfortunate that, given the choice, she would still rather not have heard it in the first place…

'Mum!' The excited shout echoed down the hallway as the front door was flung open and the sound of feet thundered towards the kitchen.

'You'll never guess what we've found!'

Ruby looked up at her son's excited face. 'No, I probably won't, you're right.' She grinned at him, delighted to see his cheeks red from the fresh air, and a light in his eyes that certainly hadn't been there this morning. 'Why don't you tell me?'

Behind him, Angus had just come into the room.

'Ladies,' he said, dipping his head. His bulk nearly filled the remaining space.

Jem moved around the table to stand beside her. 'Well, first… first we went into the woodland, and we didn't see the deer, but we nearly did! And then Angus showed me where to go so that I don't get lost… There's a tree with a big hole in it, and one shaped like the letter "Y", and then there's a huge conker tree which Angus said is really good for climbing… We saw baby shoots… erm…' He looked to Angus for confirmation.

'Snowdrops,' he prompted.

'Yeah, snowdrops, and then when we got to the Hall we had to load up all the wood and carry it to the truck, and then…' He stopped to catch his breath. 'And then… that's not even the best bit. Trixie made us lunch and hot chocolate and we were just drinking it when there was a really funny noise which I didn't hear the first time but Angus did and then the next time we both heard it…'

His sentence had run together in one big jumble and Ruby nodded her head trying to keep up with what he was saying. She laughed. 'Hey, slow down a bit!'

Jem's eyes grew even wider. 'Oh, Mum, we found kittens, *four* kittens!'

Ruby's eyes found Angus's, his face creased into a smile.

'It would seem that Rumpus the farm cat has been making friends,' he said with a raise of his eyebrows. 'We found her in the garden rooms that Clara and I use, starving hungry but otherwise fine, and yes, the proud mum of four ginger balls of fluff.'

'Can I look after them, Mum, please? Can I?'

Ruby hesitated. 'What exactly do you mean by look after them?' she asked, thinking about the state of her house and what it would look like with four tiny kittens roaming around it.

'We've given Rumpus a box by the stove in there,' said Angus. 'So she's happy enough for the moment.' He directed a look towards Clara. 'And snuggled her into one of your old fleeces, sorry, Clara. But, the thing is we can't leave the door to the place open, so if Jem could pop and see her every now and again, take her some food, check she's all right, that kind of thing…'

'I could go in the morning, and then when I get back from school… before bedtime too… Please, Mum.'

Ruby couldn't remember the last time she had seen Jem so animated, and it was clear that Angus was the reason for the change in her son's behaviour. The thought prickled uncomfortably.

She smiled at Jem, trying to think fast. The last thing she wanted to do was deflate his mood. 'I think that's a brilliant idea,' she said. 'You can take her a blanket too if you like, later on. As long as it's an old one, of course.'

Jem threw his arms around her. 'Ah, thanks, Mum!' He released her just as quickly and went to stand beside Angus, catching hold of his sleeve. 'Come on, we've still got all the logs to do,' he said. 'And then when we get back, can Angus stay for tea?'

Ruby was caught. What on earth could she say in front of everyone? Particularly with the weight of Clara's gaze settling on her.

'I don't see why not… If he wants to, that is.'

Angus threw a helpless look around the room and then shrugged, following Jem who was already halfway down the hallway. He stuck his head back around the door at the last minute.

'See you later,' he said to Ruby.

Daisy let out a long sigh. 'Well,' she said. 'Is it me, or is it hot in here?'

Ruby put a hand to her cheek. She did feel rather warm, but it wasn't desire that had caused it.

★

'Well, that's Darcie finally in the land of nod,' said Ruby, coming back down the stairs for the second time in the last half-hour. 'Although quite how long it's going to last I'm not sure. I think her first tooth is making itself known. Poor little mite; her cheeks are really flushed and I think all the excitement here today has probably worn her out too.'

'And her mum,' said Angus. 'You look tired.'

'I feel exhausted,' she admitted, longing to settle herself into the chair opposite Angus beside the fire. Instead she bit her lip. 'In fact… I'm really sorry, Angus, I was going to suggest a cup of tea but… would you mind if we cut the evening short? Jem will be back from putting Rumpus to bed soon, and I think I might be in for rather an unsettled night. It might be wise to get to bed early.'

It sounded plausible enough under the circumstances, and she'd tried to behave as normally as possible all through tea. She doubted Angus had even noticed any change in her behaviour.

He levered himself out of the chair. 'Of course I don't mind,' he said, moving through into the kitchen. He paused by the table. 'It's been a very productive day one way or another. And from what I could see, you're well on your way to finishing all the bows. They look absolutely beautiful, Ruby. You should be very proud of what you've done.'

She blushed, his generous words highlighting how conflicted she was feeling. She stared up at his open face. He was a nice man and he didn't deserve her mistrust. Allowing her own baggage to colour her opinion of him when the rumours about his past had been clearly explained to her was simply not fair. She knew that, but right now it didn't seem to be making any difference...

'Thank you,' she said. 'But it really was a team effort.' She swallowed, uncertain what else to say. Now that he was on his feet she just wanted him to leave.

The seconds stretched out into the space around them.

'Right, well, I'll be off then,' he said, after a moment when it was clear she wasn't going to say anything else.

She nodded, watching as he removed his jumper from the back of one of the chairs where he had discarded it earlier and pulled it back over his head.

'Night, Ruby.' He smiled, straightening the sweater over his shoulders. 'And say cheerio to Jem for me, won't you?'

He turned towards the door.

'Oh…' She'd caught sight of the label sticking out of the back of his sweater. 'Angus, you've put your jumper on inside out.'

He stretched out the bottom hem, checking the seams, and then grinned.

'You'd think I'd have learned how to get dressed properly by now, wouldn't you?' he said, pulling the jumper back over his head, and accidentally pulling up his tee shirt with it as he did so. He turned back around, hastily trying to tug it back down where it had rucked up, but not before Ruby caught sight of the broad expanse of his back beneath it.

Her breath caught in her throat. Not because of the sight of his slim hips above the tan belt of his jeans, or the smooth arc of his muscles that stretched around his strong shoulders, but because of the three round marks just slightly left of centre, halfway down his back. She knew what they were. She had seen them before.

Chapter 17

Ruby peered under the bed, but there was no sign of it there either. She could understand it better if the weather was warm, but the night before had been bitterly cold and Jem always slept with his blanket on the bed; he had done for years.

She checked the wardrobe, just in case, but it was nowhere to be seen. She might as well give up, there were very few other places it could be, after all. She would ask him about it later, but for now she had other things on her mind. In less than half an hour's time she would be meeting Trixie to go and have a look around the empty shop that she really had no place to be looking around. It was a lovely idea, but, really, how on earth could she possibly take on a venture like that? She had more chance of flying to the moon.

With another quick glance at her watch, she began to strip the duvet cover from Jem's bed ready to wash. She tugged at the bottom sheet to remove that too and retrieved the pillows from the floor where they had fallen. She reached down again to pick up what she thought was a tissue, tutting as she remembered the time one had got caught up in the wash and shredded itself all over her clothes. She was about to tuck it in her pocket to throw away later, when she realised it was a proper cotton handkerchief, and she stared at it for a moment. Jem didn't own such a thing, and neither did she. Judging by where she had found it, it must have been tucked under his pillow.

She turned the white square in her hands, feeling something rough beneath her fingertips. In one corner was a small embroidered 'A'. Her heart began to beat a little faster as she stared at the cloth. She could understand easily enough how Jem had come by it. He had been out with Angus for most of the day, and there could be any number of reasons why he might have needed a hanky. He could have got dirty, have been crying even, although given the coldness of the day it was more likely he simply needed to blow his nose. And Angus was old-fashioned. He was the sort who would put a clean square in his pocket every day, ready for just such an occasion. But what didn't make sense was why Jem had put it under his pillow.

She shook her head. There couldn't be anything sinister in it. She was just spooking herself, a stupid notion brought on by ridiculous village gossip that she had got drawn into at the weekend. In fact, hearing it had made part of her feel for the gentle giant. She could imagine that he would have been absolutely distraught over the allegation, made by a woman out of spite when she discovered that his morals were superior to hers. So, knowing this, why did finding the hanky still make her feel uneasy?

Ruby sat on the edge of the bed a moment. She knew exactly why it made her feel uneasy. Who was she kidding? She could pretend to herself all she liked but, in an incredibly short space of time, she had got used to having Angus around. He was beginning to make her feel safe and, up until last night, if he had been sweet enough to lend her a hanky, then she probably would have slept with it under her pillow too; a talisman against the dark. But she had been wrong and so very foolish, because what she had heard about him yesterday and what she had seen last night when he had taken off his sweater in her kitchen had made her realise that there was nothing safe about Angus at all. Because, extraordinary though it might seem under the circumstances, Angus had been where she had, and it was a time and place she never wanted to go back to. And that scared her more than anything.

With a jolt she remembered what she was supposed to be doing and hastily finished the task in hand, jogging back down the stairs with an armful of bed linen and shoving it into the washing machine. Then she dragged a brush through her thick tawny curls, snatched up her handbag from the back of a chair and began to unclip Darcie from her highchair. She frowned slightly at her daughter's mucky face and reached for the packet of wet wipes on the side. This was madness, all of it.

★

Noah was already waiting when they arrived in Penny Lane, and he waved a set of keys at them as he saw them approach.

'Morning!' He grinned at Ruby. 'Good to see you again. I've heard a lot about you since the other day and, from what Trixie's said, I'm really hoping that you're going to say yes to this place. The good folk of this town have been starved of somewhere to satisfy their creative urges for far too long, and I have it on good authority that you'll be on to a real winner if you do take on the shop.'

Ruby exchanged a glance with Trixie, not entirely sure what had been said about her. It was far from being a simple case of saying yes or no, whatever she thought about the shop. She simply didn't have the means at her disposal to make those kind of decisions. She was about to make a non-committal remark when something else occurred to her. She narrowed her eyes at Noah, slightly confused.

'Hang on a minute. On whose authority am I on to a winner? Apart from us, no one knows what I had in mind for the shop.'

Noah looked a little sheepish. 'Ah, well they do actually… Although in my defence for talking to everyone I could possibly think of about what you're planning…' he coughed slightly, '… and getting Lottie to do the same… it *is* really good news.'

'Lottie…?' Ruby was becoming more and more confused by the minute.

Noah looked at Trixie for affirmation. 'Yes, my sister? From the tearoom… Well we thought, or rather I thought, that there's no better place to sound out how people feel about an idea than by doing it in the one place where folks congregate to natter and exchange gossip.' He looked up at Ruby through his lashes. 'And it, er, seems to have done the trick. They've been flat out busy over the last few days, and everyone she's spoken to seems to be really excited at the prospect of having a woolly shop in the town.'

Trixie sniggered. 'A woolly shop?' she said. 'What on earth is one of those?'

Noah raised a helpless hand. 'Well, I don't know what they're called, do I?' He looked at Ruby again. 'What *do* you call a shop that sells wool?'

She couldn't help but laugh. Noah was so endearing. 'Er, a wool shop?' she suggested.

Noah shook his head. 'Nope, I think a woolly shop sounds better.'

Ruby stared at him. 'Do you know I think I do too… It kind of works both ways, doesn't it? The Woolly Shop. A shop that sells wool, and woollies too, because of course I'd still be making and selling my jackets and jumpers.'

Trixie beamed at her, and then Noah too. 'I think that's brilliant! And people really are keen for that sort of thing?'

'They are… and I spread the word a bit at the market too, and got pretty much the same response…' He trailed off as he saw the looks on their faces. 'What?'

Trixie shook her head, laughing, but not at him, with him. 'Oh, you're priceless, Noah, you really are.'

'But it's market research, that's all. You need good market research.'

Trixie linked her arm through his. 'Come on, let's go inside. I can't wait to see what it's like.' She gave Ruby a thumbs up, grinning.

Ruby returned the smile. It really was very kind of Noah to have gone to so much trouble, and his sister too, but listening to him she was only too aware that a huge swell of excitement was rising inside her, and she mustn't let it continue. It would be all too easy to get her hopes up and allow it to influence her. Besides, it was all sounding far too much like a done deal for her liking and it really was anything but. She tried to dampen down her excitement although, looking down the passageway at the lights and the festive displays, it was hard; everything looked so pretty and the thought that this time next year she could be a part of this was drawing her in like a magnet.

Noah held out his hand, the keys across his palm.

'Would you like to do the honours?' he said.

Ruby was about to take them, but then she hesitated, stepping back. 'No,' she said. 'You do it. You go first.'

Noah raised his eyebrows, giving her a little space to change her mind if she wanted, but when he could see that she wasn't going to, stepped forward and popped the key into the lock.

'I haven't been in here myself yet, so I'm as much in the dark as you.'

In the dark was right, thought Ruby. The shop was very small, that much was obvious from the front. The wooden door, painted a smart navy blue, was to the left of a single curving bay window, a deep wide sill all that could be seen. Behind it a piece of cloth had been hung, presumably to hide any tools or other items which might have been left in the shop while it was being renovated, but it hid any impression of what the shop was like inside. It also blocked out most of the light.

She waited while Noah pushed open the door and felt around for the light switch. He flicked it on and, with a deep intake of breath, she followed him inside.

'Oh...'

The voice was Trixie's, coming from somewhere over her shoulder. It was full of disappointment. Although much bigger than Ruby had thought it would be, the space looked more like someone's front room rather than a shop, and it was totally impractical.

'Ah, right... Well, I guess that explains why it hasn't been snapped up yet,' said Noah. He looked as disappointed as Trixie had sounded. 'I'm so sorry, Ruby, I really didn't think it would be like this.'

Ruby looked around her. The wall to her right held a small cast-iron fireplace, with two tall thin alcoves on either side. A window was set low into the back wall to accommodate the steeply sloping ceiling, while to the left two doors broke up the only flat wall in the room. There would be little or no room to display anything. She crossed to the furthest of the doors and pulled it open. Inside was a small kitchen area, lit by another small window in another sloping roof. The second door revealed a wide deep cupboard which she guessed must go underneath somebody's stairs.

She walked back out to the centre of the room, spinning slowly, taking in everything she could see, her thoughts whirling around her head. She really hadn't expected this. She had thought about what she would find, but it hadn't been this. She was aware that Trixie and Noah were watching her, exchanging glances between themselves. It was a settled matter as far as they were concerned and there really was only one conclusion for her too. She turned to face them.

'Oh my God, I absolutely love it!' she squealed. 'I don't care what I have to do, but I have to have it. I'll sell my soul if necessary; you have no idea how perfect this is!' She grinned at their bewildered faces. 'Ever since I was a little girl, I've dreamed of having a shop of my own, and in every single one of those dreams it looked exactly like this. I can't believe it.'

'But Ruby, there's nowhere to put anything,' said Trixie. 'You need space to display things surely? How else are you going to sell them?'

She turned around, grinning at them. 'But don't you see, that's why it's so perfect. Wool loves being thrown in baskets, or stuffed onto shelves wedged in any little nook or cranny. My jumpers can be pinned to the sloping walls… I could have a chair beside the fire, a coffee table full of patterns…' She crossed to the cupboard space. 'And this, I saw it in a magazine once, kitted out with those sort of sliding larder cupboards that pull forwards. If I had something like that I could get masses of stock on those.'

Noah came forwards. 'I think I'm beginning to see what you mean. You don't need display cabinets or shelving as such, what you need is just built-in storage.' He looked at Trixie's perplexed face. 'Think of those glossy magazines you've seen where hand-built fitted cupboards transform awkward-shaped spaces, providing storage from floor to ceiling all shelved out so that there are multiple compartments. That's what you'd need here, but it wouldn't need to be very deep or elaborate because the wool itself is part of the decoration.' He looked around him as if searching for the words to describe what he was thinking. 'When all the wool was in place it would be just like having really colourful wallpaper.'

Trixie began to nod her head in understanding. 'So actually all you might need to make this happen is to find someone who's a really good carpenter…' She grinned at Ruby. 'Such a shame we don't know *anyone* like that…'

Ruby's hand flew to her mouth. 'Oh, no, I couldn't ask Angus. I mean, why on earth would he want to do something like this? He has more than enough to do already.'

'Ruby,' said Trixie in a plaintive voice. 'You do know that Angus would pretty much do anything for you, don't you?'

That might be true, but she couldn't let it happen.

'No,' she said, firmly. 'That would be taking advantage of him.'

She turned around so that Trixie wouldn't see her face as she crossed to the window for a minute on the pretext of looking out. It gave her a moment to collect her thoughts and thrust any involving Angus from her head. Running a shop like this would provide far more of a stable future for her and her children than she had ever thought possible. Not only that, but it would allow her to build a network of contacts; other business people, suppliers, customers, friends even; people who she didn't have to hide from. She was currently standing right in the middle of a tiny shop filled with a huge amount of possibility. Tantalisingly close, she could nearly touch it; in a few short months it could be hers.

Her throat tightened as a wave of emotion threatened to engulf her. She had once thought that she was brave, that she had done everything she could to protect her children. Surely that meant that she was strong, that she was resourceful? But time had proved her wrong, had shown her that what she had thought of as bravery was in fact weakness. All she had done in the past was run, like a coward with their tail between their legs, and she had kept on running. The brave thing to do would have been to face up to things, to ask for help and stand her ground.

To fight for what she knew was right. And with a sudden clarity that had come from nowhere, she suddenly understood that right here was a place where she could do exactly that.

She felt a gentle touch on her shoulder.

'Ruby?' She turned to see Trixie's anxious face. 'Is everything okay?'

She pushed down the fear that was her constant companion, and tried to grasp the slender thread of hope that was dangling in front of her.

She nodded, feeling Trixie's arms go around her. 'Will you help me?' she whispered.

★

A few minutes later they were standing in the passageway once more, a keen wind buffeting them. Ruby gave a sudden shiver. She felt more hopeful than she could remember feeling in a long while, but she was scared too. It was a massive step to be taking, but at least this time she wouldn't be taking it on her own.

Trixie was still watching her with concern. 'Perhaps we should go and get a coffee or something before we go back to Joy's Acre,' she said. 'It will give you a chance to get your head around things a little. I imagine your brain must be doing somersaults.'

Noah smiled sympathetically. 'I was just about to suggest the same thing,' he said. 'Come on, Lottie will sort us out. Something hot and something sweet, that's what we need.' He gave Ruby a meaningful look. 'It also wouldn't hurt to have a chat with the landlord's wife…'

The tearoom was surprisingly busy for a Monday morning, but Ruby took a seat with Trixie while she waited for Noah to get their drinks. The room was full of festive cheer, from the cheesy Christmas soundtrack that was playing in the background, to the homemade paper decorations that hung from the ceiling; green and red spotted paperchains that were just as dotty as Lottie herself. A buzz of happy conversation surrounded her. It was perfect; she didn't want to be alone with her thoughts and the chatter gave her a great excuse for ignoring them. There would be time enough later on.

'You can tell me to mind my own business if you like,' said Trixie. 'And I understand your needing some help with practical things, or the business side of running a shop, but back there when you asked for help, it was almost as if there was something else... Something much bigger that you needed help with.' She broke off for a moment. 'I'm not quite sure how to put this... I'm a nosey bugger, too much of the ex-barmaid still in me, and I do have a tendency to be a bit... blunt, shall we say. But are you really all right, Ruby? You're not in any kind of trouble, are you?'

Ruby's heart sank. She had quickly glossed over her earlier cry for help by trying to clarify what she had meant. After all, she was a novice where renting a shop was concerned and there were a lot of things she might need assistance with. But she might have known that Trixie would see through her attempt to cover up how she was really feeling.

'What? Single mum, ups sticks a few weeks before Christmas, moves miles away from home, and is obviously looking for a fresh start? That kind of thing?' But she smiled to let Trixie know she wasn't angry at her question. 'I can see how it looks,' she added. 'And you're right, things haven't been easy of late... There are things I'm keen to leave behind, but no, I'm not in any kind of trouble, just a failed relationship behind me and all the accompanying baggage that brings with it.' She smiled as warmly as she could. 'You've all been so generous with your time and friendship since I arrived though,' she said. 'Maybe one day I'll tell you all the gory details.' She broke off as she saw Noah coming back towards them. 'But I doubt whether Noah really wants to listen to all that, so another time perhaps?'

Noah plonked himself down. 'Lottie's going to bring our cake and drinks over in a few minutes and then join us, if that's okay? She can answer some of your questions and has promised to have a chat with Jake later on.' He frowned a little. 'She did, however, mention that there was someone else in here earlier this morning asking about the shop.'

Trixie exchanged a look with Ruby. 'Oh no, did she think they were serious?'

'Lottie wasn't really sure. She'd never seen the woman before, but she was asking lots of questions about the rent and so on, what type of lease it was. Quite well-informed questions apparently, as if she knew what she was talking about.'

'Oh, well that's that then,' said Ruby. 'I knew it was too good to be true.'

'Now don't go jumping to conclusions,' admonished Trixie. 'It could have been just a casual enquiry.'

Noah nodded. 'Lottie obviously didn't tell the woman she was the landlord's wife, but suggested she contact the agent for more details instead. She didn't comment either way apparently. But don't forget that we got in first. Even if this woman did want to find out more, that still doesn't detract from your interest.'

'Do you know what she looked like, Noah? Could it have been someone from the market?'

'I don't think so. From the description she didn't sound familiar, and Lottie said she was really pretty. No offence, but, apart from your good selves, I can't think of anyone that fits that description.'

Trixie blushed. 'Oh, go on with you,' she said, and then grinned. 'What else did Lottie say?'

'Just that she was very pretty and was wearing a gorgeous black biker jacket, not the cheap and nasty plastic sort, mind, but a really nice quality one, and boots to match; legs up to her armpits, that kind of thing.' He rolled his eyes. 'If I said something like that I'd get into so much trouble.'

Trixie stared at him. 'Never mind that,' she said, turning to look at Ruby. 'Are you thinking what I'm thinking?'

'I could well be,' she replied, frowning. 'But why would Louise be looking at the shop?'

Chapter 18

Angus lowered his arm quickly, feeling more than a little self-conscious. He had thought that Ruby had seen him, but his wave had gone unanswered so he must have been mistaken; her early morning greetings were usually very friendly.

As he watched, he realised that she was making her way across the gardens to the store room where Rumpus's kittens were growing bigger by the day. He had seen Jem go in there earlier, fulfilling his morning duty of care before school. So far, he had not missed a single day and kept up at least twice-daily visits, but a quick check on his watch confirmed that this morning Jem was in danger of being late for school.

He began to make his way around the outside of the garden. The task he had been working on wasn't quite finished but he could get back to it later; the front yard needed sweeping and it was a job he liked to do early in preparation for the coming day. It also meant that he could give Jem a cheery wave as he left for school, as had become something of a habit.

This morning though, it took a full ten minutes before Jem appeared, trailing behind Ruby with an unusually fractious Darcie in her arms. Jem's head was down and his whole demeanour mirrored that of his first few days at Joy's Acre. Not since the day they had discovered Rumpus and her kittens had Angus seen Jem looking so low; the change in his behaviour for the better had been quite marked, but something must have happened now to cause his current bad mood.

He took a few steps across the yard.

'Morning!' he called as cheerfully as he could.

'We're running late, Angus,' said Ruby.

It wasn't a greeting, it was a dismissal.

Angus stopped in his tracks. Neither Ruby nor Jem had even looked at him – well, a fleeting glance from Ruby perhaps, but nothing from Jem at all. It was as if the boy hadn't even seen him. He was about to call again and wish Jem a good day at school when he realised that it would achieve nothing. Hurt, he turned away to carry on with his sweeping.

He had heard from Trixie that Ruby had made some serious enquiries about taking on a shop in the town. Surely, when it looked as if her dream might be coming true after all, she should look overjoyed and full of excitement, not stressed and preoccupied. Perhaps she had encountered some problems with the lease, or things with Jem were not as good as he had thought. Then again, Darcie had looked unusually upset too; perhaps with her teething they'd all had rather an unsettled night. He slowed his pace. He had no idea how long Ruby would be out for, but it wouldn't hurt to be around when she got back.

As it happened, he didn't have to wait long. Ruby arrived back at the farm a scant fifteen minutes after she had left. It was clearly not a morning for hanging around talking to the other mums at the school gate. He watched as she unbuckled Darcie's car seat and marched through the gate at the far end of the yard.

'Still sweeping that yard, Angus?' she said as she passed.

He had been about to speak and, instead, clamped his mouth shut in surprise; there was a tone to her voice that he had never heard before. Was it sarcasm? She clearly didn't want to talk to him, that much was blindingly obvious. Angus wasn't about to let it go, however; that was twice now that she had dismissed him and that wasn't like the Ruby he had come to know.

He picked up his pace so that by the time she reached the kitchen window he would intersect her path.

'Have I done something to offend you, Ruby?' he asked quietly.

Her big blue eyes swivelled to meet his, before dropping to stare at the floor. Now that he was closer, he could see how exhausted she looked. She stopped for a moment, adjusting her grip on the car seat.

'I haven't had much sleep,' she said. 'Darcie's been teething and we've been up for most of the night.'

And the night before that by the look of things, thought Angus, aware she hadn't exactly answered his question.

He smiled sympathetically. 'Then perhaps now that she's asleep it wouldn't hurt for you to head back to bed yourself.'

'I have things to do,' she replied.

'I'm sure you do. You have a busy life, but that doesn't mean you should wear yourself out. People don't cope so well with things when they're tired either.'

Her eyes flashed. 'And how would you know about that? You don't have any children.'

He held her look. 'True, I don't. I am just your basic big, bluff woodcutter; as thick as the planks of wood I rip apart with my bare hands.' He took a firmer grip on his broom and took a step back. 'How could I possibly notice that you look like you have the weight of the world on your shoulders, or that Jem looks as unhappy as the first day you arrived, as miserable as I've ever seen him in fact.' He turned away. 'I'll let you get on with your day,' he said, stiffly. He hadn't even taken a single step before her voice came from behind him.

'Don't you dare bring Jem into this! What on earth gives you the right to comment on how I parent my child, or how I choose to discipline him. You don't even know what he's done!' Her hands were white as she gripped the handle of Darcie's car seat, her eyes boring into his.

'No, I don't.' He glared back at her, confused but feeling the heat of his hurt and anger flare. 'So why don't you tell me? I never even mentioned your parenting skills so don't go accusing me of things I've never said. In fact, it sounds to me as if you're the one who's calling them into question, not me. Just because you've got a guilty conscience, don't go trying to heap it all on me!'

He thought for a moment that Ruby might be about to burst into tears, but then her anger got the better of her too, and her face tightened even further. 'Right, well if you're such a bloody know-it-all, you can come and see what he's done.'

She turned on her heel and marched off before Angus could even try and stop her. This really wasn't what he wanted at all and he felt all the anger slide out of him as quickly as it had arrived. He wanted to make her feel better, not worse, but he had no chance at all of doing that unless he caught up with her. He followed her around the corner of the house as quickly as he could, looking up with a grimace as a few flakes of snow blew in a sudden squall; as if reading the mood, the sky had grown suspiciously dark.

To his surprise, he realised that they were going to the garden rooms. Ruby unceremoniously yanked open the door, marching inside without a backwards glance, leaving him to follow meekly behind.

Approaching the box where Rumpus was curled up with her kittens, she placed Darcie's car seat on the ground before finally turning around to face him. The cat stood and stretched when she saw them, picking her way over her babies and to Angus's extended hand. Rumpus rubbed herself against it in ecstasy, a full-throated purr filling the awkward silence in the room.

The four kittens wriggled and mewed, temporarily bereft of their warm mother, eyes still tight shut, blind and helpless. Underneath them was a bright coloured blanket that had been tucked tightly into all the corners of the box to guard against draughts.

Angus had a feeling he knew what was coming next.

'When Jem was born I stitched him a blanket,' began Ruby. 'It was made with some of my old jumpers, some wool from a cot blanket that my grandma had made for me, but most of all from love. He was too little to have it on his bed straight away, and so I packed it away carefully in tissue paper like the most precious jewel, and as soon as Jem was old enough to have a proper bed, I brought it out for him. It's been on his bed every day since. Right up until a few days ago when it went missing. I thought he loved this blanket. It's been with him everywhere and he's never been able to sleep without it before. And look here, now he's just thrown it away. It's like he's thrown *me* away. Because of you, this wonderful, precious thing, full of love, is being used as a litter tray.'

The force of her accusation hit him full in the chest. 'Hey, now wait a minute, why is this my fault, Ruby?'

'Because you encouraged him to look after the kittens. You couldn't just leave Jem alone, could you? And now you've given him false hope too, something else to love that I'm only going to end up taking away from him, like I always do! I feel bad enough already without having to see this wonderful reminder of how little my son thinks of me.'

Her voice cracked as she finished, but her head was held at a defiant angle, blue eyes flashing in anger as she poured out her hurt. But Angus was hurting too, wounded by the barbs she had thrown at him. They had landed right where she'd intended them to.

'That's not what this is about and you know it,' he snapped. 'I think you need to take a long hard look at yourself, Ruby, before you go blaming other people for your own insecurities. You're so fixated on seeing Jem's behaviour as moody or aggressive that you can't even see when he does something out of love.'

He inhaled a deep breath, warming to his theme. 'In fact, that's what this is really all about, isn't it? Your fear that Jem is going to turn out just like his father? Don't you know that children love uncondition-ally? Did it never even occur to you that Jem might have had another very obvious reason for using his treasured blanket for Rumpus and her kittens?'

Ruby opened her mouth to speak, but then closed it again. She held his look for a moment, before dropping her eyes to the floor.

'No, you don't want to hear it, do you…? Have you ever actually seen Jem in here?' he demanded. 'I mean properly seen him, watched him while he's looking after the kittens? How he cares for them, talks to them, tells them that they're going to be okay and that he'll look after them?' He waited until she shook her head, her eyes still on the ground. 'I imagine he learnt all that from you.'

Ruby raised her head a little.

'I've seen the angry little boy, the one who lashed out without thinking of other people, the one who was sulky and rude. But now I've also seen the boy who knows what it is to love unconditionally, to care for something with little or no reward, and who can sit still for hours just so that he can keep watch on his little charges, wanting only to help them. So, far from throwing the blanket away, what he actually did was look around in his life for the one thing that meant something to him, the one thing that spoke of love like nothing else could. And when he found it, he gave that love to another, just as you did all those years ago when you made the blanket for Jem. He hasn't thrown you away, Ruby, he's paid you the biggest compliment there is… except that you're so blinded by your own past you can't even see it.' He took a step backwards, his throat tightening with emotion as he turned to go.

'Angus… I—'

'No, Ruby, don't say another word.'

He turned his back on her and took another couple of steps.

'Do you know what really hurts?' he said, suddenly spinning around. 'The fact that I thought we understood one another. I thought we were friends, and although I could see what a difficult time you were having, that maybe I could help. Instead, it's very clear by the way you've spoken to me, the way you've inferred… things… that you've listened to gossip from the village.'

He threw up his hands. 'And even though I'm assuming that you've also heard that everything I'm supposed to have done in the past was built around a pack of lies told by someone with the morals of an alley cat, I even get why that matters to you. Why you, more than most people, would be reluctant to let anyone get close to you. But you couldn't even do me the courtesy of asking me about what happened, could you? Instead you just jumped to conclusions… You threw *me* away, Ruby.'

And with that he walked from the room.

Chapter 19

'Well, thank heavens for that, that's all I can say.'

Trixie looked up, startled, as Maddie came into the kitchen, and scurried across the kitchen to shut the pantry door, with a pointed look at her friend.

'I thought we'd agreed you were going to knock if the kitchen door was closed,' she said.

Maddie pulled a face, having forgotten their agreement. She didn't really want to catch an early glimpse of her wedding cake, but her head was so full of other things at the moment.

'Oops,' she said, grinning. 'Anyway, it wasn't completely closed.'

Trixie still gave her an exasperated look. 'So, what are you thanking the heavens for then?' she asked.

'The snow,' said Maddie. 'It's very pretty and Christmassy, but I was scared it wasn't going to stop.' She crossed to the window and stared at the lowering sky, the colour of putty. 'But it has and now it just looks like it's going to rain instead. I was beginning to worry it would ruin all our plans.'

Trixie collected her notebook from where it lay beside the cooker, this time exchanging a glance with Clara who was sitting at the table.

'What?' asked Maddie, catching her look.

Trixie sighed. 'If I said "nothing" would you believe me?'

'Go on…' said Maddie slowly, an ominous feeling settling into the pit of her stomach.

'Well for one, those aren't rain clouds, they're full of snow… and two, I just caught the end of the weather forecast and it's not looking good. The wind has changed from something or other to something else, and well, the upshot of it is that the snow is now predicted to dump right on top of us.' She grimaced. 'Although, they could be wrong of course…'

Maddie groaned. 'I think I liked the "nothing" option better.' The mild sense of panic she had felt on first seeing the snow again this morning had now risen by several notches. 'Is it too early to have hysterics?' she asked.

'Much,' replied Trixie. 'There's nothing we can do about it and so I suggest we just get on with stuff while we still can.'

'Notebooks at the ready?' said Maddie, brandishing the one she was carrying.

'Indeed… It's going to be a busy day.'

'Right then, ladies, are you all set?' Maddie grinned. 'Among other things, we've got a barn to decorate.'

★

The tree for the barn had arrived earlier that morning, on the back of a lorry that Angus had borrowed from a mate. It had taken Seth, Tom, Angus and his friend just to carry it into the barn, and Maddie declared that she couldn't watch, retreating into the slightly calmer atmosphere of the house. Now though, word had it that the tree had finally been coaxed up into position and was ready for viewing.

No sooner had the three of them closed the back door behind them than Seth appeared running down the path, flagging them down.

'Hang on a minute!' He grinned breathlessly, and with a flourish pulled a scarf from his coat pocket. 'You didn't think I was just going to let you walk in there, did you?' He held the scarf up to Maddie's eyes. 'You have to put this on,' he said.

Trixie giggled. 'And no peeking.' She helped Seth to tie the blindfold firmly and then spun Maddie around for good measure until she groaned.

'Oh, don't, I'll be sick,' she said.

Seth took her arm and, with a backwards wink at Trixie, led Maddie carefully back up the path. He stopped her at the barn's threshold and soon there were three of them, forming a mini conga, all with eyes shut tight, hanging onto the back of one another. They hobbled into the barn, hampered, not just by their strange positions, but also by their laughter.

Maddie was brought to a sudden stop. She could smell the tree, its evocative pine scent hanging in the air, and this alone was enough to set the butterflies in her stomach dancing. It took her right back to her childhood: the smell of the tree, as she and her mum teased the sparkling decorations over its branches while her dad laughed at their delight, taking photos and occasionally lifting Maddie up so that she could place a bauble higher up the tree. There was always a big tin of sweets on the go and, as she unwrapped them, she would hold the coloured cellophane wrappers up to the fire to let the light shine through them. She breathed deeply, feeling the magic gathering in the air.

Two hands gently turned her around until she was facing in the other direction. Trixie had let go of the back of her coat and, as she felt a hand slip into hers, she realised that the other two were standing by her side.

'Keep your eyes closed now,' came Tom's voice. 'Just for a moment longer.'

There was the sound of footsteps and a rustling noise.

'On three now, ladies,' said Seth. 'One, two—'

'Three!' shouted Maddie.

There was a sharp intake of breath beside her and she opened her eyes.

No one said a word and the stunned silence stretched out as they stared at the sight in front of them.

'I think we're going to need more bows…' she said, and then snorted with laughter. 'Oh my God, Angus, it's huge!'

He scratched his head. 'Aye, it didn't look half as big in the wood, or lying down neither…'

'Oh, but she's beautiful,' breathed Clara. 'Perfect…' She moved forward to touch one of the branches, burying her face in the pines and breathing deeply.

'She's not the only one,' came a voice from behind the tree.

'Declan!' squealed Clara, running around it and practically jumping into his arms. 'When did you get here?'

'About thirty minutes ago,' he said. 'And the van will be arriving in the next hour or so. By the end of today, I'll be your new neighbour…'

'And that's not all,' said Tom, grinning at something behind Maddie's head. Something, or someone…

Maddie slowly turned around as a figure came forward out of the light from the doorway, a scattering of snow blowing in through the opening.

'Hi, Maddie,' she said a little shyly, but then rushed forwards to throw her arms around her.

'Isobel, oh you're back!'

The two women grinned at one another. 'Well I had to be, didn't I? I mean, who else is going to play the music at your wedding? I wouldn't miss this for the world!'

Maddie took hold of Seth's hands, her eyes shining. 'Oh my God,' she said. 'Everyone's coming home... We *are* actually getting married, aren't we? It really is going to happen.'

'It really is,' said Seth. 'In less than a week's time, we'll be standing here together again, but this time as man and wife...'

Trixie heaved a sigh. 'Oh for goodness' sake... I don't know about you, Angus, but I'm beginning to feel a bit of a gooseberry...' She looked around her, grinning at the three couples. 'All this yucky lovey stuff...' She motioned putting two fingers down her throat.

Maddie slapped at her arm. 'Just you wait,' she said, grinning back. 'Noah will have his wicked way with you under the mistletoe and that will be the end of you.'

'As if...'

Clara clapped a hand to her forehead. 'Oh, bloody hell... the mistletoe... I knew I'd forgotten something!'

★

An hour later, after copious shouted instructions and a fair degree of swearing, the tree was covered in lights and the men were just beginning to hang up strings of them elsewhere in the barn. Maddie's knees felt weak just watching Angus and Tom shin up and down the huge ladders that were required to pin the bulbs to the rafters high above their heads. She was rather glad that on this occasion Seth seemed content to direct traffic from the ground, after he'd helped them to carry in all the trestle tables that had been brought over from the Hall for the occasion.

One set had been placed into a square shape and, with accompanying benches, would provide somewhere for their guests to sit if they chose, away from the area where the band would play and where hopefully dancing would take place. Another line of tables ran along the far wall, to the right of the huge tree, and she gave Trixie a sympathetic smile on seeing them. Each of these would soon need to be filled with food and anyone could see that this would be no mean feat. Lastly, a smaller square table had been brought across from the main house and placed slightly forward of the tree. It would eventually hold her wedding cake, the one thing about which she knew nothing. It was to be Trixie's present to her and Seth, and a closely guarded secret. For now she could only dream about what it would look like.

Maddie checked her watch. The small staging blocks that would provide a raised area for the band to play upon would be delivered soon. Fortunately, the annual village pantomime was not until late January and so the committee had very kindly agreed to loan them for the occasion. As soon as they were in place, the decoration could begin in earnest. If she was quick she would just have time to call in on Ruby before they arrived. She hurried out the door, pulling her coat tighter around her. The snow was coming down thicker now, huge flakes that the wind hurled against the side of the barn. Already the pathway was covered over and, although not late, the day had dimmed almost to dusk, the twinkling fairylights outside providing the only cheer against the grey sky.

She had no idea what they would have done had Ruby not chosen to stay at Joy's Acre while she was waiting for her house to become ready. Despite their best intentions, and a couple of days they had spent together to help make the bows and other decorations, the reality of caring for their other guests and the sheer number of jobs that had to be undertaken on a regular basis had meant that the majority of the work had fallen on Ruby. This wasn't the real reason why Maddie wanted to see her, however. Ruby had seemed a little down the last few days and, judging by the poorly concealed anxiety on Angus's face, Maddie had her suspicions that somehow he was involved.

She was pleased to see that Ruby looked less tired as she opened the door, although her smile didn't quite have the same radiance that it had on previous occasions.

'I saw them carry the tree in,' said Ruby straight away. 'Is it all ready?' She was already moving back down the hallway towards the kitchen. How on earth could Maddie possibly tell her that they probably hadn't made nearly enough bows? It was a week before Christmas and Ruby had two children to look after as well; her to-do list was probably huge already.

'Oh, it looks beautiful, I can't wait to see it decorated. The lights are on as well, so we can start hanging the bows any time we're ready. Clara is in charge of greenery and Trixie's disappeared back to the kitchen for a while, but the men are all around and so is Tom's girlfriend, Isobel – she's the musician I told you about – so there should be plenty of help.'

'It looked enormous,' replied Ruby. 'I managed to make another forty or so bows, but I just hope we have enough.'

Maddie nodded, and then realised what she'd said. 'You made another forty bows? Ruby, how on earth did you manage to do that?'

'Oh believe me, I was glad of something to do.' Her voice had lowered slightly, her head angled towards the living room door.

Maddie met her look. 'Ah,' she said softly. 'Are things still no better?'

Ruby glanced back towards the door. 'Hold on,' she said. She crossed the room and stuck her head around the doorway. Maddie could hear the television through the open door.

'It's okay,' said Ruby, coming back into the room. 'Jem must have gone upstairs.' She pulled a face. 'I honestly thought that we had turned a corner. His teacher said that over the last week of term she had noticed a big difference in his manner and he seemed far more settled here too, much happier. Then a couple of days before the end of term we had a silly argument. It was my fault; I jumped to conclusions about something, but even though I apologised and we sorted it out, since then he's gone back to being the surly monosyllabic child he was when we first arrived… and I have no idea why.'

'Have you spoken to Angus about it? Maybe he knows what's wrong.'

Ruby lowered her head and her face crumpled. 'I can't. Oh, Maddie, it was horrible. I was so rude to him, and now I don't think he's ever going to speak to me again. I was upset about Jem, but I allowed that stupid gossip about Angus to get the better of me. Somehow I got everything back to front; seeing things that weren't there, blaming Angus for the way that Jem had behaved when it wasn't his fault at all, it was mine. I've made such a mess of things.'

Maddie touched a hand to Ruby's arm, seeing the look of anguish on her face, and felt her heart go out to her. It didn't seem fair. Ruby was a generous soul, and thoughtful too; if she had lashed out at Angus it could only have been because she was feeling vulnerable. She was wearing another of her handmade jumpers today, a riot of colour and pattern and, although it suited her bubbly personality, perhaps her bright clothing was a subconscious prop she used to make herself feel better. It was obvious that she had had a tough time of things in the past. But if anyone could understand this, it would be Angus.

'So talk to him about it, Ruby. Angus doesn't seem the sort to bear a grudge. Everybody loses their temper from time to time and misunderstandings are the worst. If you explain, I'm sure things will be okay.'

Ruby bit her lip. 'Thank you.' She gave a wan smile. 'But I think it's a bit late for that. He's practically ignored me the last couple of days. I don't think I'm even going to get the chance to say I'm sorry.'

Maddie stared out of the window. 'Well, he's in the barn now... Nothing like striking while the iron is hot, and we're going over there anyway... Plus, everyone is in a really festive mood. It's the perfect opportunity...' She let her sentence dangle, hoping to encourage Ruby, and was relieved to see her face brighten a little.

'Do you really think so? I hate there being bad feeling between us; it's made me realise that I've never had a friend like him before,' she said. 'In fact, I've never really had friends, full stop.'

Maddie held out her arms. 'Well you do now,' she said, drawing Ruby into a hug. 'And I'm sure everything will be okay. Perhaps we're all just getting a bit tired. It's a busy time of year without all this added work I seem to have heaped on everyone.'

Ruby shook her head fiercely. 'No,' she said. 'I've enjoyed every minute of this. It's been wonderful.'

'And now, hopefully, you have the shop to look forward to as well.'

'I daren't think about it,' said Ruby, brightening a little. 'I keep pinching myself just to check I'm not dreaming.'

Maddie smiled. 'I know that feeling,' she said. 'And I can't believe you've made all those extra bows.'

'I'll go and get them, shall I? There're three big boxes up in my bedroom and then another bag with the jam-jar covers in it.'

'Let's ferry everything across to the barn and then we can decide what needs to be done first. Oh, it's so exciting!' She was about to turn away when another thought came to her. 'I'm so sorry,' she said. 'Here's me ordering you about and I'd completely forgotten about Darcie and Jem.'

Ruby smiled. 'Don't worry, I've already agreed that Jem can look after himself for a while. He knows where we are if he needs me, and Darcie, bless her, is having a proper adventure. Louise is looking after her niece today, who's only eighteen months old, and so she offered to have Darcie too. She thought it might be nice for them to "play" together and I'm afraid I bit her arm off.' She laughed. 'I don't get too many offers like that.' She looked up and peered out of the window. 'Although... if this snow keeps coming, Louise might be looking after her for longer than she bargained for. Are the roads all right, do you think?'

Maddie nodded reassuringly, as much for her own benefit as for Ruby's. 'Louise has an enormous four-by-four, she'll be fine. Anyway, I don't suppose things are that bad.'

It was what she had been telling herself all day.

Chapter 20

'Is there somebody who can get that?' yelled Trixie at no one in particular. It was the second time the phone had rung in the last five minutes, and on the last occasion she had been involved in a tricky icing manoeuvre and couldn't get there quickly enough. Now she was just about to take a tray of cakes out of the oven and there was no way she was risking them getting burnt.

After a few moments the ringing stopped and Trixie sighed. Whoever it was would just have to call again. At least the phone lines were still okay, she thought glumly; little else was working, at least not in their neck of the woods. She had turned off the radio about half an hour ago, fed up of listening to the panicked traffic reports and stories of worsening weather right across the country. It felt like the walls were closing in.

And it was still bloody snowing.

She lowered the hot tray onto the top of the oven and picked up an uncooked batch waiting on the work top. It was the fourth tray she had cooked so far and there were another six to go. On the table were the cakes she was icing, very special cakes that Maddie must not see under any circumstances, which was proving to be rather difficult. So far in the last hour Maddie had wandered through to the kitchen almost every five minutes it seemed, seeking reassurance about the weather. Trixie was trying her best, but she was running out of believable reasons for why everything would still be okay.

The phone rang again, this time her mobile, and she smiled when she saw who was calling.

'Noah, thank God,' she said. 'Please tell me everything will be okay, because I'm currently cooking over one hundred cupcakes and I'd really like them to be eaten sometime this side of Christmas, preferably at a wedding.'

There was a long pause and a burst of static.

'Noah?'

'… Hill… later…'

She stared at her phone. 'Noah,' she said again. 'I can't hear you…'

His voice was suddenly loud in her ear. 'Nothing's getting up or down the hill at the moment, maybe later but don't bank on it.'

'Noah, in what way, shape or form does that help me to think that things will be okay?'

She could hear him smile down the phone.

'Sorry,' he said. 'I bet Maddie is having kittens. What are you all going to do?'

'Well at the moment we're all trying to pretend that everything will be fine, but however much Maddie wants to believe it, I think even she is beginning to see through our rapidly depleting stock of encouraging phrases.'

'So what do you need?'

'What, apart from a miracle and some rain to melt the snow followed by bright sunshine?' Trixie didn't even know where to begin. 'Well for one, we're not even sure how Maddie is going to get to the church… plus she's supposed to be having someone from town come and do her hair and make-up. Then there's the small matter of how any of the guests are going to get here, or how all the food is going to be delivered, or the flowers. I've got stuff over at the Hall to pick up and there's also the band coming in and Isobel's violinist friends…'

Trixie checked the display on her phone when she realised the line had gone suspiciously quiet. Call Failed. Noah had already gone.

She quietly laid her phone back down on the table and picked up a cupcake that was not quite cool yet. She peeled back the paper casing and shoved it into her mouth. Stuff it.

★

'So only three more days left before Christmas,' said Angus cheerfully. 'I bet you're getting excited now?'

There was no reply from Jem, who was trudging along by his side. Angus tried a different tack.

'At least we don't need to worry about Father Christmas not being able to get through because of all the snow. I think he's used to that up at the North Pole.'

He got a shrug in reply.

There was nothing for it.

'Jem, if you don't want to help me deliver logs any more you just need to say, okay? I know it's cold, and you'd probably much rather be inside watching the television. I won't be cross, you know.'

They were halfway across the garden and Jem suddenly stopped. His breath frosted in the chilly air. He looked up at Angus, a sorrowful expression on his face.

'What is it, mate?' asked Angus. 'You're not still worried about that blanket thing, are you? I know your mum got angry with you about it, but it was just a bit of a misunderstanding. She got cross with me as well, but she said sorry to me too, so that's all okay.'

'Yeah, she said.'

'Well, that's good then.' He knew that Ruby had already apologised to her son for her outburst, but there was still something upsetting him. Perhaps he had taken it more to heart than either of them realised.

'So, what's bugging you?' he asked, nudging Jem's arm playfully. 'You've hardly said two words to anyone all day, and I thought we'd got past all the moodiness…'

For a moment, Angus thought that Jem wasn't going to realise he was being flippant and trying to provoke a reaction, but then he looked up and gave a rueful smile, just a tiny one. Almost immediately, though, his face fell again.

'Mum's going to kill me…' he murmured.

'No, she's not, Jem. She's cool about the blanket, honestly, although I think you might have to let her make you a new one, *and* promise not to let anything wee all over it…'

To his dismay Jem burst into noisy, choking sobs.

'I didn't mean to,' he cried. 'I just wanted to talk to him; I didn't realise what would happen.'

Angus dropped to his knee, feeling the cold wet snow seep through his jeans. He touched a hand to Jem's coat sleeve.

'Hey, come on now, it's not that bad, I'm sure.'

Jem threw his arms around him, and buried his face in Angus's broad chest. 'It is,' he sobbed. 'It is. I've made everything worse.'

Angus froze. He hadn't expected this reaction and unwittingly he had put himself in an awkward position. He really was incredibly stupid at times. Gently, he disentangled Jem's arms and reached for his hanky, realising belatedly that Jem still had it. Instead, he offered Jem the bunched-up sleeve of his jacket.

'Wipe your eyes,' he said, thinking. He couldn't take him back home but he felt an overwhelming need to be where other people were.

It was only just after lunch and everyone had probably already gone back to whatever task they were busy with, but one person would still be around, he was sure of it. Standing up, he rested a hand on Jem's shoulder. 'I tell you what, why don't we get ourselves hot drinks and you can tell me all about it.'

His hunch was right and, as they walked into the kitchen of the main house, Trixie was still there, sitting at the table, poring over her notebook, a steaming mug of something hot in front of her.

'Oh dear,' she said the minute she spotted them. 'Someone looks like they could use a hot chocolate.'

Angus flashed her a grateful smile and she gave a slight nod, recognising his difficulty. Jem stood motionless by his side, but eventually responded to Trixie's suggestion that he could have a biscuit as well.

'What's the matter, sweetheart?' she asked, as she set down a mug of frothy cocoa. 'Has someone upset you?' She looked across at Angus for a clue.

'Jem seems to think that he's done something very bad,' he explained. 'But I'm sure he hasn't really, it just seems that way.'

Trixie smiled. 'I'm sure Angus is right,' she said. 'And you know, if you tell someone about it, it usually doesn't seem half as bad. Things always feel worse when they're a big secret.'

Angus nodded. 'That's true.'

'But you'll tell Mum,' blurted Jem. 'I know you will.'

Angus's heart sank. He didn't know what to say and he looked at Trixie helplessly. How could he possibly promise not to tell Ruby? Especially when he didn't even know what kind of trouble Jem was in. He wanted to reassure the boy, but he couldn't lie to him. That would be the very worst kind of betrayal.

'Jem, I'm sorry. I can't promise not to tell your mum, that really wouldn't be a good thing to do. You see, you might tell me something that would mean you could get hurt, or someone else might, maybe Darcie for example, and one of our jobs as grown-ups is to try to make sure that those kinds of things don't happen. But…' he waited until Jem had looked up and he had his attention. 'But, like I said, maybe the thing isn't as bad as you think it is, and then I wouldn't have to tell your mum. Trouble is, I don't know which it is until you tell me, which makes it kind of difficult, doesn't it?'

Jem nodded glumly.

'So you understand why I don't want to promise?'

There was another small nod.

'But you're a big lad, and a smart one too, so maybe you can work out whether it's the kind of thing I might have to tell Mum about or not. And then you can decide whether you want to tell us, how's that?'

Jem poked a finger into the top of his hot chocolate, and lifted off some of the froth.

'What I do know though,' added Angus, 'is that it's always better to say when you've done something wrong than to let mums or dads find out for themselves. That tends to make them far more cross than if you had just owned up in the first place. And I could come with you, if you liked…?'

There was silence for a moment while Jem watched them through fearful eyes. Although Angus held his breath praying that they would soon be able to get to the bottom of this, it quickly became very obvious which kind of wrongdoing it was.

Jem shook his head. 'No, I can't,' he said. 'It's too bad.'

His head sank and nothing Angus said could get him to lift it again. Even the offer of another biscuit from Trixie was refused with a tiny shake of his head. He sipped his hot chocolate while Angus did the same as he wracked his brains trying to think of a way he could help Jem. A look at Trixie confirmed that she hadn't a clue either, and in the end he decided that sitting in the kitchen was no longer helping and the only way to cheer Jem up was to get on the move again – that and a sneaky snowball fight once they got back outside.

He swallowed the last of his drink and, rising from the table, collected both empty mugs, crossing the kitchen to leave them by the sink.

'Come on then, Jem, let's go and finish taking the logs round, people will be glad of them on a day like today. Go and pop your wellies back on.'

Jem's eyes remained downcast but he did as he was asked, leaving Angus looking beseechingly at Trixie.

'He's probably just worried Father Christmas won't bring him any presents,' whispered Trixie. 'Don't worry, I shouldn't think it's anything too serious.'

Angus smiled gratefully. Of course… That made perfect sense. He could remember quite vividly a childhood Christmas when he had accidentally knocked over a glass of blackcurrant squash in his bedroom. He'd been about nine at the time, and had sneaked the drink upstairs when his mum wasn't looking. He'd been terrified that Santa wouldn't come, trying at first to hide the stain but eventually, on Christmas Eve, unable to stand it any longer, he'd tearfully confessed.

He looked up as Jem stood in the threshold, his wet boots now back on his feet.

'Ready?' he asked.

Jem nodded, looking rather relieved to be out from under Angus and Trixie's scrutiny. Perhaps just the act of letting go of his pent-up emotion had helped.

'Right then, let's get going.' Angus paused in the doorway for a moment. 'What do you say to Trixie, Jem?'

He gave a shy smile. 'Thank you,' he said. 'The chocolate was lovely… and the biscuit.'

She beamed at him. 'Well, you're very welcome… any time.'

Angus caught her eye and she gave him a slight wink. Yes, he was sure she was right… Jem was probably just fretting over nothing…

★

Half an hour later the phone in the hall rang again, and this time it was answered within a couple of rings. Trixie cocked her head, listening for the sound of voices, one eye on the kitchen door in case she had to suddenly leap to cover her cakes from prying eyes again. After a few moments there was a gentle knock on the door.

'Trixie? It's Seth.'

A head popped round the door and Trixie immediately saw the anxiety in his eyes.

'Trouble?' she asked. 'Or should I say, *more* trouble?'

Seth gave a resigned nod of his head. 'Maddie's mum's on the phone.' He motioned with his head back towards the hallway. 'I've left Maddie talking to her, but it's not sounding good.'

'Ah.' Trixie's heart sank a few degrees lower. 'I can't say I'm not surprised, I'd kind of been expecting it, and I guess you have too, but the M40 is pretty much at a standstill, and they've just closed a huge section of it. There's no way Maddie's parents can get here safely, however much they want to.'

'I know. In fact, Maddie and I were just surmising when the phone call would come in… But that doesn't make it any easier.'

'No, of course it doesn't.' She rubbed a hand along his arm. 'I'm so sorry, Seth.'

He shook his head. 'Me and my stupid bloody ideas,' he said. 'Yes, of course let's get married at Christmas, when the whole world is frantically busy anyway, and the weather is bound to be bad. What a brilliant idea…'

'Seth, you weren't to know. I mean, when do we ever have a white Christmas? It's pretty much the one time you're almost guaranteed *not* to have snow… and besides, it was, and still is, a brilliant idea. And you did it because you know that if there was a perfect time of the year for Maddie to get married, this is it.'

'I just wanted to make her happy. The fairytale winter wedding, twinkling lights, gently falling snow…'

'Seth, you're *marrying* her… that's the most important thing, the thing that's going to make her happy. Everything else is just detail.'

He looked at her and nodded slightly. They both knew that was the truth, just as they both knew that wasn't the point.

'I'll put the kettle on,' said Trixie. There didn't seem to be anything else to do. She turned back towards the table and surveyed the racks of cakes that were sitting there. 'I'll clear these away for a bit,' she said, picking up a tray. 'And then Maddie can come in, if she wants to. I can't do any more for a moment anyway, not until I roll out some more fondant.'

'They're beautiful, Trixie.' He smiled, but it was a sad smile, a poignant smile.

Trixie swallowed and turned away, removing the cakes to the pantry one by one until they were hidden away. Then she picked up her mobile again and tapped out a quick message:

Kitchen please, if you're free… love, giggles and hugs required and you guys are the best at all of these…

She quickly removed Seth and Maddie from the group message, and then sent it on to everyone else at Joy's Acre. Then she turned back round with a bright smile to wait for Maddie.

They both heard the slow footsteps come along the hallway. Maddie didn't even bother to knock. Her eyes went straight to Seth's.

'Well, that's it,' she said. 'They're not coming.'

Seth folded his arms around her, his mouth in her hair, murmuring how sorry he was. She stayed there for a moment, and then pulled away, wiping under her eyes and visibly trying to pull herself together.

The lump in Trixie's throat was getting bigger by the minute. One day maybe she would feel like that about someone, would hear someone say her name in that tone, and the way her heart lifted wouldn't just be because she could see how much in love someone else was, but instead could feel it deep inside herself… She chased the thought away, but not before a particularly vivid image filled her head and a smile had crossed her face. *As if…*

The sound of singing floated down the hallway as Tom came through the back door and launched into a spectacularly bad version of 'Ding Dong Merrily on High'.

Seth grinned. 'Plays like an angel… sings like a duck.'

'Oi!' answered Tom, coming through the door. 'I heard that.'

'Oh, good grief, what are you wearing?' replied Seth, rolling his eyes.

'Why?' Tom answered, holding a hand over his heart. 'Don't you like it?' He paused just inside the doorway, striking a pose and turning his head this way and that so that the room's occupants could get a better view.

Trixie giggled. 'I think it's fantastic! Where on earth did you get that from?'

Tom was wearing a bright-red knitted Santa bobble hat, complete with a huge white tassel on the end. It wouldn't have looked that unusual were it not for the curly knitted 'beard' attached to it that hung down several inches below his chin.

'I'll give you three guesses,' he quipped.

Trixie and Maddie looked at one another. 'Ruby,' they chimed.

'Are you thinking what I'm thinking?' continued Trixie.

Maddie grinned. 'I expect so…'

They looked at one another expectantly but didn't have long to wait. Moments later, Clara and Angus could be heard coming through the back door, laughing at something one of them had said.

They appeared in the doorway, both of them with beaming smiles on their faces.

'Ta-dah!'

'Oh, that's just brilliant…' Maddie's eyes sought out Seth's and Trixie smiled to see the look that passed between them.

Clara was wearing an enormous Christmas pudding on her head, complete with a sprig of holly and woollen 'cream' oozing down the side, while Angus sported a towering Christmas tree with a gold satin star on its top and knitted woolly baubles dangling from its branches that waggled every time he moved his head.

'And that's not all,' said Clara, moving into the room and placing the bag she was carrying down on the table. 'I have a little present for everyone else too…' She rummaged around inside for a moment before pulling out something that she handed to Trixie. 'This one's for you…'

Trixie took the hat from her, which on first glance looked like a tree. She turned it the right way around, laughing when she saw that in fact it was Rudolph, with two button eyes, a bright red pompom for a nose, and a pair of huge brown antlers. She ran a hand over the pink spikes of her hair.

'Ah well,' she said, before pulling the hat down over her head. 'What do you think?'

Seth nodded. 'A huge improvement,' he said, soberly.

Clara snorted. 'Wait till you see yours!' she said.

Moments later the kitchen erupted into a round of applause as Seth donned his hat. It was complete with two bright red woolly legs protruding from a chimney. Santa had obviously eaten one too many pies and was well and truly stuck.

'And finally,' declared Clara, 'this one's for you…' She handed Maddie something white.

There was an expectant hush while they waited for Maddie to discover what Ruby had made for her. Her eyes were shining as she held it up; a flash of something sparkly catching the light.

'Aw… that's so lovely!' she exclaimed, turning it around so that everyone, especially Seth, could see it.

'Ruby thought it was the most appropriate,' said Clara. 'The angel on top of the tree…'

Maddie popped the hat on her head, the angel's 'skirt' adorned with twinkling crystals, and its head topped with flaxen hair and a tiny golden tiara.

'Well, ever feel like you've been well and truly set up?' said Maddie, laughing, a hand held to her chest as if to contain her emotion. 'Did you know anything about this?' She directed a look at Trixie.

'No, I didn't…Honestly, I swear.'

'Ruby just thought we could all do with cheering up,' said Clara. 'She knows what you're going through, Maddie… we all do.'

Trixie came forward and rubbed Maddie's arm. 'She's right, Mads, we do. I know the snow is causing all kinds of problems, but I've been thinking. I'm not trying to detract from how you feel about all this, and I know how awful it must be not having your mum and dad able to come to the wedding… but it's still Christmas, Maddie, there's still magic in the air…' She broke off as Maddie turned to look at her, her eyes still full of emotion at Ruby's kindness, but with something else there now as well; the teeniest spark of hope…

'I know you feel exactly the same way about Christmas as I do,' Trixie continued. 'It's a time for miracles and hope… when wonderful things happen simply because people believe they can. If we're not careful we're in danger of letting the snow smother all that magic as well as everything else. But you're getting married tomorrow, Maddie, and we'll find a way to make it happen, I promise you. After all, isn't that just what we do best? It might not be exactly the wedding you planned, or the party, but we can still make it special.'

Seth took a step forward so that he was standing by Maddie's side. The legs on his Santa hat wobbled as he walked – he looked ridiculous, but the look on his face was far from it. There was a glint in his eye as a slow smile spread across his whole face.

'What do you think, Maddie?' he said, softly.

Maddie's gaze swept from one person to the next, around the room and back again, before returning to meet Trixie's. The corners of her lips began to curve upwards.

'Then we'll just have to have another party, won't we?' she said. 'In the summer this time. And all our friends and relatives can pretend we've just got married all over again…'

'We will,' said Seth, nodding firmly. 'And then we can do it the year after and the year after that as well. I don't think I'm ever going to want to forget how it's going to feel getting married to you.'

Trixie flapped at her face. 'Oh, God, will someone please make a cup of tea before I start blubbing. I am going to be *such* a mess tomorrow…'

Chapter 21

Seth rolled over in his sleep and Maddie smiled as she studied his familiar face. Would she feel any different tomorrow, waking up as Maddie Thomas…? A bubble of excitement rose inside her at the thought and she touched his stubbled cheek softly to check she wasn't dreaming after all.

The snow had put paid to their original plan that he should stay with Tom and Isobel the night before the wedding. In fact, none of Tom, Isobel, Clara or Angus had made it home the night before and so all their spare bedrooms were full. While it was traditionally bad luck to see the groom before the wedding, it had been lovely going to bed last night knowing that all her friends were gathered around.

The house was slowly waking up around her. She could hear someone moving about downstairs and guessed it would be Trixie, making the first of what would amount to a million cups of tea as well as making preparations for their guests' breakfasts; some things continued whether there was a wedding taking place or not and, today of all days, Maddie couldn't let her do it all by herself. Looking back at Seth's sleeping form one last time, she got up, crossed over to the window, and peered out.

Her intake of breath was automatic. The sky had cleared overnight and a multitude of stars twinkled in the still inky-black sky. The cottages were in darkness but the huge Christmas tree in the centre of the lawn shone brightly. It looked nothing short of magical, and she offered up a silent prayer.

Clara and Trixie were both in the kitchen when she arrived downstairs. Yawning a good morning to them both, she headed over to the bread bin and got to work.

'What are you doing?' asked Trixie.

'Making toast?' she replied.

Trixie came across and took the knife out of her hand. 'No, you're not,' she said. 'You can't be making breakfasts today, it's not allowed.'

'But I'm up now, what am I supposed to do? Besides, it's not fair for you and Clara to have to do everything.'

Trixie stood with one hand on her hip, the other still holding the bread knife. The expression on her face clearly indicated that no discussion on the point would be entered into.

'I don't care what you do, but you're not helping in here. You'll get… flustered… or something,' said Trixie. 'Brides are supposed to be calm and serene, so go and practise being that until you're told otherwise.'

'Here,' said Clara, handing her a mug of tea. 'Go and sit in the living room until we're ready for you.'

Maddie looked at the pair of them, at their unwavering expressions, and then did as she was told.

The curtains were still drawn against the dark sky outside as she entered the room, but Angus had already been in to light the fire and its flames cast a soft flickering glow around the cosy room. The lights on the Christmas tree had been switched on too and she breathed in the quietly expectant atmosphere.

At some point tomorrow evening the jolly stockings that hung beside the fireplace would be filled with presents, one for each of them, and there they would wait, ready for Christmas Day morning. Then, later on there would be presents, the playing of silly board games, and perhaps a sneaky snooze on the sofa after the beautiful lunch that she knew Trixie had in store for them all. Most of all it would be a day filled with much love and laughter. Her first Christmas at Joy's Acre, her first as Seth's wife… She hugged the thought to her, sipping at her tea in contemplation of the day to come and the excitement ahead.

She was still staring into the fire, lost in her reverie, when Clara's head appeared around the door.

'Would Madam please make her way to the dining room,' she said, before ducking back out again.

To Maddie's surprise, Angus and Isobel were already in there, sitting self-consciously at the table, and staring with some anxiety at the pristine white tablecloth, napkins and champagne flutes.

Maddie looked around her. 'Okay…' she said slowly. 'What's going on?'

'I have no idea, but I can only assume breakfast,' said Angus.

From behind her came the sound of Seth's voice, grumbling as he came down the stairs. 'Okay, okay, I'm going… Where's the fire for goodness' sake…?' He stumbled into the room.

'Listen mate,' said Angus. 'Let me give you a word of advice… Do not under any circumstances argue with Trixie this morning.'

'Don't look at me,' said Maddie. 'I haven't the foggiest what's going on either. I was just about to make some toast when Trixie brandished the bread knife at me and told me to come in here.'

'And don't sit there either,' added Angus. 'I was explicitly instructed to make sure you two sit at the heads of the table.'

'Oh…' Seth got up, and began to move, throwing her a helpless look.

One by one they each took their seats. No one dared speak, until Maddie, feeling like a naughty school child, began to giggle.

'Glad you're all in here enjoying yourself,' said Trixie, bustling into the room. 'Some of us have been up for hours, slaving away…' But she flashed Maddie a cheeky smile and laid down a large covered dish on the table.

Clara was hot on her heels, a jug of orange juice balanced on a tray, alongside a basket of croissants, a dish of butter and two toast racks, stuffed full of thick slices. While she unloaded these, Trixie moved smoothly behind her and opened the door of the huge dresser that ran along one wall. Moments later an ice bucket complete with champagne had joined the other dishes.

'Scrambled eggs with smoked salmon, toast, croissants, orange juice and champagne… Well, if there's going to be a wedding, there's got to be a wedding breakfast…' She took the lid off the dish. 'Come on, dig in,' she said, glancing around the room. 'No, hang on a minute, we're not all here; where's Tom?'

'Just gone to check the lie of the land,' replied Angus. 'He'll be back any minute.'

Trixie frowned. 'He better had, everything's going to get cold.'

The tail end of her sentence was drowned out by the sound of the front door banging shut, followed by the staccato stamping of boots on the tiled floor to loosen the snow.

'Ah, talk of the devil,' said Maddie. 'Shame though, you know what a bugger Tom is for croissants. I thought if he wasn't here maybe the rest of us would get a look in.'

She knew he would hear her and fully expected him to make some witty riposte as he came into the room, but instead there was silence. The cheeky grin she expected to see was also absent. His face was pinched with cold, and he looked wary, avoiding eye contact with anyone other than Angus who, now that she looked, had echoes of the same expression on his face too.

'Tom…?' It was Seth, half getting to his feet, but halted by a hand on his arm.

'I'll go,' said Angus. 'You guys just carry on, we won't be long.'

And as quickly as he had appeared, Tom had gone, followed swiftly by Angus, leaving an anxious air in his wake.

Maddie looked at Seth, but the reassurance that she hoped to see faltered as he stared after the two men. He got to his feet and with a fleeting glance left the room, the likelihood of anyone carrying on with their breakfast going with him.

The four women stared at one another, then, without a word, they stood as one, and followed Seth into the hallway to don boots and coats, gloves and scarves.

A thick silence cloaked them as soon as they opened the front door. It was as if the world had gone to sleep and forgotten to wake up, or been swallowed whole into the belly of a beast. Maddie looked uneasily at Seth as Tom took off across the snowy expanse, leading them out across the yard to the very edge of the farm boundary where it adjoined the road.

'I don't understand,' she said, turning to Tom. 'I looked out my window this morning and the gardens looked nothing like this. They were perfect, like something from a Christmas card, a fairytale… not this… this is a nightmare.'

She could feel her breath begin to catch in her throat as she stared out past the cars and the roadway beyond, or at least where she thought the roadway began. It had completely disappeared, buried beneath a drift of snow that must have been ten feet high. The farm was completely cut off.

'Aye,' said Angus. 'The estate walls have protected the garden and the cottages, but not here, where it's open to the wind. It must have come suddenly in the night, and then blown itself out by the look of things.'

Seth's face was grim. 'How bad is it?' he asked.

'I've walked the length of the field,' replied Tom. 'I've no idea what the main road is like down to the village, but our lane is about a mile long and it's all like this…' He swallowed as he trailed off, looking for the first time straight at Maddie. 'I don't know what to say,' he said. 'I'm so sorry…'

Maddie was aware that one by one her friends had come to stand a little closer, their noses already pink from the cold, their bright scarves and hats vivid against the blanketed white of the landscape. If she didn't know better she would have thought that they were the only people alive in the world. She suddenly felt incredibly alone.

A sudden shrill ringing pierced the quiet and, with a beating heart, she reluctantly drew her phone from out of her pocket. On a day like today, a phone call could only be bad news. She listened for a few moments.

'No, I quite understand,' she said eventually. 'Thanks for all your help… No, I'm not sure either. I guess we'll be in touch. Thanks again.'

She ended the call, staring at the screen for a moment before finding Seth's eyes with her own.

'That was the florist,' she said. 'Unfortunately, she's unable to get to us or the church, so we won't have any flowers today.'

Seth's fingers found hers, entwining them tightly in his.

'Let's go back inside,' he said, a desolate look on his face. There was no point saying anything else. They both knew the score.

Maddie walked beside him, trying to bite back her tears. Her emotions had been so up and down for the last few days, but not once had she imagined that the wedding wouldn't even be able to go ahead. It was the final, cruellest blow to have come this close and then have all her dreams dashed at the last minute.

She excused herself the moment they got in through the door, saying she needed to use the bathroom, but in truth she needed a few moments by herself, away from the sudden claustrophobia of sympathetic looks. They were her closest friends but sometimes misery was better tasted alone.

Upstairs, she stood in their room, looking out across the garden which still bore no signs of the chaos beyond the walls, and took several deep breaths. There was a pressure behind her eyes and a tightness in her throat from holding back the tears and with a shuddering sob she released them at last. What was the point of anything if you didn't feel it? Life at Joy's Acre had taught her that.

In fact, living here had taught her many things, and she thought back nine months to when she had first arrived at the farm, and when she had cried herself to sleep because things hadn't turned out the way she had expected. And yet, in such a short space of time, they had turned out better than she could ever have imagined. All it needed was friendship and love…

She wiped a tear from the end of her chin as she watched a sparrow darting to and from the bird table and, as the tiny bird sought sustenance in the bleak landscape, she realised that it was only through despair that she would ever be able to measure her happiness. And, as sure as night followed day, you could never have one without the other. She was only crying now because she was grieving for the amazing way she had been feeling, thinking it was lost, but she was wrong, it would come again… or perhaps it had never gone away…

Across the fields she could just see the tip of the church spire, standing tall above the houses in the village. When you thought about it, the church wasn't that far away, not as the crow flew… Maybe, just maybe, with a little luck, and a healthy dollop of Trixie's Christmas spirit, they might still be in with a chance.

Sniffing madly, she fished about in her pocket for a tissue to scrub hurriedly at her eyes. Leaving the room, she crossed the landing to the spare bedroom where Clara had spent the night. Hanging on the wardrobe door was her wedding dress, safe in its protective cover. She carefully undid the zip, and touched her fingers to the fabric lightly, remembering how it felt to wear it, how she looked when she tried it on, how she would look when her wedding day finally arrived. A soft smile spread over her face. What was more important, the dress, or getting married?

Walking back along the landing she heard a soft ping from her phone and, pulling it from her pocket, she checked the display. It was from the hairdresser, apologising profusely but cancelling their appointment; the road up to the farm was impassable. It was followed swiftly by another from the photographer saying the same thing. She took a very deep breath and went downstairs.

The dining room was quiet when she re-entered the room. Everyone had resumed their places but the food lay untouched in front of them, a tangible sadness hanging in the air above their heads. Maddie plonked herself down and picked up the jug of orange juice.

'Would everyone like a drink?' she asked. 'Just to be going on with while I go and make some fresh toast.' She nodded towards the dish of scrambled eggs. 'Not sure about these though, Trixie, what do you reckon? Can we make more? I'm not sure I can stomach them cold.'

Trixie stared at Maddie in disbelief as all heads swivelled towards her in astonishment. Trixie's mouth opened, but then she closed it again, clearly lost for words.

Maddie grinned, sweeping her gaze around the table until it came to rest on Seth's confused face.

'Well, this is a wedding breakfast, right?' she said. 'So the breakfast should at least be edible…'

She looked around her at the expectant faces, no one quite sure yet how she was feeling, or why there seemed to be a sudden change of mood, but none of them willing to risk saying something and being the one to put their foot in it.

Still holding the jug, Maddie got to her feet and moved so that she was behind Seth, pouring juice into his glass from over his shoulder. Then she set the jug down and knelt beside him.

'I've been thinking about the vicar,' she said. 'He lives pretty close to the church, doesn't he?' She didn't wait for the reply. 'So, presumably, barring another natural disaster that we're not aware of, he can still get to the church this afternoon…'

'Yes, but—'

'So, if we still want to get married today, then all we have to do is get there too…' She trailed off as she slipped her hand into Seth's. 'I know I won't have flowers, or a photographer, that my hair will look a mess, and it may well be a silent walk up the aisle without music, but dammit Seth, I'll get married to you in my jeans and wellies if necessary, I don't care.'

Seth swallowed, and she saw the hope flare inside him. 'I'll bloody carry you across the fields if I have to,' he said.

She looked up into the faces of her friends: Trixie who had cooked and baked her heart out over the last few weeks, and almost single-handedly organised the whole of the catering for the wedding and tomorrow's party; Clara who had spent days making the floral decorations for the church and the barn, and Tom and Angus, who had hefted and carried, fetched and moved anything and everything for her. And all of this, all the time, all the care, all the love, might possibly go to waste if they did as she suggested. As she looked at their smiling faces, she knew that none of them would mind one single jot, and that, if asked, they would do it all over again. All they wanted was for her and Seth to be happy.

Maddie grinned. 'Seth Thomas, would you do me the very great honour of marrying me… today?'

'I will, Maddie Porter…' He paused a moment as his voice cracked with emotion. 'Now, get up off your knees and give me a kiss.' And so she did.

Trixie squealed and from the other end of the table Tom snatched the champagne from the bucket.

'Quick, let's get this open,' he said, 'before she changes her mind.'

'Oh, I'm not going to change my mind…' She screwed up her face. 'But what colour jeans do I wear? Perhaps they could be my something blue…'

Chapter 22

'It's no use, it won't budge,' said Seth. 'We'll have to go over it.'
He had been trying to push open the gate into the field behind the
Gardener's Cottage but the snow was so deep on the other side that
it wouldn't move. He swept a hand along the topmost rail to remove
the settled snow and, grasping hold of it, placed a boot firmly on one
of the struts. He swung his body weight up and over in one carefully
controlled smooth movement, landing on the other side up to his
knees in the drift.

'Blimey, that's cold!' he cried, his voice several octaves higher than
normal as a chunk of snow slipped inside his welly. He grinned, holding
out his gloved hand. 'Ladies, when you're ready.'

Maddie took his hand to steady her as she climbed over the gate,
laughing when he lifted her up and swung her round before gently
setting her down. She stood watching while Trixie, Clara and Isobel
did the same. Isobel's violin came next, passed by Tom, who hopped
over the gate as if it were only a foot high, taking back the instrument
the moment he landed and holding it to him as if it were made of
glass. Finally came Angus, bringing up the rear. They stood, looking
at one another for a moment before bursting into peals of laughter.

'What on earth do we look like?' asked Trixie, waggling her head
so that the antlers on her hat wobbled precariously.

'I don't know what you're suggesting,' replied Tom. 'Because there's nothing wrong with the way I look at all.' He stared at her, trying with all his might to keep a straight face. He managed it for all of five seconds before he broke into a grin, although much of it was hidden by the huge curly white 'beard' of his hat.

'At least you get to have a warm face,' said Maddie, as she reached out a hand to touch the angel on her own head to check it was in place. She turned to Seth. 'We look like we're on a staff outing from the novelty Christmas shop,' she said.

As soon as Ruby had heard what they were planning she had arrived with yet more woollen accessories. With two children in tow it had been impossible for her to accompany them, but even so there was no reason why they shouldn't at least go in style and Maddie had never seen so many colourful scarves, gloves or socks. Her bright red coat had also been pinned with several knitted flower corsages in lieu of a bouquet.

'Well, we'll be easy to spot if anyone is looking for us, that's for sure,' Seth replied. 'In fact, they'll see us coming a mile off.'

'I'm banking on it,' murmured Tom. 'If we need rescuing, I sincerely hope they send a St Bernard with a very large flask of brandy.'

It was a light-hearted comment, but not without a grain of truth. They had a way to go yet, and the snow lay in thick swathes around them. They would have to walk the perimeter of the field to avoid the drifts, but even so there was no doubt that when they arrived at the church they would be cold and wet, despite their layers of warm clothing.

'Right then,' said Seth, grinning at Maddie. 'Before we get going, could I just mention that when I said I would carry you across the fields if I had to, I'm not sure if I mentioned my sore arm…'

Maddie playfully punched him. 'Which one?' she asked innocently.

He leaned forward and kissed her nose, practically the only bit of her not covered up. 'Right then,' he said. 'Let's go get married.'

Twenty minutes later their colourful party ground to a halt, and Maddie caught hold of Seth's sleeve, panting for breath.

'Blinking hell, I didn't think it was going to be this hard,' she gasped. 'I'm going to need oxygen when we get to the church.'

Seth nodded, his breath coming in fast pants that clouded in the air. 'And I thought I was fit,' he groaned. Even Angus, whose legs were longer than anyone's, was puffing hard.

'Christ, we're not even halfway yet!' Trixie was leaning against Clara, a pained expression on her face.

'Okay,' said Tom. 'Let's have a breather for a minute. We've left ourselves plenty of time to get there, so there's no panic.' He scanned the field in front of them. 'It's the effort of lifting our feet clear of the snow that's crippling us, but in the absence of a sledge and some huskies I don't see that we have much choice.' He turned to look at Isobel, offering her his hand. Suddenly, he withdrew it. 'Wait a minute,' he said, banging the heel of his hand against his head. 'We may not have any huskies, but I might be able to rustle up the next best thing.' He stared at Seth. 'Blimey, why didn't I think of this before?'

He pulled off one of his gloves, holding it in his teeth for a moment while he removed the other and undid the zip of his coat. Fishing about in his inside pocket, he pulled out his mobile.

'Please God, let there be a signal,' he said, followed by a resounding 'Yess!' as he peered at the screen. He tapped the screen a few times and then held the phone to his ear. His face brightened as he heard a voice at the other end.

'Jack?' He turned to Seth and gave him a thumbs up. 'Listen mate, I hope you're at home and not doing anything in particular, because it's just possible you could save my life…'

A couple of minutes later he hung up, a huge smile on his face. 'Right, last one to the end of the field's a cissy!'

Maddie stood up straight, shaking out her legs to try to ease the burning in her calf muscles. 'I know it's the bride's prerogative to be late to the wedding,' she said. 'But we've broken every other tradition, we might as well throw that one out of the window as well.' She straightened her hat, took a deep breath and led out the line of friends across the remainder of the field.

By the time she neared the bottom hedge she could already hear a low rumbling in the distance. She would have broken into a run if she could, but it was simply impossible. Instead, she turned and gave an excited wave to the others.

'Come on,' she cried. 'He's nearly here!'

By the time they had all gathered at the gate, the huge green tractor was only a few feet away, making slow and bumpy progress, but more importantly pulling behind it a wooden trailer. Despite its rustic appearance, it was such a welcome sight that it could have been made from solid gold.

As it pulled level with them, the engine was cut with a loud rumble and the cab door opened. A figure clad in blue overalls jumped down.

'I was in the pub when you rang,' said Jack, with a look at Tom. 'Me and half the village actually. I mean, there's not much else to do, is there? Everywhere is shut.'

Maddie gave Tom a sideways glance, but he just grinned and came forward to greet the big burly farmer. He could have been anywhere from his late thirties to his early sixties, with his red weatherworn face and greying hair.

'Jack, you're a lifesaver.'

He beamed. 'Well, I don't reckon I've been called that before.' He stood back, for the first time registering their exuberant attire. 'Not the most likely looking of wedding parties, but then again it was a long time ago my missus made an honest man of me, I'm not right up with these modern traditions. Now which one of you lovely ladies is the blushing bride?'

Maddie raised her hand slightly, only to be immediately crushed in a rough embrace.

'Seth, you old dog, you! You've landed a good un here.' He patted Seth on the shoulder. 'We were all talking about your wedding back in the pub as it happens, saying how sad it was that it wouldn't be happening. When I told 'em it looked most likely it was, you've never seen folks move so quick. I think there might well be a bit of a welcoming committee by the time we get there.'

Seth's arm went around Maddie's waist. 'We shall be forever in your debt…'

The farmer bowed slightly. 'Don't reckon I've ever had anyone in my debt either,' he said, chuckling. 'What a day this is turning out to be.'

Seth exchanged a look with Tom. 'You got that right,' he said.

'We'd best be going then,' said Jack. 'Don't want you to be late…'

He moved to the rear of the trailer and undid the bolts at either side to lower the tailgate. 'Got no seats, I'm afraid… No nothing really… 'cept mud maybe.' He stared at Maddie. 'Sorry about that.'

Maddie couldn't care less. If it meant she didn't have to wade through any more snow, then she didn't mind how they got to the church. She watched while Jack hopped up into the trailer bed as if it were only a foot off the ground instead of the rather alarming five it actually was. She looked at Seth.

'Erm, I'm not entirely sure how we're going to do this,' she said, but in an instant Angus was by her side. Before she had time to realise what he was about to do, she felt herself lifted up, one strong arm under her legs and the other around her back.

'Here you are then, Jack, catch…'

He didn't exactly throw her, but there was a certain momentum to her upwards movement before Jack's equally strong arms grabbed hold of her and hauled her the rest of the way into the trailer.

'Where there's a will there's a way,' muttered Tom, smiling at Isobel, who looked horrified, cradling her violin case as if it were a newborn baby.

'Who's next?' grinned Angus.

A few minutes later they were all safely on board, perching on the trailer sides and hanging on for grim death as the tractor slowly rumbled into life, moving off slowly across the ground. The sound of Jack singing gustily at the top of his lungs could be heard from the cab's open window.

Trixie tapped Isobel on the knee. 'That's "The Holly and the Ivy",' she said, but Isobel was already trying to get her violin out of its case. She handed it to Tom.

'Don't whatever you do let me fall over the side of this thing,' she said, grinning at him as she readied herself. 'Ladies and gentlemen, on three…' And with a nod of her head, she counted them in.

It was perhaps the strangest wedding procession ever, a rickety trailer making its way slowly through the snowy whitescape, full of folk dressed in a riot of colourful clothes, singing at the tops of their voices and wearing novelty Christmas hats, but by the time they reached the edge of the field that bordered the churchyard Maddie was laughing so hard that tears were pouring down her cheeks.

They tumbled out of the trailer into an untidy giggling heap, slightly muddy, with wet legs and snow-encrusted boots.

'Oh, that was the best fun!' exclaimed Maddie, running over to Jack and throwing her arms around him. 'Thank you so much!' She kissed him on the cheek, much to his embarrassment. 'You'll have to come to the wedding now.'

He blushed furiously, looking down at his overalls and thick woolly coat which had a split down one seam.

Seth slapped him on the back. 'As you can see, we've somewhat abandoned the dress code today, you're perfect as you are. In any case, if it's all right with you, we'd quite like to book you for the return journey…' He checked his watch. 'I said to the vicar we might be a little late, but we've still got twenty minutes to spare. With any luck he's already at the church.'

'Aye, he will be,' said Jack, grinning. 'He were in the pub with me, before. I told you, half the village was in there.'

There was a sudden loud shout and, turning around, Maddie saw two figures standing by the gate into the churchyard.

'They're here!' came the shout again.

With a look at Seth, she took his hand and, making sure that everyone was following, they began to pick their way through the snow and on towards the church. As they neared, the gate was pulled open for them, and she could see that a path had been hastily cleared. A huge cheer went up, followed by a spontaneous and enthusiastic round of applause.

A sudden lump caught in Maddie's throat. There, in front of her, and for some distance on either side, stood what seemed like the entire village, not a posh wedding outfit or hat to be seen, but instead, faces wreathed with smiles, hands waving and clapping in an outpouring of simple happiness for two people, who against the odds had still managed to get to the church for their wedding. And standing right at the front of the crowd were Louise and Peter, she in one of her usual eclectic outfits, and he wearing his vicar's robes; a dark suit with a white surplice on top. He held out his hands, smiling at her less-than-orthodox appearance.

'Welcome,' he said simply, before turning to take Seth's hands also.

On his cue, a surge of people came forward, hugging, shaking hands, laughing at their hats and congratulating them. It didn't stop for a good ten minutes or so until Peter suddenly clapped his hands together.

'I think it's time we married these good people, don't you?' he shouted above the excited noise.

There was an even bigger shout in reply, and Peter took hold of Seth's hand once more. 'Time to go inside,' he said. 'Perhaps you… and Tom… in fact everyone, except for you, Maddie, and your bridesmaids of course.'

Louise beamed at Clara and Trixie, who moved to stand beside Maddie. 'We'll let you know when we're ready for you.'

Seth's lips lingered on hers for just a moment, before Tom pulled him away. 'I'll see you soon,' he whispered, the emotion catching at his throat.

And then, it was just the three of them, standing among the snow, eyes shining and hearts beating. Maddie pulled them into a hug.

'Are you okay?' asked Clara once they had pulled away.

'Oh, yes,' replied Maddie. 'I'm very okay. In fact, I don't think I've ever been more okay in my life.'

'We're not going to forget this day in a hurry, that's for sure,' added Trixie.

Maddie looked around her. The solid stone of the church gleamed a pale yellow against the whiteness surrounding them, the light within shining out through the stained-glass windows. A deep-green yew hedge bordered the churchyard and through the lych gate beyond she could see the houses further along the lane, smoke curling from their chimneys, their doors festooned with wreaths, eaves sparkling with twinkling lights. And all around, the snow had lent its own special magic to the scene. It was absolutely perfect.

They made their way into the church porch where Maddie tugged at her clothes. She looked down at her black wellies with pink spots, her black jeans now pretty much soaked through, and her cherry-red coat. 'Do I look all right?' she asked, suddenly a little nervous.

Clara gently removed her hat and scarf, laying them on the bench inside, then, using her fingers, she fluffed up Maddie's hair. 'Pink cheeks, sparkling eyes… you look like every bride should on their wedding day. Beautiful.'

Behind them, the door to the rear of the church opened and Louise's smiling face appeared. 'We're all set,' she said. 'Take your time, but whenever you're ready…'

Maddie nodded, and with one last look at Clara and Trixie, turned to make her way forward. There was a sudden shout from behind her.

'Wait! Hang on a minute!'

Surprised, Maddie spun around to see an elderly lady making her way up the path towards them. Despite her age and the still snowy paths, she made quick progress, her face never dropping its wide smile. In her hands was a large carrier bag.

'I suddenly thought,' she said on reaching them. 'Jim and I have been married fifty years, and well, I'm lucky, he always has been a romantic bugger, but like I said to him, your need is greater than mine, and I knew he'd agree.'

She opened the handles of the bag allowing Maddie to see a glimpse of white inside.

'It's not right to get married without a bouquet, and Jim always buys me white roses, never red ones, on account of how I had white ones when we were married.' She held out the bag to Maddie. 'I've wrapped the ends in tin foil, so they don't drip down your hands when you're holding them.'

Maddie took the bag as Clara came forward to help and, between them, they eased out the mass of blooms. There must have been two dozen roses inside, a perfect pearly white, with just a hint of creaminess at their centres. She looked up at the woman's crinkled face, not having the faintest idea who she was.

'You've brought your anniversary flowers for *me*?' she asked incredulously, the woman's generosity of spirit suddenly releasing a wave of emotion in Maddie. Her hand went to her throat. 'I don't know what to say… I don't even know your name,' she added.

There was a shy smile. 'It's Edith, but, well, it's like I said, what's the world coming to if a girl can't have a bouquet when she gets married? It's only what's right…'

'They are absolutely beautiful, as are you, Edith. Your Jim is a lucky man… Thank you,' she said. 'You've made my day.'

The old lady beamed as Louise offered to take her arm, and together they went on through the door. She turned and waved at the last minute. 'You can come in now,' she said.

Trixie and Clara moved to stand behind Maddie as she positioned the flowers. 'Right then, ladies,' she said. 'You heard Edith. Let's go do this.'

Maddie had dreamed about this moment for so long, dreamed about what she would see, how she would feel, but nothing had prepared her for how it would really be, walking down the aisle on her way to marry Seth. It was as if the air was dancing in front of her, as if she could almost see all the love and happiness surrounding her in a shimmery light. Anyone else would probably have said it was the sudden streak of sunlight that broke from behind a cloud and slanted through the window to her left, but the day had already proved that the magic and spirit of Christmas was with her, and so that was exactly what Maddie saw.

The soaring notes of Isobel's violin floated up to join it, and beyond the sea of smiling faces at the far end of the aisle was Seth, the man she had loved from, if not quite the first time she had set eyes on him, then pretty soon after. A man who had been constantly by her side and in her thoughts from that day onwards, and who would soon be hers, to have and to hold until only death parted them.

His eyes drew her towards him, and dressed in jeans and wellies, just like her, he smiled as if she were the most beautiful woman in the world and, at that moment, she felt like it. His hand reached out as she came to rest beside him.

'Hello, you,' he said.

And then she looked up at Peter who gave a gentle nod.

'Are you ready?' he asked softly.

She looked back into Seth's eyes, brimming with love. 'Oh, yes,' she said. 'I'm ready.'

Chapter 23

Ruby laid her head back down on the pillow and smiled. The clock showed seven thirty am, but she was going to enjoy another half-hour of dozing before she even contemplated getting up. Darcie was still quiet, and Jem would no doubt be fast asleep as well. After the amount of champagne that had been drunk yesterday she didn't think anyone in the main house would be up that early either. One thing was sure, when they did all finally surface it would be another day of frantic activity, and no one would begrudge her a little extra sleep. She closed her eyes.

Moments later they flew open again. It was Christmas Eve! The day of the party, except that… would there even be a party? The road had still been impassable when they finally got to bed last night. The thought reverberated around Ruby's head. She was happy, sad, excited and anguished all at the same time, how could she even think about sleep? And then it hit her, what all of this actually meant. It was in stark contrast to the Christmas before when she had been heavily pregnant with Darcie and living in a constant state of watchful fear. Even a month ago she hadn't dared to hope that things could be so different, but now her thoughts of the days, weeks and months ahead were wrapped in positivity.

Last night had been filled with the joyous celebrations of Maddie and Seth's wedding and, even though things hadn't turned out at all the way they had planned, it had still been an incredibly special day. Although she hadn't been able to go to the wedding itself, simply due to the difficulties of taking her two children through all that snow, as soon as everyone had arrived back at Joy's Acre, there had been a knock at her door. It had been Trixie, asking for her help with a few arrangements back at the main house so that an impromptu party could be put together for the happy couple. And happy it had certainly been. Ruby couldn't remember a time when she'd had so much fun, or felt, finally, as if she belonged to something.

She flung the bedclothes back and rushed to the window, looking out onto the wintry scene below. Tomorrow, on Christmas Day, she would enjoy a lazy morning with Darcie and Jem, opening presents, eating chocolate and playing games before joining everyone at lunchtime for mulled wine, nibbles and, according to Tom, the snowman-building competition to end all snowman-building competitions. Trixie would undoubtedly provide more hot chocolate and then, in the evening, they would celebrate the day with a traditional Christmas dinner. The delicious anticipation of it all was a wonderful feeling, and she hugged the thought to her. For now, though, there were other things to attend to, and first on the list would be to see what was happening about today. She couldn't believe that after all that had occurred that the party couldn't go ahead, but the way things had been looking last night, they would need a miracle.

Wide awake now, and feeling full of energy, Ruby felt for her slippers. She would have a cup of tea first and then, once they were all up and dressed, she would head over to the house and see what the plans were.

She paused in the lounge for a moment, smiling at the twinkling tree and the stockings still hanging by the fireplace, which she would fill before she went to bed that evening. The log basket would need replenishing soon, but there was enough to get the fire going again this morning, and doubtless Angus would soon appear with a fresh load. She picked up some of the morning sticks and laid them on the bed of hot ashes just as Angus had shown her, then, taking the poker, she parted the ashes gently to introduce some air and went to make the tea. By the time she returned the wood should have caught and she could add some of the larger logs.

Darcie was just beginning to burble as she carried Jem's juice up to him, but she knew that she would happily lie in her cot for a little while longer while Ruby got dressed. She tapped lightly on Jem's door and pushed it open. His bedclothes were a heaped jumble just as they always were when he got up, but of him there was no sign. Ruby hadn't heard him get up and go to the bathroom but she supposed his excitement at the day was getting the better of him too. She set the glass of orange down on his bedside table and went to find some clothes.

Ruby had already settled Darcie in her highchair and was halfway through preparing her breakfast when she realised that Jem still hadn't appeared to have his toast. She went back through to the lounge and called up the stairs but there was no response. Jem wasn't used to late nights either, so perhaps he had gone back to sleep after all. No matter, she would eat his breakfast and make some fresh toast for him when he did appear.

She smiled when the customary three-beat knock came at the front door. Angus was a little early this morning, but then she supposed, like everyone else, he had a long list of things to do. She went to let him in. At his feet was the expected basket of logs and in his arms were three gifts in brightly coloured wrapping.

'Ho, ho, ho,' he said, grinning. 'I know I'm not supposed to come until this evening, but I wasn't sure I'd get the chance and I wanted you to have these, ready for the morning.'

She stood back to let him in. After yesterday evening's get together following the wedding, things between them had been pretty much back to normal, and she was glad and very relieved. The more she thought about what had happened, the more she realised how badly she had behaved. She had completely overreacted when Jem had taken his blanket for the kittens and Angus had been right: her judgement about so many things, not just her son's behaviour, had been entirely misplaced. It was time to start trusting people again; Angus had, despite what had happened to him, and it was about time she did too, otherwise her past would always continue to haunt her. And here he was, showing her that he had forgiven her. Now it was her turn.

'Angus, you didn't have to do that…' Her hand went to her mouth. 'And I haven't even wrapped your present yet.'

He grinned. 'Have you really got me a present?' he asked, looking oddly touched. 'I don't usually get presents.'

She didn't really want to admit that she didn't either.

'Do you want to go and put them under the tree? Yours will be the first ones there,' she said, leading the way up the hallway. 'I'll go and give Jem a shout, he's still lazing in bed.'

Angus gave her a quizzical look. 'Oh, I thought he'd already gone out,' he said. 'Look.' He stood back from the doorway and sure enough, as well as his own large footprints through the snow, there was another, smaller set.

Ruby glanced down, only now noticing that Jem's wellies were gone from their place by the front door. She smiled.

'Gone to feed Rumpus, I expect,' she said. 'You're right, I've never seen him so devoted to anything before.'

'The kittens are just beginning to open their eyes,' Angus replied. 'Jem noticed when we got back yesterday, so I expect he couldn't wait to go and see them this morning. Rumpus will really have her hands full once they begin to move about.'

'And in another few weeks I'm going to have to seriously think about whether we can keep one of them,' said Ruby, sighing. 'I know Jem would love it. He hasn't actually asked me yet, but I would imagine it's only a matter of time.'

'It's done him good, having something to care for.'

'I know,' said Ruby. 'And I have you to thank for that... I would love to be able to keep one. The only drawback is that if the shop does go ahead, we'll all be out for most of the day, which wouldn't be fair at all, not while it's still a kitten anyway.'

'Perhaps you could have a shop cat?' suggested Angus. 'Imagine the fun it would have with all those balls of wool.'

Ruby rolled her eyes. 'I *can* imagine,' she said. 'That's the trouble. Anyway, we've time to think about it, the kittens won't be ready to leave their mum for a while yet.'

Angus nodded. 'I'm sure we'll think of something.'

She looked up at his smiling face. She rather liked his use of the word *we*.

'Would you like a drink?' she asked, as they walked through into the kitchen and on into the living room.

Angus glanced at his watch. 'I'd better not,' he said. 'Folks will be wanting their logs good and early this morning.' He leant down and placed his presents under the tree. 'I'll just top yours up and then I'll get going. We might not know what's happening today, but no doubt Maddie or Trixie will still have a list of jobs for me.'

'Hmm, I'm going over myself in a bit once Jem gets back so I can see what the plan is.'

Angus picked up her log basket. 'I'll scoop Jem up for you if it will help. He can come and help me with the rest of the logs.'

'Oh, would you? I'm sure he'd much rather do that than tag along with me.'

Angus gave a satisfied look at his gifts nestled under the tree. 'And when we've done that there's always the hugely exciting job of clearing the paths... again...' He gave her a shy smile. 'Although we might have time for the odd snowball fight...'

Ruby stared out of the window. 'Surely there can't be any more snow left to come down? I mean, it looks lovely, but I think we might have had enough of it by now.'

'I'm not sure it works quite like that,' said Angus, moving back through to the kitchen. 'I'll catch up with you later.'

Darcie was still chewing at her toast soldiers, her fingers a buttery mess. 'Right then, Miss,' said Ruby. 'Let's get you sorted and then we can crack on.'

★

The atmosphere in the main house's kitchen could only be described as hungover. In fact, there was still a bottle of champagne sitting in the middle of the table, which Tom was staring at idly as if he wasn't sure whether drinking it was a good idea, or perhaps more to the point whether drinking it *had* been a good idea.

Ruby didn't even bother going around to the front door today, but let herself and Darcie in through the back, shouting a greeting as she walked up the hallway. Trixie was the only one standing as she entered the room; everyone else was sitting down in various slumped positions that spoke either of tiredness or sore heads.

Tom got up as she entered, though, and offered her his seat, taking his mug with him and refilling it from the jug of coffee Trixie had just taken from the percolator.

'The road still looks blocked,' he said, as soon as Ruby was seated. 'Which, given our collective state, may not be such a bad thing. The thought of putting on a party tonight isn't hugely appealing just at the moment.'

'Ah, I did wonder,' Ruby replied. 'But I thought it better to come and check what was happening in case it was all systems go.'

'Yeah, and the phone lines seem to be down as well, mobiles at least, and the house phone is intermittent at best, so no idea what the outside world is doing either…'

'The good news though,' put in Trixie, 'is that we won't starve. There are approximately one hundred and seventy-five cupcakes which need eating.'

Maddie rolled her eyes and snorted. 'And now I don't need to worry about fitting into my dress, I'm planning on eating most of those.' She grinned. 'That sounds dreadful, doesn't it? It's not supposed to. As you can see, we are pretty chilled this morning…'

'Well, that's one word for it anyway,' said Ruby, raising her eyebrows. 'But I'm glad you're managing to smile about it all.'

'There's no point in doing otherwise,' she replied. 'We all had the best day yesterday. In the end it was just perfect, so there's no point in getting upset over what might have happened today. We can have a party some other time. In fact, we will, we've all agreed – Seth has even offered to marry me again if necessary.'

'Just the once, mind,' he quipped. 'I wouldn't want to make a habit of it.'

The laughter had only just died down when the sound of loud tooting came from somewhere outside.

For a few seconds nobody moved until, as one, they all realised what the tooting sound actually meant. Someone outside was trying to attract their attention…

They stared at one another until Trixie suddenly turned, leaning over the sink to see out the corner of the window.

'Oh my bleeping God, it bloody is! It's Noah!'

Moments later they were all on their feet, straining for a look. A huge tractor filled most of the forecourt, and Noah was already climbing down from the cab.

'What on earth…?' said Maddie.

'Well, we all prayed for a miracle before,' said Trixie. 'And I think he may just have arrived…'

Maddie went to the front door, pulling it wide open as everyone piled into the hallway. 'I don't believe it!' she yelled as not one, but two figures approached. 'It's the florist!'

The young woman waved from across the courtyard.

'Well, this is a first,' she said, when she reached them. 'I don't think I've ever arrived at a client's house quite like this before, but this man can be quite persuasive, you know. And it did seem such a shame for all the flowers to go to waste.'

'I told her we'd give her a good testimonial,' said Noah, coming up behind her. 'You know… *Patsy went above and beyond the call of duty for my recent wedding, and I couldn't have been happier with the result. She really was my fairy godmother*… even if she was a day late.' He caught hold of Maddie's hand and smiled. 'Very nice,' he said, touching her wedding ring. 'I heard it happened after all, and even though you won't be needing your bouquet today, I'm sure you'll find a home for the rest of the flowers.'

Maddie laughed. 'So how much did you bring with you?'

Patsy smiled at her. 'Well, all of it of course!'

Clara drew in a sharp breath. 'You brought *all* the wedding flowers, the garlands as well? Everything?' She shot a glance at Ruby.

'Well, it seemed stupid not to,' replied Patsy. 'There was room on the trailer after all…'

'Then we could decorate the barn,' said Clara, a little breathlessly.

Ruby caught her excitement. If the florist had been able to get up here, then maybe other people could too, with food… and perhaps the members of the band could get here too… and the villagers.

'Are you thinking what I'm thinking?' said Trixie, backing up the hallway and into the kitchen. 'I'll put the kettle on, we need to do some serious thinking…'

'Oh my God…' said Maddie, her hands on her cheeks as the penny dropped.

Noah grinned at them. 'I've got as many people on standby as I can, and most of them were happy to hang on this morning even if it is Christmas Eve.' He pulled a face. 'All except Geoff of course, who's a miserable bugger and has already shut up shop, so, no fish for the party I'm afraid, but I think I can get most of the rest of what was ordered up here. It's just a question of shuttling backwards and forwards.'

'I can't believe you even managed to get up here,' said Tom. 'I thought the road was blocked solid?'

'Nothing that several hours' hard labour and two tractors couldn't sort. I'm only sorry we couldn't get to you yesterday, but time got the better of us, so we started again at first light.'

Seth came forward. 'Wait a minute, let me get this straight… Did you say you've spent the best part of a day trying to get to us?'

Noah nodded. 'We tried to get in touch to tell you, but the phones are out, didn't you know?'

'And you did all that for us…'

Trixie squealed. 'I told you all how amazing he was!'

Seth winked at Maddie. 'And evidently not just his cheese…' he murmured, but he came over to shake Noah's hand, and then, laughing, pulled him into a hug instead. 'I don't know what to say,' he said. 'Thank you doesn't really seem to do it justice…'

'Not required,' said Noah. 'Really, I was happy to do it.' He gave Trixie a wide smile. 'Just give me an invite to the party,' he added. 'There's someone I'd rather like a dance with.'

'Blinkin' hell, the party!' exclaimed Trixie, jumping away from Noah's hopeful arms in her excitement. 'Oh my goodness, there's so much to do…' She fanned her face.

'Well, that's the whole reason I came over here in the first place,' said Ruby. 'Just tell me what needs doing.'

She looked at Trixie, who looked at Clara who, in turn, looked at Maddie. It would seem that Noah's one-man taxi service would need to be in operation for most of the day, ferrying food, people, and anything else they could think of. However, after yesterday, when they really had proved that anything was possible, one thing was for certain, the party tonight was going ahead come what may.

★

The barn already looked stunning. Every single one of the extra bows Ruby had made had been needed to dress the tree, but even in the daylight it looked amazing. The elegant theme had been echoed all around the room in the decorations that Clara had made; tall tripods made from canes bound together and interwoven with ivy and holly, wide gold curling ribbon and huge gold baubles finished with twinkly lights. They stood about five metres apart around the entire perimeter of the barn, with two slightly taller ones standing at the front corner of the staging area where the band would play.

Now that the party was going ahead, the trestle tables were being brought in and dressed with pristine cream cloths, then trailed with ivy and glittery confetti. The simple jam jars, which Ruby had transformed with her sparkly lacy jackets, were being placed at intervals along them. Now that they had all the wedding flowers too, some of these jars would be stuffed full of the same white anemones and ranunculus that Maddie would have had in her wedding bouquet, while others would be left to hold tea lights that they could light later on. To finish the table decorations, tall pyramids of heavenly scented oranges would be placed to stand in between everything else, studded with cloves and wound with trailing curls of ribbon. The garlands of flowers, which had originally been planned for the church porch and the altar table, were also being put to good use by Tom and Clara, who were currently hanging them around the table where the wedding cake would stand.

Ruby stood back to survey their handiwork thus far and she could see the same glow of satisfaction on the faces of everyone else that she knew was written all over her own. They had worked like Trojans the last couple of hours, but threaded through everything they did was the friendship and community spirit that bound them all together. And there wasn't a price you could put on that.

She looked up as Louise came to stand by her side. She had arrived about an hour ago on one of Noah's 'transports' up from the village, and so far had been helping Declan ferry across the chairs from the

Hall. Now stacks of them were waiting to be placed around the tables and dressed with the posies that would have graced the pew ends in the church. They were going to look so pretty.

'Right, don't move,' said Louise, mysteriously. 'I've been dying to get you on your own to talk about something for days, but all this snow rather put paid to that. And yesterday was impossible for all sorts of reasons.' She took Ruby's arm and led her away from the centre of the room.

'It's taken me a bit longer than I thought to get this all sorted out, probably because of Christmas and all that, everyone is so busy, but that's why I wanted to speak to you today if possible.'

Ruby leant in towards her. 'You're sounding a bit like a secret agent,' she whispered. 'And I haven't got a clue what you're talking about…'

Louise grinned. 'Oh, God, sorry. I forget sometimes that not everyone knows what's in my head… But I'm talking about the shop.'

'The shop?' Ruby frowned, completely blank for a moment. 'What shop?'

'The wool shop,' replied Louise. 'Well, it's not a wool shop yet of course, but I hope it can be…'

So much seemed to have happened in the last few days that it was hard for Ruby to remember the day she went to look at the empty shop, but then she suddenly recalled the comment that Lottie had made to Noah about another person who had been interested in it. A person who, judging by Lottie's description, had sounded suspiciously like Louise. She felt her stomach churn with anxiety.

'I knew it was too good to be true,' she said, her face falling.

'Why, what do you mean?'

Ruby hesitated. She hadn't meant to sound petulant; Louise had just as much right as she did to have the shop, and if that *were* the case would be every bit as excited as she was. It would be unfair of Ruby to pour cold water on Louise's dreams just because they happened to coincide with hers.

'I'm sorry, Louise, that didn't come out quite the way I intended. Of course you must have the shop if you want it. I haven't really got my act together yet and I wouldn't want to stand in your way, I—'

A flash of disappointment crossed Louise's face. 'Oh, have you changed your mind?' she asked.

Now Ruby was really confused. 'No, but… well, we both can't have it, can we?'

Louise shook her head, smiling at the same time. 'I think I'm as confused as you are,' she said. 'Maybe I need to start again, at the beginning this time…' She glanced around the room. 'You see, I've known for quite some time that I wasn't cut out to be just a vicar's wife. That sounds awful, doesn't it? I don't mean it to, but ever since Peter found out that he'd got the parish, we've been talking about what I should do. We moved from an inner-city environment to Summersmeade, which I absolutely adore, but the role of vicar's wife here is very different. I love what I do, but I have a degree in business administration that's just gathering dust in a box under the bed. I'd like to blow the cobwebs off it and put it to good use at some point. And what I'd really like to do is have my own business…'

'I see,' said Ruby, quietly, mustering a smile. 'Well, that makes perfect sense.'

Louise reached out a hand towards her. 'It does, but I don't think you're quite getting it yet,' she said. 'I can't give up being a vicar's wife and all that it entails, I wouldn't want to. So what I need is a business that I can be a part of, but something which doesn't require me to clock on and off every day, and that's not as easy as it sounds. Of course the ideal scenario would be one where I could go into partnership with someone, maybe even provide the financial backing, but then have the other person manage the business on a day-to-day level…' She let the end of her sentence hang for a moment, a warm smile slipping over her face.

Ruby caught the glint in her eye, and in the next second her stomach gave a sudden jolt of excitement. 'Are we still talking about the wool shop?' she asked, a shy smile on her face.

'Well, I am if you are,' replied Louise. 'What do you think? Do you reckon we could work together? I'd leave all the day-to-day stuff to you, after all I know nothing really about knitting and the like, but what I can do is source suppliers and look after the administrative side of things, both in setting up, and then on an ongoing basis. Just so long as I can pop in every now and again and get my fix of being something other than the vicar's wife.' She pulled a face. 'I swear some people have even forgotten I have a name.'

Ruby knew what it was like to feel invisible. She also knew that since arriving at Joy's Acre she had begun to feel less so, that little by little her body was gaining substance and she could feel herself returning from the place where she had hidden. The only way she had kept sight of herself had been by wearing her brightly coloured clothes, the vibrant hues a reminder of the person inside. Louise was just the same. She epitomised the archetypal vicar's wife – kind, caring, generous to a fault – but her clothes revealed something of a deeper edge to her character. An adventurer, an intelligent, forthright woman with views of her own and, by refusing to dress the way custom dictated, she was able to hold onto her own view of herself, even if no one else could. Ruby had a feeling that they would work together very well indeed.

'I can't think of anything I'd like more,' she said. 'I'm so full of ideas for the creative side of the shop, but the thought of all the responsibility terrifies me, and I'd be hopeless at all the legal and financial stuff. Having someone's hand to hold would be the perfect solution.'

Louise beamed at her, and then threw her arms around her. 'That's exactly what I was hoping to hear,' she said, squeezing Ruby tight, before pulling away. 'Oh, God, now I really am excited. This is the best Christmas present ever!' She looked up as Angus entered the barn. 'This probably isn't the best time to be talking about all this, I know, but the suspense was killing me, I had to know how you felt before I left today.' She glanced at her watch. 'I've got to get back home soon and get my own Christmas started, but as soon as the festivities are over I'll be straight on the phone to my accountant, just so you know.'

'I can't believe after all the work you've done that you won't be at the party tonight.'

Louise smiled. 'Midnight Mass,' she said, a look of real pleasure crossing her face. 'I love a good party, but I wouldn't miss that for the world.'

Ruby gave her a sheepish look in reply. 'I fear we may be taking away some of your flock this evening though,' she said.

'One or two perhaps, but Peter won't mind in the slightest. Wedding celebrations are the next best thing, after all, and after yesterday, Maddie, Seth and everyone here will most definitely have his blessing, you can be sure of it.' She started to back away with a wave. 'I'll catch you later!'

Ruby was still smiling as Angus came across to her. 'You look happy,' he commented, watching Louise go. 'I like Louise. I had cause to get to know her quite well not long after they first came to the village and she's one of the most genuine people you could ever wish to meet.'

'I think so too. In fact, I'm hoping to get to know her an awful lot better soon.'

She shook her head at Angus's quizzical look. 'I'll tell you later,' she said, as a sudden thought came to her. 'Has Jem sloped off back home?' she asked. 'I might pop and get him so he can come and help keep an eye on Darcie. How she's fallen asleep with everyone bustling around I'll never know, but she won't stay that way for too much longer.'

A stricken expression came over Angus's face. 'Isn't he with you?' he asked, searching her face. 'He wasn't there when I went to check on Rumpus, so I thought he must have doubled back to the cottage and I'd missed him.'

Ruby's heart began to pound in her chest. 'I thought he was with you...' She looked wildly around the room. 'Angus, I haven't seen him all morning.' Her eyes continued to scour the room before they met his, suddenly fearful. 'Oh, dear God...' she said slowly. 'Where is he?'

Chapter 24

Angus stared at her in horror. 'I don't know Ruby; I haven't seen him either.'

His face paled as the reality of both their words sank in. He reached out an arm for her, but she had already begun to turn away.

'Stay here,' she hissed. 'And keep an eye on Darcie.'

'No! Ruby, wait!'

She retraced the couple of steps she had taken. 'I'm going to look for my son, Angus. What bit of that is unclear?'

'But I can help you.'

'I already thought you were,' she snarled. 'But it turns out I was wrong.'

She didn't give him a chance to speak this time, but turned and ran from the barn. How could Angus have been so stupid? Where on earth did he think that Jem had gone? There was nowhere to double back to. He was either with Rumpus, on the path back to the cottage, or in the cottage, it was as simple as that. Angus hadn't missed him, he had simply forgotten about him, and he should have checked where he was. She slowed down as she hit the path. The snow had been cleared, but it was still slick, and the last thing she needed was to twist an ankle. She stopped completely then, shaking her head angrily. How could *she* have been so stupid?

Jem wasn't Angus's responsibility, he was hers, and she had totally failed him. She had torn him away from a home which was… well, a home, nonetheless. It was a familiar place, with familiar things and familiar people, and instead she had brought him to a place where he knew no one and had to start all over again. Worse, she had encouraged his friendship with a relative stranger, bestowing upon Angus a mantle of safety and trustworthiness in the process, when she should have provided those things herself. She had been gullible and foolish, allowing herself to be seduced by the lure of friendship. She should have known better.

She flung open the door to the cottage, racing through the empty kitchen to the living room. The silent television screen mocked her, the twinkling lights from the tree a false jollity.

'Jem!' she shouted, taking the stairs two at a time, but she knew before she reached his bedroom that the cottage was empty. She could feel it. A hard silence filled the harsh whiteness of his room.

She checked her own bedroom and the bathroom before retracing her steps through the house, forcing herself not to panic. There were plenty of other places he could be. But another check on Rumpus, followed by a trip to the main house, two of the most likely places, proved fruitless, and she made her way back through the garden with a growing feeling of unease. Where had Jem gone, but just as importantly, why? Her unease changed to fury as she saw Angus coming towards her.

'I thought I asked you to look after Darcie!' she shouted, but then she broke off. 'No, I don't want you to do that either.'

Angus looked like he'd been slapped, but he moved to stand in her way, his bulk blocking the path.

'Ruby,' he said, softly. 'Please stop.' His hands hung limply by his sides. 'You can't look for Jem while you have Darcie with you, and she's in safe hands, Clara and Maddie are looking after her.'

She glared at him, moving to one side, but he stepped back into her path.

'Get out of my way,' she hissed.

'No,' he said, calmly. 'Let me help you. I know you're upset, but two heads are better than one.'

She took another step but he mirrored it, forcing her to stand where she was.

'Please, Ruby. I don't want to stand in your way—'

'Then don't—'

'But I'm begging you, let me help.' His voice cracked as he stood there, his face pale against the darkening sky.

'Move!'

He stared at her, his mouth moving but no sound coming out. Neither did he stand aside.

She took a step towards him. 'Angus…' she said, her voice dropping by several octaves. She made no effort to disguise the threat in her voice.

'Ruby, your fight is not with me, let me help you.'

'It is,' she shouted. 'Right now it is with you! We're wasting time here, Angus.' She gave him a second to respond, but when he made no move to, she shoved him, hard.

The moment her hands met his chest she knew she had made a terrible mistake. Oh dear Lord, what had she done? Angus's body recoiled, absorbing the blow that by rights he should hardly have felt. A gasp of anguish left him and the look of pain on his face was one that she didn't think she would ever forget. Her head sagged as her fury left her as quickly as it had come, replaced by a deep shame at her actions. Violence was never the answer, but she didn't know what else to do. Jem was still missing and, for now, everything else would have to wait. The tears that so far she had managed to keep at bay began to well up, and she blinked hard to clear her vision, pushing past Angus and on towards her cottage.

She flew inside, leaving the door wide open. The space on the floor where Jem's wellies usually lived was still empty and for the second time she ran up the stairs to his bedroom. Forcing herself to calm down and think rationally, she opened the wardrobe door. She knew that he was wearing his wellies, but the jumper and jeans that he had on yesterday, and which were gone from the end of his bed, would not provide enough warmth against the cold outside. Rifling through his things, she was relieved to see that he had taken his thick winter coat. Not only that, but none of his other belongings seemed to have gone. If he had run away for some reason, he would have taken more stuff with him, surely?

Another thought occurred to her and she crossed to Jem's bed, hastily throwing aside his pillows. There was nothing there. The handkerchief that had once belonged to Angus had gone. Wherever he was, Jem had taken it with him. She didn't know whether that made her feel better or worse.

A further check through his drawers and other belongings confirmed that nothing else was missing, so he hadn't gone far. But why had he gone at all? She picked up his pillow and held it to her face, breathing him in, trying as she had done so many times in the past to see inside her son's head. Maybe she was jumping to conclusions...

Things had been going well. There was no reason at all to suppose that he had run off, and it was Christmas Eve; he had been excited at the prospect of opening his presents. Only last night they had snuggled up together before bed, talking about what Father Christmas might be leaving for him in his stocking. Jem had been tired, but it had been a long day for them all and she hadn't thought any more of it. He must just be somewhere else, somewhere obvious that they hadn't thought of, and any minute he'd appear as if nothing had happened.

She looked up at a sudden creak on the landing outside Jem's room. But it was Angus, standing silently looking at her, a fearful expression on his face. And then she knew without a shadow of a doubt that this was real. Jem had gone.

'He said something to me, the day before the wedding, but I'd forgotten about it, or at least… I thought Jem had. He seemed much happier yesterday.' Angus's head was bowed by the time he finished his sentence, his voice almost a whisper.

Ruby marched over to him. 'What do you know?' she asked, her anger rising again. 'Tell me.'

'We were out delivering logs and he seemed upset. I thought he was still being moody about the whole blanket thing, so I asked—'

'I know he was upset, I apologised.' Her eyes blazed as she held his look and then widened. 'Oh, my God… You think this is my fault?' she asserted. 'You're saying that I drove him away?'

'No, Ruby, no, I'm not… Please, just listen.' He held out a hand towards her. It was shaking. 'He said that he'd made everything worse, and that it was all his fault. It was nothing that you'd done; Jem was feeling bad because of something he thought he had done.'

'So what had he done?'

Angus swallowed. 'I don't know. I couldn't get him to open up. He was terrified that I'd tell you and that he'd be in all sorts of trouble.'

'And you didn't think to let me know about any of this?' Her voice had risen again.

'I know… Ruby, I'm sorry. I should have done. I know that now, but at the time… I honestly didn't think it was that serious, just something he didn't want to own up to so close to Christmas. Besides, look what happened the last time I tried to help, I was accused of interfering and you bit my head off! Believe me, I wasn't overly keen to repeat the experience.'

'Oh, for goodness' sake, you're not a child. How could you!'

'How could I not?' He lifted his head and she saw a glint of his own defiance at last. 'You can't gain anyone's trust by lying to them, Ruby. I would have thought that you at least would know that!'

'What's that supposed to mean?'

'You know exactly what it means, Ruby. How stupid do you think I am? You haven't arrived here, on your own with two young children in tow, because everything in your life is wonderful. You haven't got a son who when you arrived swung between burning anger and absolute withdrawal because everything is wonderful. And that expression you wear most of the time, when you look at your children and you think no one is looking – that haunted, hunted look didn't get there because everything in your life is wonderful, so don't you dare pretend otherwise.'

A cry stuck in her throat. How dare he accuse her of…? Of what, exactly? She stared at him, at the stoop of his shoulders, his expression, the pain in his eyes, the pain of a shared hurt. And she thought back to the marks she had seen on his skin. He knew. Somehow he knew. Angus wasn't her enemy; he was a victim, just like she was.

She put out a hand to steady herself as her legs suddenly no longer seemed capable of holding her up, and she would have fallen had a strong arm not reached out for her.

'Sit down,' said Angus gently. 'Come and sit down.'

He sat beside her on the edge of the bed, rubbing his head. 'I'm trying to remember what he said, but I can't, my head, it's too full…'

And she suddenly realised that he was finding all this just as hard as she was. Her hand went out to him and she took his fingers in hers. 'Just breathe,' she said. 'Calm. Softly… in, and out.'

He gulped, snatching in lungfuls of air, but after a few moments he sat a little straighter.

'Jem said that he didn't realise what would happen, that he just wanted to talk to him…' He looked up suddenly, eyes widening. 'Oh, God,' he said. 'I've just realised what that meant…'

His fear transferred itself to Ruby in an instant, and she knew immediately what had happened. How had she been so stupid? She jumped up, pulling Angus with her.

'No, no, no,' she muttered. 'Please let him not have found it…' But even as she reached her bedroom and pulled open the drawer that contained her jumpers she knew that her hiding place had been found. She rooted under the pile, feeling with her fingers until they made contact with the hard, shiny casing of her old phone. She pulled it out and pressed the button that would bring the screen to life. And there, in bright green speech bubbles, was everything she had feared the most. Her husband had found her. They were no longer hidden.

A choking sob of panic rose in her throat.

'We've got to find them!' she cried. 'He doesn't care about Jem, he never has, but it's how he controls me. He knows I'll do anything to keep them safe.' Her hand went to her mouth as a sudden wave of nausea flowed over her.

Angus took the phone from her, quickly checking the screen, seeing for himself what they were facing.

'I'll call the police,' he said.

The last outgoing message was brief. It was a name. Joy's Acre.

'No,' she said. 'Wait a minute… let me think.'

Her eyes searched Angus's as she forced herself to stay calm. Jem had seen the message and had seen his dad's reply which had arrived only yesterday. And there was no way that his dad could have come to the farm. No one could. They had been cut off, and up until a few hours ago they still were…

'I don't think it's what we first thought,' she said. 'It can't be. The road was blocked so there's no way that Jem's dad could have made it up here. If Jem has realised this, then I think he's done the only thing that would make sense to him. He's run away before his dad can find him.'

Angus's head swivelled to the window. 'Then he could be anywhere,' he said.

Ruby wasn't sure what was worse: the thought of Jem being on his own, or the thought of him being with his dad.

Angus turned back. 'No,' he said, slowly. 'He won't be just anywhere… he's a clever lad. He'll have gone somewhere he knows, and there are lots of hiding places around the farm.' He grabbed at her hand. 'Come on,' he said. 'We need to go and find everyone. And then we need to go and find Jem.'

They hurried out of the cottage, Angus looking anxiously at the sky. Please dear God, let it not start snowing again. Noah was just making his way across the garden with Trixie in tow, both of them carrying trays.

'You go on to the barn,' he said to Ruby. 'Check on Darcie, and then I'll meet you there. Let me speak with Noah first. If he's been back and forth to the village, then he might have seen something, he still might.'

Ruby nodded, an overwhelming desire to see her daughter pushing at her. She hurried down the path, even now harbouring hope that when she walked into the barn she would find Jem, helping out in some way as if nothing had happened.

Miraculously, Darcie was still asleep, the hubbub around her acting like white noise. Her chair was in the middle of the staging area while Clara moved around, decorating the sides of the stage with ribbons and greenery, but of Jem there was no sign. She smiled brightly as Ruby approached.

'So where was he then? Curled up with Rumpus? I bet he gave you a heart attack.' But then she stopped. 'Ruby…? Is everything okay?' She glanced down at Darcie and then back up, her gaze slowly swinging past Ruby to the entrance of the barn.

'Ruby?' She jumped down off the stage. 'What's going on?'

Ruby turned around to see Angus and Trixie enter the barn and make their way steadily towards her. It was as if a loudhailer had just made a public service announcement. Bit by bit the conversations stopped and faces turned to look in their direction. Whether it was the hushed voices, or the anxious expressions, Ruby didn't know. Or maybe it was just the introduction of the sombre atmosphere that she and Angus carried into an otherwise happy space, but within moments everyone had stopped what they were doing and come to stand beside them.

Trixie came forward to hug Ruby, her hand stroking her hair in comfort.

'We'll find him, Ruby, don't worry. Noah hasn't seen anything, but he sits high up in the tractor, and it's surprising what you can see from there. If either of them are around on the roads, Noah will spot them.'

Ruby didn't know what to say. Maddie was just making her way over, with Seth by her side. They had been married for just a day. And now Ruby was going to utterly ruin their celebrations. She saw Angus step forward, putting out a hand to take Maddie's arm, leading them off to one side to speak in hushed, urgent tones, and within minutes it seemed he had communicated the same message to everyone inside the barn. What he said she didn't know, but she was grateful that she didn't have to utter the words that her son was missing. She didn't think she could bear to say them out loud.

Five minutes later and it was all organised. Seth and Maddie would search the main house, Clara and Declan would search the gardens and the outbuildings, Tom and Isobel would visit all the other cottages, and Trixie would stay with Ruby, maintaining constant contact with Noah and everyone else, as far as their mobile signals would allow. Only Angus would leave Joy's Acre for now, making his way across the fields via the gate that lay at the back of the cottages. Apart from brief conversations about their course of action, no one said a word. No one needed to. The time for talking would come later. But one by one, as they left, they each gave Ruby a hug to let her know that everything would be okay.

She walked forward with Trixie to the big double doors at the entrance to the barn and watched as they all went out, heading their separate ways, but connected by a common cause. But none of their comforting and help could ever make a difference to how she was feeling.

Her son was lost in the snow, and it was all her fault.

Chapter 25

Angus stared at the field in front of him, at the thick blanket of white that stretched out into the distance, and he cursed his stupidity once more. Any tracks that might have been made this morning were now almost obliterated; the snow was still churned up from where they had walked yesterday, but the wind had also changed direction and was blowing across the tops of the drifts already there, altering their shape, making it impossible to see if someone had passed by.

He should have been on his guard from the moment Jem had first confided his fears that he had done something wrong. Not realising that the boy had been referring to contacting his father was a poor excuse; he *should* have realised. He knew that Ruby had run from something, the signs were clear enough, but he had wanted to protect her from further hurt, and in doing so he had pretended that everything was okay. With the excitement of the wedding yesterday he had forgotten about Jem's confession, or at least relegated it to the back of his mind. Dear God, he hoped that none of them, least of all Jem, would pay the price.

A check on his watch confirmed that it was now well past lunchtime. Supposing that Jem had left the house around seven that morning, not only would it have been dark, but bitterly cold as well. The glow of the snow would have given off some light to see by, but it would have been very easy to become disorientated; the usual landscape markers would have been hidden and nothing would have looked familiar. Unless Jem had found somewhere to shelter, he could have been outside for six hours now. Angus shivered, scanning the field for any signs of movement.

Common sense should have told Jem to follow the line of the hedgerow. It would have provided some shelter from the wind, and given him a guide. But which way would he have travelled? Angus stopped, trying to put himself in Jem's shoes. If he was afraid that his dad was coming to the farm, then he would probably have tried to put as much distance between them as possible. But he was also a sensible lad, he would have known that the roads were cut off, which meant that if anyone wanted to reach them they would have had to walk up from the village across the fields, or beg a lift from a passing tractor. And Jem had no way of knowing when his dad might arrive.

Angus shook his head, trying to clear it. There was something there, a thought, something important, and then it came to him; perhaps Jem was keeping watch so that he could raise the alarm if he needed to, but to do that he would need to get to the village. He looked up, just making out the rise of the church spire in the distant gloom. He had once told Jem how to get to the village from here and it was just possible that he could still follow the path they had all taken the day before. Picking up his pace, he began to stride down the slope of the field towards the stile in the far corner.

Even with his long legs, it took Angus the best part of half an hour to reach the second field, the one that adjoined the churchyard, and without the luxury of a lift from Jack and his trailer he hurried across it, his feet and trousers soaking wet, his legs burning from the exertion of battling through the drifts. How on earth had Jem managed it? He prayed that once he got to the church he would find Jem taking shelter there; a little chilly in the empty stone building, but otherwise okay. The door, however, was locked when he reached it. Louise and her husband would be there later on for Midnight Mass of course, but that was hours away yet. He carried on down the path and through the lych gate into the street beyond.

As he neared the school he could see a gathering of people already there, Noah's tractor parked up by the side of the road. He hurried across.

'Any news?' he asked breathlessly.

But Noah shook his head. 'No one's seen anything,' he said. 'But nothing's moving in or out of the village, Angus. The buses aren't running, and the trains into town on the Birmingham line have all been cancelled too. If Jem's dad has arrived over the last day or two I can't see how he got here, not unless he parachuted in. And he hasn't stayed anywhere locally either. The pub has had all its room bookings cancelled because folks can't travel, and Sally, who runs the B&B up at the far end, hasn't got anyone staying either. We've drawn a blank, Angus, I'm afraid. In fact, I was just about to go back up to the farm to let them know.'

Angus looked at the faces around him, every single one known to him. One of his neighbours came forward.

'We'll search the village in the meantime, but I don't think the lad came this way. More likely he's hiding up at the farm somewhere, thinking he's in a whole heap of trouble.'

Now that Angus was actually in the village he could see that this made sense. It wasn't just the farm that had been cut off, but the whole area. Getting in and out of the place was extremely difficult and to some extent it put his mind at rest. Surely Jem would have realised this if he had made it this far. In fact, now that he thought about it, his neighbour was right. Wouldn't it make far more sense if Jem had simply panicked at the thought of what he had done and hidden because he was scared of the repercussions?

'Aye, you're probably right, but thank you, for all you're doing. I'll let Jem's mum know that you're all keeping an eye out for her son. I know she'll be incredibly grateful, especially today of all days.'

'A child's gone missing, Angus, the day matters not one jot. Keep in touch…'

'I will… in fact, I'm sure that when I get back to the farm, he'll already be tucked up somewhere warm.' He looked up at Noah, an almost overwhelming urge to return to Joy's Acre coming over him. He was wasting his time down here. 'Can you give me a lift?' he asked, glancing down at his soaked clothing. 'I don't fancy the walk back somehow.'

Noah nodded, heading towards his tractor. 'Let's get going,' he said to Angus before turning around to face the villagers. 'And then I want to see you all dressed up in your glad rags later on, 'cause I'll be back to pick you all up.'

Angus had almost forgotten that there was supposed to be a party later on. He glanced at Noah. Neither of them wanted to think about the possibility that it might have to be cancelled, or why…

He pulled himself up into the cab, moving a bundle of letters off the seat.

'I'm adding postman to my job description,' said Noah with a small smile. 'The woman from the post office was pulling her hair out this morning. It's the last delivery before Christmas.'

'It's hard to imagine that the world keeps turning at times like this, isn't it?' said Angus. 'But I hope you know how grateful we all are to you. Not just for today…'

To his surprise, Noah smiled. 'People are what makes the world go around, Angus, and as long as people help other people, it keeps turning. That's all we can do, other than stacking the odds in our favour of course, that never hurts.' He turned the key in the ignition and the tractor rumbled into life. 'It will be okay, Angus, I'm sure of it.'

Angus stared at him in amazement. He had said that very thing to Ruby, the first day he had met her, when everything in her world had been new and scary. Hearing his own words, repeated back to him, made him realise the power of them when said by another person. Suddenly, all he wanted was to be with her, to make everything all right for her, whatever it took. He turned his gaze to the road ahead and willed the miles to pass quickly.

Even at the slow speed they were travelling, the journey had taken no longer than ten minutes by the time they arrived back at Joy's Acre. They had seen no one else on the roads. The land was cold and white, but he still fully expected to see everyone waiting for them at the gate to the farm, waiting to bring them news that Jem had been found. The forecourt was empty, however, the mobile phone in his hand still lifeless.

He scrambled down from the cab, picking his way carefully along the frozen ruts of snow until he reached the path and could move more quickly towards the house. He peered through the kitchen window, but the room beyond was empty. Glancing at Noah, the two of them practically ran around the side of the house and into the rear courtyard, but there was not a sound to be heard. Even when they reached the garden path the space in front of them was clean and empty; nothing appeared to have altered at all. It surprised Angus – somehow he'd expected it all to have changed.

By the time they reached the barn, his heart was in his mouth. Everything would depend on the scene he found when he opened the doors. He took a deep breath and pulled one open, stepping into the warmth of the space beyond. Except, as he did so, his worst fears were confirmed. All his friends were sitting in a group at one of the tables, huddled together as if this very act would help to provide the support they so desperately sought to give. There, in the middle, was Ruby, her head bowed as she leaned into Maddie beside her. The room was silent.

The noise of their entrance was like a shotgun going off, and all heads rapidly turned in their direction. Angus tried to brighten his expression, but then he realised he didn't know what for and his face fell again. Wordlessly, Ruby got to her feet and crossed the space towards him. Her eyes stayed on his the whole time and she got to within twelve feet of him before her face crumpled and she reached out. She gave his face one more searching look before she succumbed to his silent embrace as he folded her tiny frame beneath his arms. One hand held her head against his chest and the other splayed across her back to calm her trembling body.

He heard Noah move past him, but Angus's eyes remained closed as he listened to Seth impart the news from Joy's Acre in a quiet voice, Noah sharing their own update once he had finished. There was detail about the number of times they had searched, the places, thoughts and opinions, but the simple fact remained that Jem was nowhere to be found.

Eventually, Ruby gave a shuddering sigh and began to pull away. Her face was wet with tears, but she ran her hands down Angus's arms.

'You're cold,' she said. 'Come and sit down, there's tea.'

He let himself be led to the table where a gap magically materialised so that he could sit beside Ruby. He divested himself of the post from his jacket pocket before taking his seat, pushing the pile of letters towards Maddie with a weak smile. There were cards among them, he could tell, either season's greetings or perhaps well wishes for their wedding, which had arrived slightly later than planned. It all seemed so incongruous now.

Maddie poured him a drink and slid it towards him before pouring another so that Noah might also have something hot. Angus wrapped his hands around his mug gratefully. He wasn't sure he could drink anything, but the heat was very welcome. He helped himself to milk while Maddie absentmindedly pulled the pile of post towards her and started to sort through the letters. It was something to do, something to occupy a tiny fragment of time while they all waited.

He stared into his drink, knowing that someone needed to ask the question. It might as well be him. 'So what do we do now?' he asked.

Seth held his look. 'I know that no one wants to admit it, but it's been several hours now, and there still hasn't been any clue as to where Jem might have gone. I think the only sensible course of action is to turn it over to the professionals and call the police.'

'I agree.' Ruby's voice was firm. 'It feels like we've failed, I feel like I've failed. I've ruined your wedding celebrations and the last thing I want to do is become the type of hysterical mother you see on the television wasting police time, but right now I don't know what else to do. I should know where my son is, but I don't and it's Christmas Eve for God's sake, I just want Jem home. Whatever he thinks he's done, I don't care, I just want him home.'

Angus took her hand in his and squeezed it, but after a second she pulled it away and pounced on an envelope that Maddie had slid across the table to her, ripping it open.

Seth nodded, looking first at Angus and then everyone else in turn. He didn't need their agreement, but it was clear how everyone felt. He rose wearily to his feet.

'I'll go and make the call,' he said.

He had only taken two steps before Ruby's head shot up, her voice a loud retort in the room.

'No, wait!' Her hand grabbed Angus's. 'Read this,' she said breathlessly. 'I need to think.' She shoved the card towards him, eyes boring a hole in the side of his face as he read the message inside.

He looked up, startled. 'This is from Jem's dad.'

'Yes,' she said, snatching up the envelope and studying it. 'And look… The postmark says Coventry and it was franked two days ago…'

'But why has he sent a card if he—' He broke off, seeing the same question he was just about to ask reflected in Ruby's eyes.

'Exactly!' she said. 'Why send a card if he was planning to come here? And you've all told me that the roads are totally impassable. I don't think he's here at all. I don't think he was ever planning on coming here, he simply wanted the address to send this, but Jem doesn't know that…' She put her hand to her mouth as a sob escaped. 'Oh God, I've done this,' she said. 'I've let my own fear taint Jem's life too, and he's run away because of it.'

Angus took her hands, covering them both with one of his own. 'No,' he said, gently drawing a thumb under her eyes. 'No blame, no one's at fault here.' His heart began to hammer in his chest. 'But we need to think smart… There's been something about all this that's been bugging me from the start. Something that doesn't fit with the Jem I know.' He searched Ruby's face.

'I know things were tough for him when he first came here, but all that's improved since. He's got to know us all, to trust us, maybe even think of us as his friends. So, if he thought he was in trouble, or needed help, wouldn't he have come to one of us?'

The thoughts were crashing through his head now and he was having trouble keeping up with them.

'And then there's Rumpus and her kittens… He's absolutely besotted with them and has shown a real pride and commitment to caring for them. I can't believe he'd just run away and not make some arrangements for them so that they were looked after. The same with you and Darcie; he'd do anything not to upset you.'

He looked up and around the table. 'Everything he cared about is here, so why would he want to leave?'

Ruby was staring at him, a stunned expression on her face. 'Oh my God,' she said slowly. 'That's it…'

Angus nodded. 'He hasn't run away because he was scared,' he said. 'Instead he wanted to protect the things he loved by keeping them safe… and the only way he could do that was if he knew when his dad was coming…'

'But I don't understand,' said Maddie.

'No, but I do,' replied Angus, a surge of adrenaline hitting his body like a shock wave.

He jumped up from his chair with such speed that the violence of his movement sent it crashing to the floor.

'I know where he is!' he shouted, already running for the door. 'Dear God, I know where he is!'

Chapter 26

As Angus ran, he prayed that he was right. He had come this way over an hour ago, but stupidly turned in the wrong direction, going down the field towards the village instead of across it and into the woodland. The sky was growing darker by the minute and in among the trees it would be darker still and by the time Jem got here, he would already be cold and wet… Angus practically vaulted the gate into the field.

How much would Jem have remembered? Would he have taken the right path? Everything looked so different in the snow; how could he possibly have distinguished one landmark from another when the landmarks themselves had disappeared? And the snow was deeper here; it lay in huge drifts disguising the natural dips and troughs of the landscape. In places it was past his knees and Jem was much smaller than he was. Angus didn't stop running until he reached the first line of trees, braking suddenly, bent almost in half from the exertion of pushing through the drifts. He looked up through the clearing ahead of him, squinting at the shapes, shaking his head at the change in the view. He might as well be somewhere else entirely for all the familiarity it afforded him.

Angus forced himself to breathe, to calm himself to the point where he could think more rationally. He was now only minutes away but he must slow down. What use would he be to the boy if he had no strength left of his own? He had no idea what he would find when he reached him, and this was not going to be a simple walk in the woods, common sense told him that. He straightened, feeling the burn in his lungs as they coped with the freezing air. He measured where he was, centring himself in his surroundings, and repeated his instructions in his head, over and over like a mantra:

Tree with a hollow in the bottom,
Tree on the right,
Tree shaped like a letter of the alphabet,
Holly bush,
Chimneys, stile and the conker tree…

The first would have been almost impossible for Jem to find. Angus knew where it was but he needed to trust in faith and the determination of a young lad who had only one thing on his mind. Jem would have found it, he must have.

Angus reached the holly bush.

'Jem!' he shouted, hearing the sound race away from him. He cocked his head to the air, listening for any echo returning to him. He had to be right. He had to be.

'Jem!'

Nothing. The air was dead and still.

He reached the spot where the chimneys came into view.

'Jem!'

And then the line of the fence.

'Jem!' He broke into a furious bout of coughing, the air catching at his hoarse throat. He looked up at the darkening sky, relieved to see that dusk hadn't yet fallen above the cover of the trees. He offered up a silent thank you.

And finally he stood beneath the huge horse chestnut tree that he had climbed so many times as a child. The same tree where he had spied on people coming to the house, the same tree he had told Jem about, and where he now prayed with all his might that Jem was hiding.

He rested his hands upon the rough bark as if seeking to draw power of his own from the enormous strength of the tree, and he stared up through the canopy of branches, his face wet with tears, and shouted with all his might.

'Jem! It's Angus… It's okay… I promise you, everything's okay!'

It might have been a rustle on the wind, the slight shift in sound that could have been an animal, or a fall of snow, or a slight movement that caught Angus's ears. He shouted again, and this time he heard it, a faint but unmistakable cry.

Seconds later he was climbing.

Angus's boots were thick, with cumbersome soles, and his gloves were made for warmth not for gripping, but Angus had spent a good deal of his life in among the trees and he could climb with the best of them. His muscles were strong and powerful, and where he could not find purchase on the slippery bark, his arms simply hauled his body up the tree. And all the while he called out a steady stream of comforting chatter.

'I can't get down…' Jem's voice was almost a whimper.

'I'm nearly there.'

'I didn't think anyone was coming…'

'We'd never leave you.'

'I can't see you!'

'I'm almost with you, don't look down.'

Angus had climbed almost halfway when he realised with a sudden jolt of memory why he couldn't see Jem either. It wasn't just the thick branches that were blocking his view, but the platform he had built one summer. Only two planks wide, it wasn't huge, but it was wide enough for a young boy to sit on. It was wedged between two huge branches which made a natural 'V' shape so that once on it you had a trunk at your back for support, and another close by to hold onto. If Jem had made it to the platform he would have been relatively safe, as long as the planks… Angus pushed the thought from his mind. The platform would be sound. Jem would be fine.

He altered his course slightly so that he would come level with Jem from just in front of him and not directly underneath.

'I'm nearly there, just sit still.'

Jem was crying harder now, the sudden realisation that he was no longer alone rising up as tears of relief, a release from having had to be brave for so long.

With one final pull, Angus's head rose above the level of the platform and he and Jem came face-to-face. A sob of his own broke free from his throat at the sight that met him.

Jem was sitting, as expected, with his back to the tree trunk, but through the gloom Angus could see that his body was wrapped in a thick fleecy blanket. A rucksack lay on his lap and from its open top shiny foil wrappers from the chocolates on the Christmas tree could clearly be seen. Angus had never dreamed for one minute that Jem would need to know how to look after himself outdoors, how to make fires or shelters, to climb trees, and use the landmarks around him to reveal his location. He had simply talked about such things to share his love of being outdoors, to forge a connection with the troubled but inquisitive boy. But Jem had listened, to every word, and the proof was right there in front of him. It might have even saved his life.

Carefully and slowly, Angus made his way across to Jem, testing his weight on the branches before crouching beside him as best he could. He reached out a hand to take Jem's tiny one in his own.

'It's okay,' he murmured. 'It's okay.'

Jem was shivering and Angus realised that he would now have to act very quickly indeed. Despite the blankets and the warm clothing he was wearing, Jem had been outside in the cold for hours, his energy had been spent keeping his body warm and movement now would soon deplete what reserves he had left.

He glanced down at the ground far below them and tried to think logically.

'If I take the blanket, Jem, can you get onto your hands and knees for me?'

The boy shook his head, a look of real panic in his eyes. 'I can't move. I'm going to fall.'

'I've got you, Jem, just remember that. No one is going to fall, okay?'

There was a tiny nod.

'Can you point at the way you climbed up?'

Another shake of the head.

Angus swallowed, and he reached forward with his hand again. This time to stroke the side of Jem's face. They locked eyes.

'Do you trust me, Jem?'

A nod.

'Then I need you to do exactly as I say, do you understand?' He didn't wait for a reply. 'I don't need to tell you that we need to get down out of this tree, but I'm not going to lie, it's going to be a little tricky... But we can do it, that's important to remember. You got up, so we can get down, okay?'

Another nod.

'But I need you to trust me, and if you can do that I promise we will soon be on the ground. We're going to do it bit by bit, one foot after the other...'

He gave the best reassuring smile he could muster. He had never lied to Jem and he really hoped he didn't have to start now, but the truth of it was that he had absolutely no idea how they were going to get down.

Angus braced his legs against the branch he was standing on and leant forwards as far as he could.

'Take my hand, Jem. That's it… and now the other. You're going to shuffle, okay?' He smiled and nodded. 'Towards me, a bit at a time, and I've got you, don't forget, you won't fall, I've got you.'

He let Jem inch along the boards towards him, until he was close enough to get a better grip, hauling him the last of the way. Angus's arms wrapped around Jem's shivering body as he frantically tried to think about their options. As everybody knew, climbing up a tree was far easier than climbing down, and Angus couldn't let Jem go first. The only way would be for Angus to start down, leaving Jem above him. That way he could guide Jem, tell him where to place his feet, help him if he needed it. But Jem was terrified and freezing cold; Angus wasn't even sure he would be able to make it off the ledge on which he was sitting.

He looked down at the blackness beneath them; they had too far to go, and not enough time to do it in. And what if Jem fell, or slipped? Angus would never be able to hold the boy's weight. He had no way to tie them together, no way to… He shook his head. He was out of time, he had to make a decision, and suddenly he realised there was only one way that he would ever get Jem down. He would have to carry him.

With Jem now sitting on the edge of the planks and facing towards him, Angus pulled off the blanket that was around him and stuffed it into Jem's rucksack. He would need it, but right now the bag was just extra baggage that he couldn't afford. Lifting it clear from the edge of the planks, he threw it downwards with as much force as he could muster.

If luck was on his side it would reach the ground, and Angus could retrieve it later. If not… he forced the thought from his head. Jem was now without the layer of relative warmth that had been surrounding him and it was now or never. He took hold of Jem's shoulders.

'We need to move, Jem,' he said. 'So I want you to listen. I'm going to turn around slightly, and when I do, I want you to put both arms around my neck. Lock your hands together and then get your legs around my waist. I'm going to give you a piggy-back down, okay? All you need to do is hold on.'

Jem made a sound in his throat, but Angus couldn't hear what he said. 'Come on, do it now.'

He waited a second or two. 'You need to do it now, Jem,' he repeated in a firmer voice. 'Come on, you can do it. Just reach up… shuffle closer, lean onto my back, hands up… that's right…' He leaned back slightly. 'Good, now both hands, that's it… I've got you… Now your legs. Do the same with your legs, Jem.'

He grabbed hold of Jem's knees and pulled the boy closer to him, feeling his muscles hugging him tight.

'That's perfect, Jem, well done. Now we're going to move, okay, which is going to feel weird, but I promise you it won't be long until we're down.' He felt the boy's head nod against his back.

'Now, Jem, you need to promise me three things, okay? And they're really important, they're things which are going to help me out so I want to hear you say yes, so that I know you've understood?'

There was another nod.

'So the first thing is that I want you to hang on, just concentrate on that, you don't need to do anything else. You're not going to hurt me, so I want you to grip as tight as you can, okay?'

'Yes…'

'Good lad. Now the second thing is that when you're hanging on, I want you to try and lean into me… don't lean backwards, that's really important. Have you got that too?'

Jem nodded. 'Yes.'

'Great stuff… and now lastly, I want you to shut your eyes, really tight, all the way down. And don't open them until I tell you, okay? So that's the last thing I need you to promise. Is that all right?'

'Promise…'

'Okay then… let's go.'

Angus edged himself further around, feeling Jem's grip instinctively tighten. He closed his eyes briefly and swallowed. Then he gingerly began to lower one leg.

It was the hardest thing he had ever done in his life. His view below was very limited and if he leaned to one side to see better, Jem's arms dug into the side of his throat even more. His breath was coming in shallow rasps as it was, and any movement away from centre only made this worse. All he could do was keep moving, no thought beyond where his next move would be. Testing his footholds, feeling with his feet inch by inch until he found one, his hands clawing at the tree trunk, grasping with all his might onto anything that would take his weight.

The pain in his shoulders and legs became all-consuming, a warm ache, then a burning sensation and finally like a white-hot poker searing his skin. But still he moved on.

They say that at moments like this time seems to stand still, and Angus had no idea how long it was before his feet finally touched the ground. Every muscle in his body was on fire, but they were down, they were safe! He slid Jem from his back, gently lowering him to the ground before dropping to his haunches to bring his face to the same level as his. He reached out a hand to touch Jem's cheek before pulling him into a fierce hug, emotion shaking both their bodies as they clung together.

'Are we going home now…?'

It was a croak and it was all Jem could manage, but Angus's heart soared and a new strength surged through him. He had made a promise to Ruby, and he intended to keep it.

'Aye, Jem, as fast as we can. Don't you worry. Your mum will be waiting for you, and so will Darcie… and everyone else. Trixie might even have one of her very special hot chocolates ready for you, what do you think to that?'

Jem gave a slight smile. 'Will she have made one for you too? If she hasn't you can have half of mine.' He slipped his hand into Angus's, his bottom lip beginning to tremble. 'I don't like the dark,' he said.

Angus didn't either. The night had fallen during their climb down and the temperature was dropping all the while. He would need to get Jem home as quickly as possible and he hastily cast about for the discarded rucksack, praying that it had dropped to the ground instead of becoming snagged on a branch. He found it a few feet away, the grinning face of a cartoon character on the front staring up at him, and he pulled the blanket from it, not caring what else flew from the bag in his hurry.

Hoisting the rucksack onto his back, Angus threw the blanket around Jem and then picked him up, pulling the fleece material around him and tucking in his hands and feet as best he could. Then Angus tested his legs experimentally, which still felt like jelly, and set off at a run.

'I've got you, Jem. I've got you. We'll be home soon…'

★

'Oh!'

The exclamation was automatic as, all around them, the lights in the barn suddenly went out. A wail went up from Darcie as they were plunged into darkness.

Seconds later Tom's face lit up as he pulled out his mobile phone, switching on the torch. Within moments everyone else had done the same.

'I wouldn't mind betting that the snow has brought down a power line somewhere,' muttered Tom. 'That's all we bloody need.'

'There's a box of candles in the pantry back at the house,' said Trixie. 'Can someone come with me?' She had got halfway to her feet when she suddenly stopped. 'What am I talking about?'

Using her phone to light the way, she picked her way down the table to the far end where no one was sitting. She picked up a box of matches that was lying there and gave it a rattle. Ruby heard a match flare and after a moment she saw the brighter flame of a taper. Then, one by one, Trixie began to light the small candles at the base of each of the jam jars which lined the centres of the tables. When she had finished, a square of light flickered in the darkness. Despite the occasion, it was a beautiful sight.

Ruby stared at it for a few moments, entranced by the way the flames twinkled through the lacy coverings of the jam jars. It was extraordinary how much comfort could be gleaned from such a simple thing. And then she suddenly turned, her head swivelling to face the doors. The lights in the cottages would have gone out, as would the fairylights all over the site and those of the Christmas tree which stood in the centre of the garden. There would be no light anywhere, nothing to light the way for Angus coming through the snow, nothing to welcome him and her son home...

She jumped up. 'I can't sit here,' she said. 'Not when they're still out there. I've got to go and wait for them no matter how long it takes.' She took up one of the jam jars. If she could protect it from the wind, perhaps she could keep the flame alive.

Maddie took one look at her and then did the same, followed by Trixie, and then without a word, so did everyone else. All except for Clara who clutched Darcie to her, holding Ruby's look in a way that told her all she needed to know: her daughter was in safe hands. They paused for a few moments to put on more layers, and hats and scarves, with Trixie snatching up the matches at the last minute, and then the procession of light, of hope, made its way out into the darkness.

★

Angus had only travelled a few yards before he realised how dark it was. Too dark. He should be passing the Hall just now, but the place was just a black outline against the sky and, as he stared around him, there was not a single light to be seen. He pressed on, crashing through the paths, moving as fast as he dared on the snow-covered uneven ground.

They reached the clearing after a few more minutes and Angus grunted to a halt. 'Just give me a minute,' he said, lowering Jem gently to the ground. 'Just a minute.' His breath was coming in painful gasps, the burning in his arms and back like hot metal against his skin.

'I can walk,' Jem replied. 'Honestly…' But he faltered after only a couple of steps, all his energy sapped by the cold.

'No, it's okay, I'm fine now,' replied Angus, picking Jem up again and hitching him a little higher to get a better grip. 'Right now, let's go.'

They were out in the field now, but there was still no sign of light. They should be able to see those at Joy's Acre now, or at the very least a faint glow in the sky. Angus felt fear grip him as he wondered fleetingly if they had completely lost their way and had run in the wrong direction but, as he stared about him, he knew that they were right. And nearly home.

He stumbled, catching his foot in a furrow that was hidden by the snow and, as he lurched upright, he thought he caught a flicker of something. He stopped, listening, but there was nothing, just his imagination. The hedgerow was a dark presence to his right but he was grateful for it, and he ploughed on, keeping his eyes resolutely on the way ahead.

He stopped again, looking around him; he had definitely heard something that time.

'Here! We're here!' Angus lifted his head and tried to home in on the sound as Jem wriggled in his arms. He had heard it too.

'Look!' he said, pointing, and as Angus's eyes focused, he heard the shouts again.

'Jem! Oh, Jem!' And suddenly he spotted a figure running towards him, a line of lights in the darkness, guiding them home.

Angus ran blindly, tears pouring down his face, until he was surrounded by dancing lights, with people, with faces, arms and hugs. The weight lifted and was gone from his body. He reached out, feeling himself float away, too light, untethered, and then as he saw Ruby hugging Jem she looked straight at him and their eyes met. It was a look he would never forget, and as he felt Seth's arms go around him, his legs buckled and he sank to his knees in the snow. They were home.

Chapter 27

Ruby didn't think she had ever seen anything more beautiful. The power had eventually come back on about half an hour ago, but Angus hadn't even noticed when the lights flickered back into life. He and Jem were fast asleep, Jem tucked into the crook of his arm, and they had been that way for the last two hours.

The lighting was soft, with just the warm glow from the fire and the gentle twinkle from the fairylights on the tree casting a golden light onto Angus's face. He was finally at peace, the anguish of the day behind him, smoothing the tiredness and emotion from his features. She followed the contour of his jaw, his burnished cheeks, thick dark eyelashes and the slight wrinkles at the corners of his eyes; eyes that, when he laughed, seemed to follow her around the room. It was a face she would never tire of looking at.

Jem too looked at peace, snuffling gently every now and again, his mouth twitching slightly, his fingers curling and uncurling around the soft fold of jumper covering Angus's chest. Miraculously, the doctor had pronounced that there was no lasting damage done. Possibly mild hypothermia but the precautions Jem had taken, together with Angus's swift action once he had found him, had prevented it developing any further. He needed warmth, sugar, sleep, and a lot of love and attention. Ruby didn't think she could possibly love anyone more.

Jem had recovered remarkably quickly from his ordeal and, once his mind had been put very firmly at rest that his dad was not about to appear any time soon, he had almost revelled in the recounting of his adventures during the day. How he had packed his bag ready for any eventuality; Angus had taught him that. How he had climbed the tree, totally unafraid because he knew that Angus had climbed it before. How he had sat, watching, in case his dad had appeared, at which point he knew exactly how long it would take him to run home and raise the alarm. Except, of course, that he hadn't banked on his dad not showing up, or how cold it would get, or how frightened he would become when he realised that climbing up had been very much easier than climbing down. But Ruby didn't mind about any of this. She had let him chatter, relishing the sound of his voice and the thought that he was home. That Angus had brought him back to her, in more ways than one.

Later they would go across to the party, which had been in full swing now for the last couple of hours, and raise a toast to the happy couple. But for now Ruby was right where she should be, and the only place she wanted to be.

As she watched, Angus opened one eye and blinked sleepily, stretching out his leg carefully so as not to wake Jem. He caught her watching him and a lazy smile lit his face.

'Morning…' he said.

'It isn't yet,' she said. 'Still Christmas Eve. Still plenty of time for more miracles.'

But they both knew that the biggest one of them all had already taken place.

The smile grew bigger. 'Not that I'm complaining or anything, but I think I might have lost all feeling in my legs…'

She laughed. 'I'm not surprised,' she said. 'I don't think either of you have moved since you fell asleep.'

'What time is it?'

'A little after nine.'

Angus groaned softly. 'Past my bedtime,' he whispered.

Ruby looked at Jem, still fast asleep. 'I'll take him upstairs,' she said. 'Are you hungry? Perhaps we should have something to eat?'

He nodded. 'Starving…'

She reached down to take Jem in her arms, lifting him just as she had when he was a baby, her hands sliding around his back, against Angus's warm chest. She blushed as their arms touched. Jem murmured, clinging to her neck. She had forgotten how heavy he was and only just managed to lift him, determined that Angus should stay where he was. Slowly, she began to climb the stairs.

Passing across the landing she glanced in at Darcie, lying flat on her back, fast asleep, her thumb firmly in her mouth. Totally oblivious to all the drama, she had been an absolute star.

She laid Jem down in his bed, pulling the bedclothes up around him and tucking them in. A new blanket now covered his bed and she pulled this over him also, watching him snuggle in deeper. She was about to turn on his night light when she heard the landing creak behind her.

Angus was standing there, one of the brightly wrapped gifts from under the tree in his hand.

'I wondered if perhaps Jem might like this tonight,' he said. 'I know he should have it in the morning, really, but if he wakes in the night, I'd like it to be there.' He held out the present a little shyly. 'You could open it for him.'

Ruby took the gift, feeling the solid weight of it in her hand. Whatever it was, it was important to Angus and she couldn't possibly refuse.

She peeled back the paper, slowly revealing the gift inside. She gasped when she saw it, flicking an anxious glance at Jem in case she had woken him, but then, eyes shining, smiled her gratitude at Angus.

Inside the wrapping was a wooden night light, beautifully carved, and polished until it gleamed. Its base was a solid tree trunk, above, a curved veneer shade had been decorated with cut-outs of more trees, some deer, the moon. She quietly unplugged the old light and placed the new one down on his bedside table, angling the shade towards Jem so that he would see it if he woke, then switched it on. The soft glow from behind the shade lit up the forest scene it depicted. It was incredible.

'You made this?' she whispered.

There was an almost imperceptible nod.

'It's the most perfect thing I've ever seen,' she said. 'And I know that Jem will think so too.' She reached out her hand towards Angus. 'Come on,' she said, 'let's go back downstairs.'

'Are you sure you don't want anything more to eat?' asked Ruby a little while later, handing Angus a mug.

He shook his head. 'I don't think I can,' he replied. 'It feels like I've eaten my body weight in food as it is.'

'Then come and sit back down again.'

She followed him into the living room where he placed his mug on the coffee table. The room was cosy and inviting and, with the fire having been deliberately built up earlier, very warm.

'I think I could afford to shed a layer now,' he joked. 'Never mind hypothermia, I'm in danger of getting heatstroke.'

Ruby bent down to pick up the blanket from the chair and began to fold it. It was a flippant comment, but they both knew how close-

run a thing it had been, and for some reason she couldn't look at him
directly. She didn't entirely trust herself. She kept busy tidying away
the throw, turning around just as Angus pulled his jumper over his
head, his back towards her. The breath caught in her throat as it had
done once before.

'Angus?' she said softly. 'Are you going to tell me what happened
to you now?'

He turned back to her, his eyes on hers, suddenly full of pain.

'How did you know?' he asked.

She moved towards him, coming to stand in front of him as he
towered above her. Very gently she slid a hand inside his tee shirt, and
around his waist, relishing the feel of his warm, smooth skin. She ran
her hand lightly up his spine, eliciting a soft groan before she let it
rest, halfway up his back, on the topmost cigarette burn of the three
that she had seen once before. He shuddered.

'Do they hurt?' she whispered, flattening her hand against his skin.

'Not any more,' he said. 'At least, not on the outside.'

She stared up into his eyes, seeing her own story reflected there.
Years of accumulated pain, of feeling worthless, the constant erosion
of confidence, the doubt, the guilt…

'Tell me,' she said, pulling him down to the sofa.

It was a while before he could speak.

'My father worked hard, and in many ways provided well for us,
but he was controlling. My mother was never allowed to work outside
of the home and, despite the money he earned, he made sure that what
she received in housekeeping money from him was never quite enough.
It meant that she was forever beholden to him, forced to scrimp and
save to make ends meet, but the minute she served up a lacklustre meal,
or made some other economy that affected his comfort, he would lash

out at her; fists, his belt, it rarely mattered. But of course he only ever hit her in a place where no one would see the bruises. That's how it works, isn't it?'

Ruby reached for his hand.

'Once I was old enough to work out what was going on I took the beatings for her, when I could. I would goad my father so that he turned on me instead, and I think he quite enjoyed the feeling of power it gave him. I was a big lad even as a child, but yet he could still better me. I don't think it ever occurred to him that I let him beat the crap out of me, that that was the whole point, the reason why I did it and the only way I could protect my mother.'

He rested his hand on top of hers, his eyes dark in the soft light. 'She died ten years ago from cancer, but she died full of guilt for having allowed it to happen…' He swallowed. 'But how could she possibly feel guilty when it was my father who was to blame? And yet she did; she felt guilty for what she had put me through, hating herself for failing to protect me. She never understood that I didn't do it because I pitied her, I did it because I loved her.' He sat up, clutching at her hand. 'Guilt is such a terrible thing, Ruby.'

She sat quietly for a moment, looking into the eyes of a man who was everything her husband was not. For whom kindness and generosity, friendship and love were freely given, not for any return, but because of who he was. But these things had come at a price, and he had borne the scars of that price his whole life. He deserved so much more. And she knew without doubt or fear that this was why they had come together.

She thought back to the very first day they had met, when Angus had told her that everything would be okay. She had asked herself then how he could possibly have known about her past but, somehow he had, he had always known… Suddenly it all made sense.

'That's what you saw, isn't it? When I first arrived at Joy's Acre? You saw my guilt... and worse, you saw my son living in the shadow of it.'

Angus smiled, a warm smile that came from somewhere very deep inside and which lit his whole face.

'You have to get over the guilt of being abused, Ruby. You have done nothing wrong, and yet you feel guilty for making the choices you have for your children, choices which were made out of love. These choices should set you free, not tether you to fear and guilt, and if you live with these things, you'll allow your children to bring them into their lives also.'

'I thought I'd lost Jem,' she whispered, and the look on Angus's face told her that he understood she didn't just mean today.

'You never lost him,' he said. 'What he did today was proof of how much he loves you, how much he wants to keep you safe, just as you do him.'

'My husband never touched Jem, or Darcie, but there was always the fear of it, that's the hold he had over me. I had to get them away from him, I was terrified that Jem would grow up to be just like him otherwise.'

Angus nodded. 'Often we become victims through no fault of our own, but for some people it becomes a way of life. They don't have the strength to break free from that cycle until it becomes the thing that defines them and ultimately the victim becomes the aggressor. It took me a very long time to understand that sometimes there really is no difference between the two.'

Ruby frowned. *What was he trying to tell her?*

'The scars that you saw, Ruby, the cigarette burns. They weren't caused by my father... but by my wife...'

'Your wife?' Her stomach dropped away in shock.

'I met her in the waiting room of my counsellor's office,' he said, giving a mirthless laugh. 'I should have known better. But you know how it is – I thought I would be the one to save her, to finally make her better… But, in the end, she just couldn't break free, and I had to save myself.'

'Oh, Angus…'

'That was part of the problem, you see. She hated that I just stood there and took it from her, that I would never fight back, because – oh, how she wanted me to! She wanted me to rise up and strike her too, to reinforce how much of a victim she was, to acknowledge her pain in the only way she recognised. But I'm a big bloke, Ruby, if I did what she wanted there was no telling what harm I might do. It would have been the end of me. And so, I learned to be still and be calm. I took my anger out on the trees in the woodland, anything but give in to it and become my father.'

And finally, Ruby understood what Angus had been through, why he hated violence, and had become the gentle giant he was. A man whose strength went far beyond the physical.

She turned back to look at the room around her, at the little cottage that had given her and her family so much, but also made her realise just how much she had to give too. Slowly she pulled her jumper up and over her head, leaving just her vest top underneath. She turned so that the soft light from the fire fell on her shoulder, and onto the line of burn marks that were her own scars of a life she had left behind. She wanted Angus to see it all. No secrets, no fear, no guilt, just her, and perhaps the future…

His hand glanced lightly along the skin of her arm, across her shoulder and neck, until it came to rest just lightly on the edge of her chin.

'You have all the strength you need, Ruby. You've broken free.'

'No,' she whispered, just moments before his lips met hers. 'We both have.'

Chapter 28

It was almost eleven by the time Ruby and Angus pushed open the door to the garden room and crept inside. Two of Angus's neighbours had arrived at the cottage a few moments earlier, offering to look after Jem and Darcie, so now they were on their way to join in the celebrations in the barn. First though, there was just one more thing they needed to attend to.

'Why are we whispering?' asked Ruby, giggling as they made their way into the far room. 'Jem is asleep right across the other side of the garden, there's no way he can hear us, and I don't suppose that Rumpus will mind the interruption.'

Angus grinned. 'Seeing as we've brought her a present too, I don't suppose she will,' he replied, nodding at the tuna-laden plate he was carrying. 'Happy Christmas, Rumpus,' he added.

He laid the plate on the floor just in front of the box where the cat and all four kittens were curled up together. Rumpus lifted her head, yawned and immediately stretched out her legs. She picked her way from the box and, rubbing herself first against Angus's outstretched hand, was soon tucking into her treat.

'Sorry your supper is so late,' said Ruby. 'But Jem will be over first thing in the morning with your breakfast, that I can guarantee.'

She looked up into Angus's shining eyes and thought of the hastily put together envelope under the tree with a card from Rumpus asking Jem if he would like to choose a kitten as a thank-you present for looking after them all so well. With the card was a list of a few extra presents from Ruby and Angus that they would be buying just as soon as the shops opened again: a round furry basket, two bowls, and a selection of toys; all the things in fact that a kitten would need in its new home.

'He's going to be so excited,' she added.

'Never mind Jem, *I'm* going to be excited,' said Angus. 'I can't wait to see which one he chooses.'

Ruby reached out to stroke the kittens, all squirming gently now that the warmth of their mother was temporarily gone. She touched the head of the one nearest to her, gently resting the tips of her fingers against the white 'star' on its head.

'I reckon it will be this one,' she said. 'Jem said it reminded him of Christmas.'

Angus smiled. 'I think you're right; she'd be a beautiful choice.' He handed Ruby a bright red shiny bow which he had carried in his pocket.

'Where shall we put this?' he asked.

A surge of happiness washed over her. 'I'll pop it here,' she said, sticking it to the side of the box. 'Jem will see it straight away.' And she turned over the tag so that the message would be clear to see.

Happy Christmas, Jem, it read. *With lots of love, Rumpus xxx.*

Angus took her hand. 'I think this is going to be the best present ever, don't you?'

Ruby cocked her head, a teasing grin on her face. 'Oh, I don't know… I think mine was pretty good…'

★

They could hear music from the barn from several feet away, despite heavy oak doors closed against the cold. Angus pulled one open.

'Are you ready for this?' he asked with a grin.

'Ready as I'll ever be,' replied Ruby, taking a deep breath.

The band was in full swing and a wall of sound hit them; an exhilarating mix of music, laughter and excited chatter. Ruby searched the room for her friends as she stepped inside, immediately spotting Noah and Declan standing a little way into the room, both of them looking towards the doorway. Noah caught her eye straight away and waved, coming forward to greet them.

'You're just in time,' he said. 'Maddie will be here in a minute.'

Ruby frowned. 'Sorry?' she replied, raising her voice against the noise of the band. 'I thought she was already here… Where's she gone?'

But Noah just tapped the side of his nose. 'Ah,' he intoned. 'It's a surprise.'

Ruby glanced at Angus but he just shrugged. 'Nope, I haven't a clue either,' he said, looking around him.

'Is everybody else still here, though?' she asked. 'We ought to go and say hello.'

'Ah, well Tom and Isobel are otherwise engaged,' he said, directing a nod towards the band, where Ruby could see them both smiling away as they played. 'And Seth is over at the table talking to Agatha… Clara and Trixie are… busy,' he added mysteriously.

As he spoke his eyes swivelled back towards the door. 'Oh, and speaking of which, here comes Clara now.'

'And that's my cue,' said Declan with a grin. 'I'll catch you later.'

He moved off, threading his way through the crowds of people, heading towards the table where Seth was sitting. Ruby saw him bend to whisper something in Seth's ear just as Agatha got to her feet and took his arm, a wicked grin on her face, eyes trained on the door…

Ruby followed their direction back towards Clara and, as she did so, the music suddenly stopped. A throat was cleared.

'Ladies and gentlemen…' began Tom from the stage. 'I can't express how thrilled we all are to see so many of you here tonight and, despite the weather's best efforts to thwart us, you can see there's not much that stops celebrations at Joy's Acre from going ahead. It's testimony to the amazing people who live and work here, our friends, our neighbours and all of you, the wonderful community in which we find ourselves, so our huge and heartfelt thank you to you all…'

He paused for a moment as an enthusiastic round of applause rang out.

'However, despite the fact that Maddie and Seth have already tied the knot – in their wellies and woollies, no less – we thought you might all like the opportunity to wish them all the very best for many years of absolute bliss together. So, without further ado, I give you, Mr and Mrs Thomas.'

There was an excited rustle, an audible intake of breath and then the band broke into a spirited rendition of 'Here Comes the Bride'. The double doors to the barn were both pulled open and, in the doorway, framed in a pool of light, stood Maddie in the most beautiful dress Ruby thought she had ever seen. A shimmery covering of the thinnest tulle draped elegantly over Maddie's shoulders and neckline, extending down her arms to just below her elbow. Gentle folds gathered over a satin bodice beneath, while a soft draped bow at a nipped-in waist gave way to a dreamy cascade of soft rippling layers that pooled around her feet. Her rich auburn curls were piled high on her head and accented with creamy roses and deep velvety peonies that were echoed in the bouquet she held. She looked amazing, but it was the expression of pure happiness on her face that made her truly beautiful.

The tears sprang into Ruby's eyes as she watched Maddie step forward to take Seth's hand, the look that passed between them making her throat constrict with emotion. It was just the way that Angus had looked at her earlier and, as he took her hand and squeezed it tight, an exuberant chorus of shouts and clapping rose up around them.

★

It took a while for the noise and congratulations to die down, but eventually Trixie was able to make her way back over to the tables which, despite the lateness of the hour, still groaned with food. Maddie and Seth were continuing to do rounds of the hall, giving everyone the opportunity to admire her dress and allowing the couple to say their copious thanks for all the help they had received.

Trixie didn't know why they hadn't thought about it before, but the idea for Maddie to get changed into her wedding dress had come suddenly as they were all reminiscing over the very eventful day that had just been. It was the perfect opportunity, and the most wonderful surprise for Seth who, up until now, had been denied the chance to see his bride as she had originally intended. It was a moment that Trixie didn't think she would ever forget, and one that fixed itself in her brain. All at once, she knew that there was something she wanted more than anything in her life before and, if she had read the signs right, she wasn't the only one. There was enough magic swirling in the air tonight to make anything possible, but there was only one way to make her dream come true.

'Anybody would think you hadn't eaten all day…' she said, nudging Noah's arm playfully. 'Oh, oops… you haven't, have you?'

Noah stopped chewing, eyes widening in response to her cheeky question. 'That's so unfair; sneaking up on me when I've got my mouth full and can't answer properly. Fabulous food though...' he said, winking. 'That cheese may be Gouda but this one is Feta.'

Trixie groaned. 'Oh, that's terrible. Did you go on a course or something?'

'What? In cheese making?'

'No... telling bad jokes! Honestly, Noah, what are you like?'

He grinned. 'In my defence, I think I might be a little bit hysterical. I am absolutely, one hundred percent, completely knackered.'

Trixie studied his face. In all the time she had known him, she didn't think she had ever seen him downcast or despondent. Even tonight, despite the fraught day, he had soon bounced back, but looking at him now it was obvious that events had taken their toll. He did look tired, and it suddenly occurred to her that he had only just stopped for a rest from ferrying the last of the villagers up here, or taking back home those older members of the community who had come early and wanted to leave early too. And while he might be having something to eat now, he would soon be back on the road again. She had lost count of the number of trips he had made today, and yesterday, and all the help he had given over the last few weeks; weeks when she had had more fun than she could remember in ages...

'I really don't know how we would have done any of this without you,' she said. 'A party is not much good without people, is it? Or food, or chairs and tables, or any of the other multitude of things you've fetched and carried for us.' She held a hand over his so that he would look at her for a moment. 'And I was wondering why exactly you might have done all that for us?'

Noah narrowed his eyes. 'Because I'm a nice person?' he suggested.

It was still quite dim in the barn with only the twinkling candles and fairylights to illuminate the room but, if she hadn't known better, she'd have said he was blushing.

'Oh, I see,' she said slowly. 'And that's the only reason, is it? Nothing else?'

'Well, um… you needed the help, obviously, and I—'

'So it wouldn't have been because you were trying to earn yourself any brownie points, would it…?' She let the sentence dangle. 'Because if it was, I think it would be fair to say that you've amassed quite a considerable number.'

He swallowed. 'And brownie points are a good thing in your book, is that right? Big thick chocolatey ones…'

'All gooey in the middle and then served dripping in cream.'

'Erm, yes.'

'I thought as much.' She nodded. 'And did you know that if you earn enough of these points, it entitles you to a reward of your choice, so…' She licked her lips. 'I was wondering if you'd like to claim it.'

He cleared his throat and put down the piece of bread he was holding, beginning to fumble in the back pocket of his jeans. 'Well, I was wondering…'

'Yes?'

'Well, if perhaps…' He paused to pull out the thing he had been looking for: a piece of mistletoe, rather battered and forlorn-looking.

Trixie burst out laughing. 'Oh, God, you should see your face,' she said, winking. 'Good job I came prepared, isn't it?' And with that she whipped her hand out from behind her back and brandished a massive bunch of the festive greenery. She grabbed hold of the front of his shirt and pulled him closer.

'Hello, you,' she said.

'Don't you mean Halloumi?' he replied.

'Noah?'

'Yes?'

'Shut up and kiss me.'

★

'Why are we even doing this?' asked Maddie, shouting to make herself heard over the band. 'It's utter madness!'

'Because it's fun!' shouted Trixie.

'Because it's Christmas!' yelled Clara, a string of tinsel around her neck.

'Because it's the most wonderful thing to be alive and married to you!'

'Fair enough,' replied Maddie laughing, pulling Seth in closer.

She looked around at all of her friends, the beautifully decorated room and the crowd of people who had either all been ferried in by Noah or had made their way through the snow.

'And it looks like everyone else agrees with you too.'

A few hours ago, it hadn't occurred to any of them that there could possibly be a party this evening, but now here they all were. Just moments after Ruby, Jem and Angus had returned to the cottage to recover, Noah's phone had begun to ring. It was a couple of the villagers checking to see what time he was picking them up. A hasty conference had been called and, as Maddie and Seth had looked around the room, at their friends who had all worked so hard to help them celebrate their wedding, who had helped to make Joy's Acre what it was, Seth declared that actually there was no better time for a party. After all, the barn was ready, the food and drink needed ferrying about but was all prepared, Trixie's wedding cake was waiting patiently in the pantry and the band were gathering in the village. All they needed now were people, and with a few more journeys and a trailer on the back of the tractor, Noah could certainly provide no end of those.

Since then it had been a mad, exhilarating whirl, but then, as Maddie looked around the room in wonder, this was Joy's Acre after all. Things like this tended to happen here.

She checked her watch; it was very nearly midnight. How could she possibly have dreamed all that was in store for her this year? It had been a time of highs and lows, of achievement and friendship, and most importantly, of love. They had been tested to the limits, and rewarded beyond measure, and she wouldn't have changed one single bit of it. She raised her glass just as someone in the crowd shouted merrily.

'Happy Christmas!' she echoed amid a chorus of cheerful wishes. Tom and Isobel were still up on the stage having the times of their lives by the look of things, but one by one the rest of them raised their glasses: Clara, Declan, Trixie, Noah, Ruby, Angus and Seth.

'Happy Christmas!' they chorused.

Seth kissed her nose. 'And are you happy, Mrs Thomas?'

'Oh yes!' she breathed. 'Very happy. I can't believe it though, can you? How on earth did we do all this? No, don't answer that,' she added, looking around the room. 'I know how we did it, with the help of all these wonderful, wonderful people. We really are lucky, you know.'

Seth tipped his head to one side. 'I don't know,' he said. 'Is it luck? Or do you make your own luck? By working together, through kindness, through friendship…' He laughed. 'And a lot of hard work.'

She smiled, considering his question. 'I think you might be right, but either way it's set to be the most magical Christmas after all…'

'And it's only just beginning. There's a new year right around the corner, Mrs Thomas. Let's make it a good one, shall we?'

'No,' she said as she pulled him closer still, her lips just touching his. 'Let's make it amazing…'

A Letter from Emma

So here we are, we've spent a whole year at Joy's Acre and whether you've been with me throughout the seasons, or just stopped by for a little Christmas cheer, a huge and heartfelt thank you for your company. So, for now, it's time to leave Joy's Acre behind but I'm delighted and very excited to tell you that I'm now working on a new series that I think you're going to love... I really hope you'd like to stay updated on what's coming next, so please do sign up to my newsletter here and you'll be the first to know!

www.bookouture.com/emma-davies

I can't believe that the series has come to an end, and I won't pretend I'm not sad. I've come to know and love these bunch of characters as if they were my own friends, and in a way they have been; they've been with me through rain or shine, through good times and bad, and I literally couldn't have done it without them! It's been incredibly hard work writing four books in a year, but I've received so many lovely comments from readers saying how much they have enjoyed reading these books that it has made every moment worthwhile.

Having readers take the time to get in touch really does make my day, and if you'd like to contact me then I'd love to hear from you. The easiest way to do this is by finding me on Twitter and Facebook, or you could also pop by my website where you can read about my love of Pringles among other things…

I hope to see you again very soon, and in the meantime, if you've enjoyed your visit to Joy's Acre, I would really appreciate a few minutes of your time to leave a review or post on social media. Even a recommendation to anyone who'll listen at the hairdresser's is very much appreciated!

Until next time,
Love, Emma x

 authoremmadavies

 EmDaviesAuthor

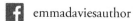 emmadaviesauthor

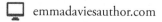 emmadaviesauthor.com

Acknowledgements

There are always a number of people during the writing of any book who have provided help, advice, encouragement and support. I'm always incredibly grateful, but it seems fitting with this book, the last one in the series, that my very special thanks should be reserved for the people who have made it all possible: my utterly fabulous publishers, Bookouture.

So a huge and heartfelt thank you for the brilliant covers, for being innovative and courageously creative, for having the best marketing team there is, behind the scenes, and on the front lines (Kim and Noelle, that's you!), for being eternally supportive, incredibly efficient and the best fun to work with. And finally, but by no means least, to Jessie, my amazing editor, who never flaps even when I do, who calmly moves deadlines when real life gets in the way of mine, and always makes me believe I can write books even when I'm convinced I can't!

Printed in Great Britain
by Amazon

39282146R00175